PRAISE FOR ROBERT GREER AND
THE DEVIL'S BACKBONE

"A must-read souvenir for city slickers whose senses are quickened by whiffs of the real West. It's all here, in rich, unflinching detail. Author Greer shares today's West with the knowledge and enthusiasm of a Zane Grey or Louis L'Amour. . . . Greer gives us a tremendous sense of place [and] introduces us to some wonderful characters, including Bobby Two Shirts's sister. She's a beauty, and so is this book."
—*Denver Post*

"Greer has a great sense of place and a knack for fixing his colorful characters in your mind, offering an unusual background of Colorado diamond mining, the rodeo, and black life in Denver."
—*Detroit News and Free Press*

"One of the crime genre's emerging stars. The Floyd series boasts an appealing African-American hero who combines toughness with charm, a wonderfully realized western setting; and, perhaps best of all, a fascinating look at a particular way of life in each adventure."
—*Booklist*

"Skillfully and excitingly paced. . . . CJ is a strong character, a pleasant addition to the growing ranks of black mystery series protagonists."
—*Cleveland Plain Dealer*

"A compelling character who will win readers' loyalty."
—*Houston Chronicle*

more. . .

THE DEVIL'S BACKBONE

By Robert Greer

The Devil's Backbone
The Devil's Red Nickel
The Devil's Hatband

THE DEVIL'S BACKBONE

ROBERT GREER

WARNER BOOKS

A Time Warner Company

The characters, events, and places that are depicted in *The Devil's Backbone* are spawned from the author's imagination. Certain Denver and Western locales are used fictitiously, and any resemblance between the novel's fictional inhabitants and actual persons living or dead is purely coincidental.

WARNER BOOKS EDITION

Copyright © 1998 by Robert O. Greer
All rights reserved.

Cover design by Rachel McClain
Cover illustration by Tom Hallmann

Warner Books, Inc.
1271 Avenue of the Americas
New York, NY 10020

Visit our Web site at
www.warnerbooks.com

W A Time Warner Company

Printed in the United States of America

Originally published in hardcover by The Mysterious Press.
First Paperback Printing: July 1999

10 9 8 7 6 5 4 3 2 1

For America's Black Rodeo Cowboys—
Past, Present, and Future

Acknowledgments

Few writers can claim to accomplish things single-handedly. This work is no exception. I am indebted to a wonderful, seasoned editor, Sara Ann Freed, who keeps me directed; and a savvy, top-notch publicist, Susan Richman, who points me in the right direction. The finished manuscript of *The Devil's Backbone* would have been an impossibility without the dedicated support, technical skill, and watchful eyes of Kathleen Hoernig and Connie Oehring.

I owe a debt of thanks to Dave Hyatt for his insight into the bail bonding business and to Chuck Bellairs for his aerial photographic expertise.

Finally, as always I am deeply grateful for the support and love of my wife, Phyllis, who always sacrifices the most when CJ Floyd begins another adventure.

"Cowboys to girls."
The Intruders

THE DEVIL'S BACKBONE

Chapter 1

During his lifetime Hambone Dolbey had developed a passionate hatred and fear of only two things: water and the smell of human excrement. In a near-death childhood incident he had nearly drowned in a three-foot-deep pool of leech-filled effluent in a neighbor's backyard cesspool. Over the years he had developed one simple method of dealing with his phobias, and that was to fortify himself with a hefty dose of ninety-proof whiskey or rum, confront the water and olfactory beasts, and pretend the incident that had initiated his fears had never occurred. It usually took a pint or so of the demon redeye to do the trick. But when fully lubricated, Hambone considered himself a worthy warrior. Hambone's aversion to water had forced him into a lifelong pattern of drinking nothing but buttermilk, malt liquor, cod-liver oil, and gin. Until his liver had started to give him fits a few years earlier, he always boasted that his good health was directly attributable to not having had a single glass of plain water in thirty years.

Considering his hatred of water, there were only two reasons why Hambone Dolbey was standing up to his navel in a chilly Colorado Rocky Mountain lake with a tow rope cinched around his waist: the taste of whiskey and the smell of money. For nearly an hour he had been partially immersed, methodically picking away at a rocky underwater ledge just in front of him with a rusty climber's pick. The grand-piano-shaped ledge was submerged just a few inches beneath the water, and in the course of an hour Hambone had plucked half a dozen golfball-sized volcanic rocks from its surface and deposited them into the creel at his side. A slender, brown-skinned woman dressed in expensive boots and fashionable form-fitting Western wear manned Hambone's lifeline: twenty yards of stout navy surplus rope undulating up from the water's edge and out onto the hillside where she was standing, ending in a modified barrel knot that Hambone had tied around the trunk of a forty-foot-tall aspen tree.

"Tighten up the slack in the GD rope, Nadine, unless you want me to slip on my ass and drown." Hambone's command to Nadine Kemp, the current woman in his lifelong string of women, was the tenth nervous order he had barked in less than two minutes. Nadine had been struggling to cope with Hambone's partial inebriation and his dead sandbag weight just as they had practiced it in the shade of the creek behind her house.

But rehearsals and the real event weren't the same. The swirling mountain winds differed from the stillness of her backyard. Their shaded practices hadn't taken into account the strength-zapping reality of the blistering Colorado high country noonday sun, and there had been no hillside to adjust to at the creek's edge. The only constant between then and now was that in order to face the water head on, Hambone had had to get himself half drunk. Nadine had been managing rope slack for so long now that the palms of both hands burned in protest. She watched as Hambone, inspired by his whiskey-and-buttermilk high, picked away at the underwater ledge that he had been boasting for months was going to be their financial salvation.

In order to protect himself from hypothermia, Hambone was wearing a pricey neoprene shell and Gore-Tex-lined wet suit. He had topped the outfit off with a bone-white diver's belt, a shark knife, and flippers in an effort to convince himself that if he did accidentally slip under the water, he would at least be prepared to ward off whatever might be lurking in the depths of the fifty-foot-deep lake.

"Give me some slack. I need to move over to a little hump I can feel in the ledge."

Nadine began slowly easing out rope until Hambone called out, "Good, hold it there." Adjusting his creel as if it were ballast, he sidestepped his way along the lake's muddy bottom toward the hump. A sudden gust of wind knifed its way out of the towering pines to the west, peppering them both with a ten-second sandblast of dust and BB-sized rocks. The gust swept across the lake, teasing up a series of whitecaps before dancing its way off the water's surface and into the rocky canyon that separated the two table mesas rising from the opposite side of the lake. The gust left Hambone snorting and spitting grit into the water. He kicked a flipper in protest and mumbled, "Shit."

He regained his composure after one last sinus-clearing snort and teased the rock pick back out from the loop in his belt as he once again began tapping along the eight-foot-long underwater shelf. The ledge was marble solid for most of its length, but the knot he had felt earlier had the consistency of dough. Hammering at the defect, he kicked up a bubbly froth until an apricot-sized knot of rock popped out and jetted up from the shelf for a split second before floating toward the bottom of the lake. Before the rock could sink, Hambone scooped it up in his hand, pulled it out of the water, and began examining it closely. "Pay dirt!" he screamed back at Nadine after a few seconds. "Damn sure pay dirt for real!"

Then, puffing out his cheeks, he blew a forceful stream of air along the jagged rock's surface. A muted luster briefly appeared from the depth of one of the rock's cupped-out defects. Hambone broke into an impish grin, carefully deposited the rock in his creel, and muttered, "Son of a bitch."

"How much longer you gonna be?" hollered Nadine from a perch she had between the knots of sagebrush on the hillside above the lake.

"Don't worry about it. Just give me some rope. I got nowhere to go but back to the Stampede."

Nadine let out another foot of rope and watched as Hambone gingerly worked his way to her left. "Why don't you just call their bluff?" She was counting on the fact that Hambone wasn't yet so drunk that he'd ignore her.

"And spoil the ride? Shit, Nadine, you must've forgot that I used to make my livin' as the only black man in the country officially sanctioned by the Professional Rodeo Cowboy Association of America itself to ride two-thousand-pound bulls. In case you didn't know, there's an old rodeo sayin' that claims the longer the ride, the better the pay." He tapped his pick along the underwater shelf several times to emphasize his point. Then, twisting in the muck at his feet, he moved to get a better working angle on the ledge. With his second step he lost his footing, dropping into a hole that sent him listing sideways into the water, flailing and gasping for air. His shoulder plunged beneath the water's surface and then his head. He screamed, sending a frothy stream of bubbles to the surface.

Nadine matched Hambone's scream with a high-pitched shriek. She yanked the slack out of the rope and pulled the rope toward her with all her strength. After a few seconds Hambone's head broke the choppy water's surface as he wheezed and snorted like a spent quarter horse. Nadine strained with the rope until her hands and face turned an unflattering shade of purple.

Waterlogged and coughing, with the rope squeezing his waist, Hambone could barely breathe. Kicking and hammering at the water, he kept telling himself, *Get back over to the shelf!* as he yelled at Nadine, "Pull to the right, pull to the right!" Suddenly he found himself kicking back and forth in the same bull-riding kind of rhythm he had used years before. When his right calf banged against the edge of the rocky shelf he had been standing on earlier, he thrashed violently, shouting, "Shit, shit, shit!" Rock sediment and bottom ooze filled his flippers as he finally cleared the shelf's edge. Nadine was still pulling, screaming, "Right, right, right!" When he realized that he was above the ledge, he made a wobbly effort to stand and found himself erect and quivering in water that was once more only just above his waist. As he stood shaking, half submerged, fear dancing through his brain, he had the feeling that at any second the lake's unstable floor might turn into a cesspool bottom that would slip out from under him once again. Carotid arteries pulsating, he stood frozen in place, slapping at the water with open palms. Finally he looked toward an equally spent Nadine, tow rope still in hand, and said almost inaudibly, "You can ease up on the rope."

He drew in a long, deep breath, loosened the tow rope, slowly wiggled his way beyond the rock ledge, and slithered out of the water back onto the safety of land. As his flippers cleared the water he felt a surge of relief matched only by that of his childhood rescue from the cesspool.

Tripping over rocks and slipping in the sandy soil and mud, Nadine raced toward him, tow rope still in one hand. She dropped to her knees in a pool of water and wrapped her arms around his legs. Stroking the backs of his calves she said, "You okay?"

Hambone looked down at her and sniffed the air. "You smell it?" he said, sniffing once again.

"No," said Nadine, looking puzzled.

Hambone began sniffing frantically until, with one long, final snort, he said, "Smells like shit."

Nadine looked at him sympathetically. "You'll be

okay," she said, moving to get back on her feet. "I'll drop you back at the Stampede. You can change out of your wet suit there."

Hambone nodded. Lost in a daze, he started sniffing the air once again.

For a couple of hours the faded white truck had been parked at the edge of one of the table mesas overlooking the muddy lakeshore where Nadine now stood stroking Hambone Dolbey's arm. The driver had angled the truck into a pocket of aging aspen, and from a distance the vehicle's front end resembled just another white aspen trunk. The truck was covered with a layer of copper-colored grit, courtesy of its low, winding trip up a dusty trail-ridge road to the top of the mesa. Clutching an expensive pair of Bausch and Lomb field binoculars, the truck's driver sat on the hood, watching Hambone Dolbey's exploits in the lake. Now the driver let out a climactic grunt and slipped off the hood, stretched out a leg cramp, walked around the pickup, and lifted a Remington .30-06 with a telescopic lens off the front seat. After a brief sigh, the driver placed the rifle on the passenger seat, set the binoculars aside, and slipped behind the wheel.

The sound of the big-block V8 turning over was muffled by the noise from thirty honkers passing overhead. The driver looked up at the geese and smiled, easing the truck out of its nesting place. "Later," said the driver, patting the rifle's wooden stock and peering over the mesa's edge back down toward the lakeside spot where Hambone Dolbey and Nadine Kemp were standing in a relieved embrace.

Chapter 2

CJ Floyd was working his way up Chokecherry Draw in the remote northwest Colorado Diamond Breaks wilderness. He was tracking a bond-skipping Acoma Indian and illegal-fireworks distributor named Bobby Two-Shirts and daydreaming about the long-overdue payday he was about to enjoy.

It was an overcast, muggy first-of-July day, and although the 6,200-foot elevation wasn't that much higher than the mile-high elevation he was used to back home in Denver, CJ was huffing and puffing like an old steam engine. Too many recent catfish and collard-green specials at Mae's Louisiana Kitchen, his favorite soul food haunt, had added fifteen extra pounds to a six-foot-three, normally 220-pound frame. The half-dozen cheroots he

smoked each day didn't help matters much, and CJ was
bound and determined that he was going to give up
smoking before the end of the summer. Stuck in low
gear, he continued gasping up the draw.

CJ was the only black bail bondsman operating on
Denver's Bail Bondsman's Row. Business hadn't been
that great lately, so he had resorted to his habit of taking
occasional bounty-hunting jobs to make ends meet. For
three days he had been tracking Bobby Two-Shirts's
rusted-out, big-block Ford pickup—and the gleaming
silver sixteen-foot Steidman horse trailer Bobby had
packed to the gills with $50,000 worth of illegal fire-
works—across Colorado's Western Slope. The crazy-
quilt journey had sent CJ switchbacking his way across
the northern Rockies, over Red Dirt Pass to Harper's
Corner, through Dinosaur National Monument, and finally to Chokecherry Draw.

Out of breath, CJ ducked behind a boulder and
shaded his eyes. Squinting into the sun and over the crest
of the knobby boulder, he watched Bobby Two-Shirts
tinker beneath the hood of his truck, which was parked
at the edge of a hay meadow forty-five yards away.

Cicero Vickers, the well-heeled bail bondsman who
operated out of the building next door, had talked CJ
into taking the job of tracking down Bobby Two-Shirts.
It hadn't been a hard sell because CJ's finances had been
on life support for months. Bobby had skipped out on a
$15,000 bond for illegal possession of fireworks and left
Cicero, a quintessential tightwad, holding the bail-bonding
bag. Too old and racked with arthritis to track down
Bobby himself, Cicero had persuaded CJ to do it for a
$3,000 finder's fee.

Bobby Two-Shirts was parked in front of two decaying turn-of-the-century homestead cabins that flanked the far edge of a grassy meadow at the blind end of Chokecherry Draw. A steep hillside dotted with boulders, piñon pine, juniper, and sagebrush rose behind the cabins.

Bobby pulled his head from beneath the truck's hood, sucking on the two tender knuckles he had burned on the overheated engine. He skirted the truck's bumper and headed purposefully for the trailer. Popping the trailer's latch, he swung the double doors open, shearing a clump of horse manure off the bumper as he did. He chuckled and kicked the dried manure into the meadow. Inside, the trailer was packed from its floor to the arched aluminum ceiling with what were known in the fireworks industry as "big-time boomers." Wooden cases of flaming fireballs with enticing names like Johnny Reds, Black Widows, and Dixie Thunder occupied a center strip down the middle of the trailer. Flanking the fireballs were smaller cardboard boxes of skyrockets, bottlebacks, and M60s. Satisfied that everything was in its place, he stepped back out of the trailer and eyed the cache of illegal assault weapons he had jammed between a couple of wooden crates, smiling as he closed the trailer doors. He stepped up on the trailer's bumper, pulled off his Resistol cowboy hat, and wiped his brow. As was his habit, he was sporting two sweat-stained University of Colorado athletic department T-shirts, seemingly in direct defiance of the sizzling 88 degree temperature.

Six feet tall and split-rail thin, Bobby had had only five years of reservation schooling, and for most of his life he had been described as *kind of slow*. Surprisingly, he had a craggy southern sharecropper's kind of face, crisscrossed with crow's feet from too many years in the sun. There was a noticeable bulge in his right pants pocket from the weight of a .357 Magnum.

Leaning his weight into the boulder he was hiding behind, CJ squinted up into the three o'clock sun and then patted his back pocket for his snub-nosed .38. He rarely carried a gun, but a weapon was mandatory when it came to bounty hunting in the Rockies. Tracking down a man like Bobby Two-Shirts without some form of fire-power would have been stupid.

Half a football field of hay meadow, a few scrubby gamble oaks, and a line of chokecherry trees separated him from the man he had been stalking. CJ slipped down into the boulder's shade and thought about his two tours as a navy swiftboat gunner's mate during Vietnam. He knew he needed a game plan for closing the gap between himself and the enemy; a plan that would be simple, without casualties, and swift. He stood back up and was considering what to do next when the unmistakable sizzling-bacon sound of a rattlesnake buzzing jarred his thoughts. He looked down to find a coiled three-foot rattlesnake less than four paces from him. Slowly he sidestepped away from the boulder. As he moved out of striking distance of the rattler, he tripped over a small rock. His mouth went dry, but the snake stayed put. After two more side steps, CJ crunched across the uncovered root of a dead juniper. The unexpected crack of dry wood startled him, and he froze in the juniper's shadow. The snake remained coiled, no longer buzzing.

Breathing quietly, CJ stood stock-still for nearly a

minute, repeatedly measuring the distance between him and the snake. Finally convinced that he had moved out of striking distance and knowing he needed a silent weapon rather than his .38, he reached up and broke off a five-foot branch from the juniper, hoping the noisy snap wouldn't alert Bobby Two-Shirts to his presence or cause the rattler to strike. It wasn't until he had the branch fully extended toward the snake that he noticed there was a gnarled, four-inch-wide cleft at one end. As he looked at the Y-shaped cleft, a plan for dealing with the snake began to take shape. He took half a step forward, easing the wishbone split toward the rattler, judging the distance between them again before pulling the juniper branch back into the web of his thumb and forefinger to check it one last time for stoutness. As he eased the branch back toward the snake's head, the snake began to rattle. In the split second before it had a chance to strike, CJ had its head trapped in the fork of the juniper branch and jammed into the ground. Uncoiled, the rattler struggled violently to escape, but it was no match for the ten-pound rock CJ had picked up and now sent crashing down on its head. As the snake continued to thrash, the seed of a plan to capture Bobby Two-Shirts suddenly emerged in CJ's head—a plan that would rely on the fact that nearly everyone harbored a deadly fear of rattlesnakes.

Colorado's Greeley Independence Stampede is the world's largest Fourth of July rodeo. The Stampede boasts over seven hundred contestants and prize money topping $300,000. The fifteen-day-long community event kicks off each July 1 at the base of the Rockies in the city seventy miles north of Denver named after Horace Greeley, famous for his visionary saying, "Go west, young man, and grow up with the country." The Stampede features a nationally acclaimed carnival midway, country-music stars, a world-class chili cook-off, art exhibits, trail rides, and a Sunday morning flapjack breakfast. The rodeo itself takes place in Greeley's Island Grove Regional Park, which for two weeks every July is transformed into a Western rodeo oasis complete with a high-rise stadium and arena with seating for fifteen thousand.

Morgan Williams, a muscular cigar stump of a black man with a shaved head and skin as smooth as a carnival Nubian's, hadn't missed a Greeley Stampede in over twenty years. Bubbling with energy and thinking about the past, Morgan strolled the Stampede midway, tipping his hat to passersby and shaking hands with those he knew. Morgan had been a champion bull rider on the pro rodeo circuit until he ruptured three lumbar vertebrae and separated his shoulder a second before completing a world-record ride on an angry bull named Piston at Cheyenne Frontier Days fifteen years earlier. Now he eked out an existence on the streets of Denver with his lifelong friend Dittier Atkins, a deaf mute and former champion rodeo clown.

Morgan was dressed in the same regalia he wore every year for the Stampede: frayed-at-the-cuff Wrangler jeans, a set of chocolate-brown leather chaps checked with age, his lucky washed-out blue chambray shirt, runover oiled leather cowhand work boots, and a Montana blocked straw Stetson. His buffed and polished six-inchwide oval Professional Rodeo Cowboy Association championship silver belt buckle, engraved with the words *Champion Bull Rider—55th Annual Greeley Stampede*, set off the outfit. Morgan still retained the distinction of being the only three-time successive bull riding champion the Greeley Stampede had ever had.

Morgan had been crisscrossing the Stampede grounds trying to find his old friend and mentor, Cletus Dolbey. Cletus, known as Hambone to his friends, had called him the night before and told him he was on the verge of striking it rich. Fifteen years older than Morgan and a rodeo circuit jack-of-all-trades, Hambone was the most recognizable black cowboy to have ever graced the circuit. He was also one of only three black cowboys in the pro rodeo Hall of Fame. He was a colorful, gregarious, athletic backslapper, whose fame was widespread enough that he still continued to pop up on regional talk radio and television.

Each year at the Stampede he was billed as a chute rooster, a goodwill ambassador who knitted together the enthusiasm of the cowboys and the fans and a bombastic wise guy who knew everyone's job. His Stampede grounds routine ranged from critiquing cowboys, judges, and announcers to pampering the livestock. Hambone wasn't paid for his activities, and some event organizers resented what they considered his brassy interference, but his notoriety, flamboyance, and crowd-pleasing shtick seemed to protect him from the hook. Whitaker Rodgers, the Stampede chairman, had approached Hambone about toning down his act, but Hambone had ignored him and seemed to enjoy giving Rodgers what he liked to call the "bull dick shaft."

By the time Morgan reached the isolated horse barn

area north of the arena, rivulets of sweat were streaming down his face from beneath his Stetson and his shirt was plastered to his back with sweat. The distant noise and laughter from inside the arena told Morgan that some rodeo clown was at work warming up the crowd. He checked the thermometer tacked outside one of the barns that faced south, directly into the sun. It was 92 degrees. Morgan stepped into the barn's welcome shade and wiped a pool of sweat from his brow. Knowing how Hambone loved passing out treats to the horses, he walked the alleyway between the stalls, hoping to locate him. Freshly cut alfalfa crackled loudly beneath his boots, its clover-sweet aroma masking the pungent smell of horse manure that always hung in the air. "You in here, Hambone?" called Morgan, stopping abruptly before turning in a circle in search of a response.

A couple of cowboys with contestant packets clutched tightly in their hands brushed past Morgan and nodded. "Hope I don't get no bad draw today," said the taller of the two men. "Bad draw luck's been doggin' me all year."

His companion, a shorter, more compact man, nodded. "I been there," he said, as they continued down the alleyway.

Morgan offered a supportive, sympathetic nod before moving on past a half-dozen more stalls, calling out Hambone's name without a response. He made a swing past the last stall, where a lone cowboy checking his horse didn't pay him any attention. He then made a quick trip back up the silent opposite side of the barn and stepped out into the sun. Disappointed, hat in hand, shading his eyes and still sweating, he decided it was

time to head back to the food court and hook up with
Dittier Atkins.

Fifteen yards from the barn's entrance, a crowd of
half a dozen people was gathered around a horse trough.
The reflection of the sunlight streaming off the galvanized lip of the trough caught Morgan's attention. He
rolled his Stetson around in a tight circle in his hand and
wiped his brow on his sleeve. He had just slipped his
Stetson back in place when Dittier Atkins broke out of
the crowd and came racing toward him. Dittier's eyes
were twice their normal size. He grabbed Morgan by the
arm and began tugging him toward the crowd. Dittier cut
his way between a buxom woman in formfitting Wran-
glers and a portly man in a $500 Stetson to the trough
where a half-jackknifed man in a diver's wet suit drifted
face up just below the water's surface. A foot-long ten-
dril of coagulated blood arched its way out of a gaping
hole in the man's left cheek, morphing into a lily pad of
blood that floated on the water's surface.

The body drifted lazily in the water, and its wide-
open eyes seemed to stare directly at Morgan. A horrified look of surprise was frozen on the dead man's face.
Dittier began tugging on Morgan's sleeve like an excited
child. Suddenly Morgan could feel every ounce of the
skinny rodeo clown's weight. Looking down at the dead
man, he whispered "Hambone" softly, as if he didn't
have the heart to say Hambone Dolbey's name out loud.

Chapter 3

It had taken CJ nearly an hour to quietly inch his way into position next to the driver's-side door of Bobby Two-Shirts's pickup. The Colorado evening sky was now peppered with stars, and coyote pups yelped in the distance. A crazy quilt of houndstooth burrs and thistle dotted the front of CJ's shirt. His Levis were soaked belt buckle to boot tops from a belly crawl through an icy mountain stream that he hadn't seen when he first charted his route across the meadow that separated him from Bobby Two-Shirts. Hugging the ground, he stopped at the left rear tire of Bobby's pickup and pulled the dark green trash bag he was dragging up next to his shoulder. He froze for a moment, listening to the intermittent guttural snores coming from the cab of the truck.

Assured that Bobby was asleep, CJ reached inside the trash bag and pulled out the dead rattler. The snake's rubber-hose pliability was gone. During the six hours that CJ had waited impatiently for darkness and for Bobby Two-Shirts to settle into his cab for the night, rigor mortis had given the rattlesnake the rigidity of a bamboo pole. Death had also left behind a nauseating God-awful smell.

During his three days of trailing Bobby Two-Shirts across the Rockies' Western Slope, CJ had methodically catalogued the frail bond skipper's habits. Each evening, after a day of hanging out in small-town gas stations and bars, bullshitting with the locals and guzzling beer, Bobby would pull into a heavily wooded U.S. Forest Service campsite, making certain there were no other vehicles or campers around, nestle his rig into a space among the trees, and then wolf down a couple of bologna sandwiches and three or four final beers. Before turning in he checked the .357 Magnum he strapped to his belt at sunset, slipped a couple of extra clips of ammo into his shirt pocket, and climbed into the cab for the night. He always left the truck's windows cracked and locked the doors before stretching out across the front seat.

CJ fished the pungent rattlesnake out of the trash bag, still puzzled at why Bobby Two-Shirts had chosen Chokecherry Draw for his third Western Slope pit stop. The draw was as isolated a spot as Bobby could have found in Colorado, but the illegal contraband he was hauling wasn't plutonium. A horse trailer full of illegal fireworks could have been exchanged on any street in Denver. CJ's gut feeling was that Bobby had to be trucking around a more dangerous commodity or that he was doing business with someone who didn't want to be seen. He was inching up on his haunches, rattler in hand, ready to spear the snake through the eight-inch window opening, when in the distance he heard a vehicle approaching. It took him a few seconds to peg the guttural sound of a tractor-trailer straining its way up the draw's seven percent grade. In the time it took for CJ to decide whether to fold his cards or complete his plan, Bobby also heard the diesel's throaty roar and inched up on his elbows in the cab.

Aiming for the window opening, CJ let the rattlesnake fly.

"Motherfuck," screamed Bobby, realizing there was a baseball-bat-length rotten-smelling animal of some sort now occupying the front seat with him. He reached for the cab light switch above his head with one hand. With the other he fumbled on the seat for his .357. Gun in hand, he burst from the cab with the barrel pointed twelve o'clock high.

His feet had barely touched the ground when CJ reached out, grabbed him around the neck and yanked him squarely to the ground.

"What the fuck?" shouted Bobby.

Before he could say another word CJ had one knee across his neck, all of his 235 pounds pressing against Bobby Two-Shirts's Adam's apple. As Bobby tried to wiggle free, CJ slipped his .38 out of his back pocket and jammed the barrel against Bobby's right nostril. "Who's in the rig heading up the draw?"

Bobby smiled. "Your mother."

A few years earlier CJ might have thought about shooting the skinny bond skipper but recently he had made a promise to himself and Mavis Sundee, the feminine soft spot in his otherwise hard-edged life, that he would learn to control his temper. He dropped his thumb on the .38's hammer. "Who's in the rig?" he said, momentarily easing the full weight of his body off Bobby Two-Shirts's neck.

"Someone who'll kill your black ass. Count on it."

CJ shot a nervous glance in the direction of the diesel. He guessed the semi was still two or three minutes away. When Bobby suddenly began wriggling violently, CJ subdued him with another knee crush to the throat. Then he reached into his back pocket and pulled out a set of handcuffs. "Over on your stomach." He eased the barrel of his .38 against Bobby's forehead.

Bobby Two-Shirts rolled over obligingly before tweaking CJ once again. "She'll kill you, whoever the shit you are," he said, now flat on his stomach.

CJ slapped the handcuffs on Bobby's bony wrists and stood up, pulling Bobby with him. "Got a date with a judge in Denver, Mr. Fireworks Kingpin. We better get going."

The headlights of the approaching semi were now dancing off the branches of the nearby chokecherry trees. "Move it," said CJ, pointing Bobby in the direction of the meadow he had crawled across earlier and toward the ravine where he had parked his Jeep.

Bobby Two-Shirts moved off slowly just as the semi reached the level ground of the old homestead, its lights darting across the mesa.

CJ pointed his .38 at the back of Bobby Two-Shirts's head. "Run," he shouted. Bobby took off across the meadow in an all-out terrified sprint, his handcuffed arms locked behind him. CJ followed, knifing through the dew-covered timothy and shooting glances back toward the semi's headlights. They were fifty yards away at the far edge of the meadow when the semi's driver set the big rig's air brakes and called out, "Bobby, you here?" The woman operating the semi swung out of the cab and onto the ground. Arcing a two-foot-long riot-gear flashlight around in a semicircle, she carved loops of light into the nearby trees until the beam froze on the grill of Bobby Two-Shirts's pickup.

Celeste Deepstream was nearly six feet tall. She had a world-class swimmer's bulky upper torso and the sculptured muscular calves of the three-time NCAA two-hundred-meter butterfly champion she had once been. Her skin had a deep winter ski-slope tan, the kind usually reserved for mountain-climbing free spirits who enjoy worshiping the sun at ten thousand feet. Celeste and Bobby Two-Shirts were more than simply brother and sister, they were fraternal twins, born exactly six minutes apart. Bobby's lifelong claim to fame was that he was the oldest. Celeste was not only younger but smarter, stronger, and better than Bobby at just about everything in the world that counted. It was as if the couplet of DNA she had sprung from had harbored all of life's rich components while Bobby's had been stripped to the bone.

Celeste stepped around the cab and into the big rig's high beams. "No games tonight, Bobby. You know I need to drop your trailerload of Chinese New Year shit off in Durango before I head for Shiprock. Get your butt out here right now."

When she didn't get an answer, she headed for her brother's pickup. She pulled the partially ajar driver's-side door fully open and shone her flashlight into the cab to find a loaf of bread and an opened pound of bologna on the front seat. Chalking the foul smell in the cab up to rancid lunchmeat, she wouldn't have noticed the dead rattlesnake on the floor if the snake's tail hadn't wedged the door open when she tried to slam it shut. She reached down, picked the snake up by its rattles, and tossed it twenty yards out into the open meadow. She wiped her hand down the front of her jeans and stepped away from the door. Then, clearing her sinuses, she spat out a wad of mucus and frowned as a bad feeling began to work its way up from her bowels. She aimed her flashlight at the ground, checking out the dusty area around the truck. The signs of a struggle were obvious, including two sets of footprints. "Shit, shit, shit." She slammed the flashlight against the truck's front quarter panel, causing the light to flicker off and on. Then she rushed around to the rear of the horse trailer. "Fucking Vickers," she mumbled. "Fucking Vickers for sure."

A week earlier Cicero Vickers had called her to make certain that she would have Bobby present at his arraignment. Within hours he had called her a second time, cursing and screaming in a voice that verged on delirium to say that he had just forfeited $15,000 because Bobby had failed to appear. Celeste had pushed the phone away from her ear and let Cicero rant. "Kiss off," she finally told Vickers, slamming down the phone. When she later heard from a Denver fence she knew that Vickers would never suffer being stiffed and that he also had the kind of money it took to track Bobby across every square inch of the West, she had called Vickers and warned him to back off on trying to bring her brother back to justice. Vickers had grunted and told her to go play with herself. Now, realizing that she had offered a challenge to a man who took money as seriously as she did, she knew the phone call had been a mistake.

Flashlight still in hand, she followed the traces of footprints and scuff marks in the dusty ground past the end of the horse trailer all the way to the edge of the grassy meadow. Frustrated, she walked back to the trailer, pondering how long it was going to take her to load a horse trailer full of fireworks into a half-full semi. The thought of facing two hours of sweaty labor made Celeste wrinkle her face into a revengeful glare. She hated to sweat. Sweating reminded her too much of the labor involved in unfulfilled love. She clicked off her flashlight and stared up into the star-filled night. "Vickers," she mumbled to herself as she swung back the horse trailer door. "Fucking asshole, I should have known."

Chapter 4

The zygoma, commonly called the cheekbone, is one of 206 distinct bones in the human skeleton, all of which are ill-designed to withstand the crushing forces of modern-day car crashes, military engagement, contact sports, or the business end of a ten-pound branding iron descending with the plunging speed of a ball-peen hammer.

According to the Weld County coroner, Cletus Hambone Dolbey's right zygoma had been shattered almost beyond recognition by the weighted end of a branding iron in a blow delivered with such force that the fractured bone had severed several arteries, punctured the right eye, punched out a portion of the thin plate of bone that separates the eye socket from the nose, and lodged itself at the base of the skull just below the brain. Hambone had died immediately from shock and blood loss as his blood pressure plummeted in less time than it took for the killer to walk from the isolated horse trough where his body was found back out to the crowded Stampede midway. Neither the Weld County sheriff's people nor the Greeley police had been able to locate the murder weapon, but the almost perfect impression of a quarter circle on Hambone's cheek was enough to convince law enforcement officials and the coroner that a branding iron had been the death instrument.

It was just past midnight when Buford Jenkins, the Weld County coroner, headed out the newly installed automatic sliding doors of the county morgue and into the brisk night air. In addition to serving as coroner, Jenkins was a professor of veterinary medicine at Colorado State University. The fact that he was a specialist in veterinary rather than human pathology had never been an impediment to ten years in the elected position.

Jenkins had gotten the call to perform an autopsy on an old cowboy who had been murdered at the Stampede in the middle of his annual North Platte River fly-fishing trip with half a dozen other Colorado county coroners. His normally jovial disposition had turned into an overstuffed pin cushion of a bad mood. The autopsy could have waited, but phone calls from the Stampede chairman, Whitaker Rodgers, two Stampede board members, including Greeley's mayor, and the Weld County sheriff were enough to persuade Jenkins to make the three-hour drive from the undercut trout banks of the North Platte back to Greeley.

It hadn't taken Jenkins more than fifteen minutes to piece together what had happened and determine the cause of death, but it had taken him until midnight to smooth the ruffled feathers of a gaggle of nervous Stampede organizers, who were all more concerned about a murder tarnishing the rodeo's reputation as a family event than about the fact that Hambone Dolbey was dead. By the time he completed the autopsy and the necessary paperwork and discussed his findings with the sheriff, it was a brand-new day. When he trudged across the morgue's parking lot toward his rusted-out Chevy Blazer, still packed to the gills with fishing gear and beer, he was surprised to find a welcoming party of Dittier Atkins, Morgan Williams, and Morgan's niece, Lisa Darley, awaiting him. Lisa, who was also a vet, had a large-animal practice forty miles south near Loveland, and Jenkins had been one of her professors. Aware of the tenuous connection between his niece and the coroner, Morgan had called Lisa for support when he had found out from the sheriff earlier in the day that his friend would probably be autopsied that evening.

Lisa stepped out of her car and into the bright halogen lights of the parking lot just as Jenkins reached the rear of his Blazer. Under orders from her, Morgan and Dittier stayed put inside her Cherokee.

"Excuse me, Dr. Jenkins," Lisa said tentatively, towering over her short, stocky former professor. Startled, Jenkins jerked his head toward her. It was several seconds before a hint of recognition spread across his face.

"Lisa Darley. I finished CSU school six years ago. I've got a large-animal practice outside Loveland."

"Yes, yes," said Jenkins, finally realizing that the tall, slim, fair-skinned, sandy-haired woman standing next to him was one of the handful of black veterinarians that CSU had produced during his twenty-year tenure. He remembered that he had thought Lisa was white until she showed up at a black student alliance meeting at which he had been invited to speak during her freshman year. He broke into a smile, reached out, and shook her hand. "One of your classmates who's now a part-time faculty member told me you were still in the area. She mentioned that you're still jumping Swedish Warmbloods," said Jenkins, pleased that he still had the capacity to remember his former students' interests.

Lisa was amazed that Jenkins recalled her passion for jumping horses and dressage, unusual avocations for a black girl who had grown up in the middle of L.A., fully immersed for most of her formative years in the bright city lights. Now that she ran a forty-acre horse farm and managed a veterinary practice outside a small mountain town at the base of the Rockies, Los Angeles seemed galaxies away.

Lisa, the only child of Morgan's widowed, college-educated sister, had never ridden a horse until Morgan had taken her to see him ride bulls at a backwater second-tier rodeo just outside Bakersfield, California, when she was fifteen. Her mother had hoped that the experience of dodging manure, inhaling the blowing Mojave Desert sand, and fighting off horseflies while she watched her uncle jar himself senseless on the back of a bull would reinforce her attempts to get Lisa to accept her more staid vision of the world. But she hadn't counted on the fact that even fifteen-year-old black girls can fall in love with horses or that Morgan, who at the time was riding the crest of his pro rodeo fame, would make a free-spirited impression on Lisa that would brand her for life.

Thirty-two years old and sunburned with what Morgan liked to call a "colored folks' tan," Lisa had a country-girl smile, penetrating hazel eyes, and the self-assured mindset of a woman determined to conquer the West. She had remained close to Morgan all her life, and when his rodeo career finally hit the skids during her first year of vet school and he ended up homeless on the Denver streets, she had demanded that he move in with her. Proud to a fault and too much of a rolling stone to take Lisa up on her offer, Morgan had begged off by saying that moving in with her would leave Dittier on the streets to fend for himself. Morgan prevailed, and in the decade since then, he and Dittier had carved out a life collecting and selling cans, peddling firewood for a good-old-boy Texan they knew from their days on the circuit, and doing odd jobs for CJ Floyd. Each month Lisa sent CJ money to be deposited into an account she called her Morgan and Dittier Catastrophic Fund. She wasn't certain whether Morgan knew about the fund, but she knew better than to ever bring it up.

Lisa cleared her throat nervously, slipping her hand out of Jenkins's grasp. "I hate to bother you now, Dr. Jenkins, but the man they found floating in the water trough this afternoon was a longtime friend of my uncle's." She nodded toward the front seat of her Cherokee and Morgan's beefy silhouette. "He's pretty upset. I was hoping you could tell us what happened." Before Jenkins could respond, she motioned for Morgan to join them. Morgan was out of the Cherokee and on his way toward them when a portly, ruddy-complected man came loping across the parking lot. He was wearing run-down but expensive handmade cowboy boots and a wide-brimmed Resistol cowboy hat with oversized fresh-air portholes on either side of the crown. The man chugged directly up to Jenkins, completely out of breath, and gave him a look of consternation.

"Buford, you're letting me down," said the man in between gasps.

Jenkins shot the man he had known most of his life an exasperated look. "It's late, Whit. How about saving your complaints until sunup?"

Whitaker Rodgers, the Stampede chairman, surveyed Lisa and Morgan before bursting forth with, "The hell I will. Any information you have about the unfortunate incident this afternoon should go through official channels before you start broadcasting it in parking lots." He eyed Lisa and Morgan again. "I hope you haven't said anything unflattering about the Stampede."

Buford Jenkins rarely lost his temper, but he was disappointed and tired, and Whitaker Rodgers had caught him at a bad time. "Whit, right now I don't give a ragged rat's ass about the image of your precious Stampede. Your little murder here frittered away a fishing trip that it took me a year to organize. I'm tired as hell, and I just finished sewing up a dead man's skull." He looked over at Lisa and then back at Rodgers. "Just for the record, I haven't disclosed anything about the autopsy findings to anyone, including the sheriff. Maybe you need to learn to let people do their jobs and have a little respect for the dead. My discussion here with Dr. Darley is none of your business unless you've suddenly developed an interest in jumping Swedish Warmblood horses or dressage."

Halfway through Jenkins's tongue-lashing, Rodgers had turned crimson. As an oil company president, he wasn't used to having his authority challenged. "I'd just like you to go through channels," he said apologetically.

Jenkins smiled. "You're at the top of my list, Whit," he said, diplomatically adding, "How about tomorrow morning?"

"Nine o'clock okay?" asked Rodgers, still flushed.

"It's as good a time as any."

"I've got a few other fires to put out right now anyway," said Whitaker, searching for a face-saving way to make an exit. "I'll see you tomorrow morning in my Stampede office. You know where it is."

"Sure do," said Jenkins with a nod.

Rodgers tipped his hat to Lisa. Then, with obvious recognition in his eye, he looked Morgan up and down, said, "Evening, Williams," and briskly walked away.

"Hyper," said Lisa, once Rodgers was out of earshot.

Jenkins smiled. "Comes from being in the oil business all his life and living on the cusp of boom and bust. Seems he recognized your uncle, though."

Lisa suddenly realized that she hadn't introduced Morgan. "I'm sorry," she said. "This is my uncle, Morgan Williams."

Jenkins gave Morgan an awestruck stare. "Not the bull rider?" he said, stumbling over his words.

"In the flesh," said Morgan, reaching out and pumping Jenkins's hand.

"It's a pleasure. A real pleasure. I saw your famous ride on Piston back in '75. Hell of a ride. They still talk about it around here. I'm embarrassed that I didn't recognize you." He finally let go of Morgan's hand. "The dead man was a friend of yours, I take it."

"Taught me everything about bull ridin' I ever knew. Even better, Hambone got me interested in doin' something with my life instead of wastin' it away."

Lisa cleared her throat, a signal to Morgan that at twelve-thirty A.M. Jenkins probably didn't want to hear his life story. Morgan got the message, cutting straight to the quick. "What happened to him, Doc? I'd sure like to know." Morgan's voice resonated with sorrow.

Jenkins stroked his chin without answering. He wasn't about to go back on his word to Whitaker Rodgers, but the pained look on Morgan's face touched him deeply. "I'm guessing you can't be here tomorrow morning for the debriefing I just set up."

"No," said Morgan, getting Jenkins's drift.

"Well, then, since you can't, I'll share a few things with you right now. Your friend bled to death from a blow to the head with a branding iron, and whoever hit him happened to target the right spot."

Morgan eyed the ground, uncomfortable with hearing the details of how Hambone had been murdered. Disconsolate and puzzled, he had a question for Jenkins that had been eating at him ever since Hambone's body had been pulled from the horse trough. "Why was he wearing a wet suit, Doc? You figure that out?"

Jenkins shrugged. "Beats me. But I do know that he was killed right there on the spot, and that the wet suit he was wearing was meant for water a hell of a lot deeper and colder than any around the Stampede."

"Any sign of where he might have been in that outfit?" asked Morgan.

"No," said Jenkins, unwilling to speculate.

Morgan frowned. "Strange. Real strange."

"Why's that?"

" 'Cause Hambone hated water, and he couldn't swim."

"I see."

"Anything else you can tell us right now?"

"Nothing else that wouldn't compromise my job as coroner."

Morgan looked at Lisa, realizing that Jenkins was through talking, and glanced toward Lisa's Cherokee. "Dittier's probably close to having a conniption by now. Think we better call it a night and rescue him."

Lisa reached out and shook Jenkins's hand. "It was good seeing you again, Dr. Jenkins. And thanks for helping my uncle out."

"No problem. After all, I'm a rodeo fan. I do have one question, though. How did you know about the autopsy or that I'd be coming out this way after I finished?"

"Easy," said Lisa. "We followed the coroner's station wagon down here and hung around the rest of the day. More importantly, I recognized your truck."

Jenkins suspected that most of his former students would have also recognized the beat-up sport utility vehicle he had driven for the past fifteen years. "One last thing," he said, turning to go.

"Shoot," said Morgan, draping his arm over Lisa's shoulder and turning her toward her Cherokee.

"This is a murder case. Sooner or later everything's

going to end up on the doorstep of the law. If I were you, I'd watch my step."

"I sort of figured that," said Morgan. "No need to worry. Got me a friend I do odd jobs for who specializes in messes like this."

Chapter 5

There was one simple reason that Whitaker Rodgers had decided to diversify his business holdings—money. He was losing too much of it. As president of Pandeco Natural Resources and Exploration, better known as Pandeco Oil and Gas, one of the largest oil and natural gas companies in the Rocky Mountain West, he had decided ten months earlier to try and sidestep the vise-grip of a financial squeeze by branching out into another form of natural resource exploration.

For almost a decade Rodgers had watched helplessly as profits from a business that his father and grandfather had taken fifty years to build dwindled away at an alarming rate each year. To aggravate matters, he had piddled away a big chunk of the family fortune five years earlier when he had tried to develop a rapid express method for carrying gas between Colorado and eastern Kansas in converted oil pipeline. The experiment had failed because of labor disputes, pressure gradient seepage from pipe that hadn't been intended to transport gas, and serious O-ring problems, leaving Pandeco teetering on the brink of bankruptcy. His mother, Pandeco's chief executive officer, had used her own personal fortune to bail the company out, with a stern warning to Whitaker that if he expected to remain president he needed to think more and experiment less. Whitaker had recovered some of the losses when the demand for natural gas outstripped supply for a couple of years, but pipeline bottlenecks continued to constrain the flow of his product to major purchasers, and Pandeco was once again flirting with an unending flow of red ink.

Whitaker had always been a bit of an eccentric and something of a gambler. Although he had attended the Colorado School of Mines and dutifully studied geology in the family tradition, he had been a renegade for most of his life. While an older brother, now dead, had suffocated in the Pandeco bureaucracy, nose to the grindstone, until the day he died, Whitaker had spent every free moment since his teens hanging out at the family cattle ranch near Greeley, playing rodeo cowboy and cattle baron. Against his father's wishes, his mother, who made no bones about the fact that she had a favorite son, had encouraged his behavior. During his summers off from college Whitaker had split his time between trying to perfect his saddle bronc riding skills at the ranch and chasing after the pro rodeo circuit. He eventually became a skilled enough rider to enter Cheyenne Frontier

Days as a rookie bronc rider one year, but he lacked the toughness, athletic skill, and eye-hand coordination to ever become a pro. And although he had risen to chairman of the Greeley Stampede, and the official Stampede program described him as not only an oilman but a saddle-bronc rider in his youth, he felt deep down that he would always be just a chubby rich boy dabbling in a real man's sport.

When his father and brother both died in the space of two years, the corporate vacuum and his mother's urging had sucked him full throttle into the business and Whitaker had ended up running a corporation that he had always hated.

It was two A.M. when he stepped into the elevator of the downtown Denver high-rise that housed the corporate headquarters of Pandeco Oil and Gas. He punched the button for the twenty-second floor, stepped back a couple of paces, and leaned wearily against the back wall. The drive from Greeley had taken him just over an hour, and all the way to Denver his stomach had gurgled reflux upward until now his mouth was a sourball of acid. Hambone Dolbey's murder had him scared. Suddenly he realized that the nauseating piped-in music that usually blared from the ceiling of the elevator twenty-four hours a day was missing. He shook his head, hoping it wasn't a further bad-luck omen. For some reason he began to think about his failures. His express-pipeline dream had been a bust. His attempt at bronc riding had failed. His tenure as Stampede chairman had been highlighted by a murder. And to top things off, ten months earlier he had been gullible enough to believe the fairy-tale ramblings of a washed-up, down-on-his-

luck bull rider named Hambone Dolbey, who had come
to him with a get-rich-quick scheme with more holes
than a Florida land-deal scam.

The elevator jerked to a stop and a loud, irritating
ding announced that he had reached the twenty-second
floor. He watched the elevator doors open as if he expected them to immediately rebound shut and make his
problems disappear. When they didn't, he stepped out
into the dimly lit hallway, brushed back his hair with one
hand the way he always did when he was upset, and
headed for his office.

Whitaker stood in the center of his office feeling
more comfortable than he had in hours. After staring at
the bookshelves for a while, he turned and headed for
the bathroom tucked into the far corner of the opposite
wall. He flicked on a light and stared at his image in the
floor-to-ceiling mirror in front of him before walking
over to the sink, turning on the water, and splashing several soothing handfuls of cool water over his face.

Frustrated and jittery, he walked back into his office
and opened the blinds. The parade of lights from the
houses that now dotted the once unspoiled western
foothills reminded him of just how much Denver had
changed. He watched the flicker of the lights for a while
before dropping into an overstuffed chair in the corner of
the room and slipping out of his cowboy boots. Massag-
ing the balls of his feet, he tried to decide on the kind of
damage-control strategy he should muster now that
Hambone was dead. He ran a few scenarios through his
head before concluding that first he'd have to deal with
Hambone's girlfriend, Nadine Kemp. She'd have to
know that Hambone was dead, and he suspected that

sooner or later she would be on his doorstep demanding money. He slipped off his socks and nervously scratched his feet before pulling a half-empty bottle of bourbon out of a drawer in the end table next to him. He uncapped the bottle and took two generous swallows as his stomach gurgled in protest. He held the bottle in his hand for a while, gritting his teeth, deciding finally that like it or not, he needed to call Evelyn Coleman, Pandeco's chief of field operations, and ask her for advice.

He walked over to the phone on his desk and punched in Evelyn's number.

Evelyn answered, "Hello," in a husky, rest-broken voice.

"It's Whit."

Evelyn slid the digital clock on her nightstand around to face her. "It's two-thirty A.M., Whit. This better be good."

"Hambone Dolbey's dead."

There was ten seconds of cold silence on the line before Evelyn responded, "What a mess."

"What should I do with the agreement Dolbey and I drew up?"

"Burn it."

"You sure?"

"Yes."

"Okay," came Rodgers's reluctant response.

Evelyn jammed three pillows behind her and sat up in bed. "Anything else I should know?"

"No."

"Then we'll discuss things tomorrow."

"Ah—there is one thing."

"Tomorrow." She hung up before Whitaker could say anything else.

With the taste of vinegar flooding his mouth, Whitaker cradled the receiver, slowly got up from his desk, and walked over to his wall of books. He ran an index finger across several leather-bound first editions on the third shelf, stopping at a plain-looking brown volume titled *A Practical Guide to Oil Extraction from Shale*. He then teased a copy of *Rock and Gem* magazine from between the pages of the larger book and flipped through the magazine until he found a single sheet of Pandeco corporate letterhead. The sheet was filled with type, and his signature and Hambone Dolbey's were scrawled a half inch from the bottom of the page, nearly kissing. He stared at both signatures for a while before tearing the paper into tiny pieces and slipping the magazine back inside the book. Then, slowly, as if sleepwalking, he walked back to the bathroom, dumped the paper scraps into the toilet, flushed it, and watched the evidence of his stupidity swirl away.

Chapter 6

It was a few minutes before four A.M. when CJ pulled up in front of Cicero Vickers's bail bonding office and home of thirty-five years. Vickers's three-story building sat next to CJ's among a cluster of six turn-of-the-century Victorians known affectionately as painted ladies. The brightly painted buildings lined the west side of Delaware Street directly across from the Denver City Jail, forming Denver's notorious Bail Bondsman's Row. The row, as it was known, never descended into darkness. The wraparound porches of the once stately Victorian dwellings now flashed neon lights in every color of the rainbow; billboard come-ons with such slogans as OPEN 24 HOURS, BAIL BONDS ANYTIME, NEVER CLOSED. A ten-foot-tall cast-iron replica of the Statue of Liberty, complete with a flashing neon crown and eyes that glowed in the dark, had recently been added to the front yard belonging to Herman Currothers, the little bug-eyed weasel of a man who operated AAA Bonding Services three buildings down from CJ. Currothers, a New York transplant, claimed the statue reminded him of home.

CJ had worked on Bondsman's Row since his return home from Vietnam, when he went to work as a runner for his drunken uncle, hustling nickel-and-dime bonds that gave second-tier hoods another chance to walk the street. When his uncle died, CJ inherited a business and a building that had seen more bad times than good. CJ lived in a converted four-room apartment on the building's second floor. His business office occupied most of the first floor except for the massive back room where he stored the precious collectibles, memorabilia, and antiques he had amassed over the years. His collections of cat's-eye marbles, one-hundred-year-old inkwells, and first-issue baseball cards were a nostalgia collector's dream. But his assemblage of mint-condition antique porcelain license plates was, very simply, world-class.

CJ had started the license plate collection during his teenage years, when his uncle's drinking had reached its peak and he needed a hobby to take the place of family in his life. He hoped the collection would eventually include at least one first-issue plate from all fifty states. The pride of his collection changed from time to time, but the current prize was his 1915 Denver municipal tag, which had been fabricated using the long-abandoned process of overlaying porcelain onto iron. He often got his tips on the whereabouts of a primo license plate from a cigar-chomping, seventy-two-year-old curmudgeon

named Mario Satoni, who ran a secondhand furniture
store in the predominantly Italian section of north Denver. Satoni hadn't called him with news of a find in
months, which had CJ stewing, wondering if the old man
had decided to freeze him out. He had been wanting to
call Satoni for weeks, but the old man preferred to be the
one who made the calls. So CJ had put his collecting
passion on hold for most of the summer, hoping a license plate bonanza might materialize in the fall.

He took a long look at Cicero Vickers's building
and then his own before checking the badly nicked
glow-in-the-dark Seiko he had worn since Vietnam. The
drive home from Chokecherry Draw had taken almost
seven hours, and he couldn't recall the last time he had
been so happy to see the flashing neon tubes rimming his
porch. Road weary, he rubbed his eyes, glanced across
the street toward the jail, and then turned to the back seat
of his Jeep. "Wake up, my man, you're almost home."
He nudged Bobby Two-Shirts's bony left knee.

Bobby was seated in the back seat, legs spread-eagled.
Both wrists were handcuffed to U-bolts that CJ had
welded to the Jeep's roll bar, and his right foot was
shackled to a U-bolt anchored in the floor. Bobby
yawned. "I need to pee," he said in a raspy, urgent voice.

"Tough shit," said CJ, frowning and rubbing the
throbbing, swollen right ear Bobby had given him a few
hours earlier. In his haste to leave Chokecherry Draw
and avoid the semi, CJ had made the mistake of hand-
cuffing only Bobby Two-Shirts's left arm and right leg to
the U-bolts. He had then nursed the Jeep along a two-
mile stretch of bumpy horse trail that ran along the edge
of a cliff. During the bumpy roller-coaster ride down the

trail, CJ had nearly bitten through his tongue. When he finally reached the safety of U.S. Highway 57, the adrenaline rush that had propelled CJ mountain-goat style down the trail began to subside. He forgot that Bobby Two-Shirts was only partially locked down in the back seat, and he was feeling guilty about having to get so physical with the skinny bond skipper.

His feelings of compassion disappeared after Bobby, who had been begging him every five minutes to stop and let him pee, got his wish just west of the mineral springs health spa mountain community of Glenwood Springs. Thinking a skinny, slow-talking man who couldn't have weighed more than 160 pounds was no match for someone his size, CJ had stopped along the highway shoulder, unshackled Bobby's wrist, and said, "Do your business, and make it quick." He had freed Bobby's handcuffed left wrist from the U-bolt, and he was about to slip the loose end of the cuffs onto his own wrist when Bobby lunged at him, gave him a fierce head butt, and bit him in the right ear. CJ let out an agonized scream just as a semi rolled by. In the flash of the semi's lights he saw the glint of the blade of the penknife Bobby had pulled from his pants cuff heading toward his face. He cocked his arm in defense, and the blade plunged into the fleshy part of his palm. He grunted in pain as he sent an elbow flying into Bobby Two-Shirts's temple that dropped Bobby like a rock, leaving him groaning, stuporous, and floundering like a spent fish until they started up the seven percent grade toward the Eisenhower Tunnel. When Bobby finally came to, he found himself secured to every one of the Jeep's U-bolts, and he still needed to pee.

Now, parked safely in front of his house in Denver with his .38 pointed directly at Bobby's nose, CJ carefully unlocked the handcuffs anchoring Bobby's right arm to the roll bar and slapped the open cuff onto his own wrist, knowing better than to take any more chances with his bounty.

"Just don't pee in my Jeep," he said, reaching across Bobby to undo the other wrist. "I'd hate to have to drive around constantly smelling your scent."

"Won't be no drivin' where you're headed, colored boy. You'll find out soon enough."

"That so?" CJ unlocked Bobby's leg irons and motioned for him to get out of the Jeep. He couldn't help but wonder just how much of his bad talk Bobby Two-Shirts could actually back up. "Trouble is, Mr. Big, for right now we're both headed for the same place." CJ pointed toward Cicero Vickers's building. "After that you're headed over there." He smiled and nodded across the street toward the city jail. "Hit the sidewalk, firecracker man, and try holding your piss until you're inside."

People in need of Cicero Vickers's services usually called ahead, but CJ knew Cicero had accommodated four A.M. clients before. He leaned into Cicero's front door buzzer, listening to its unfriendly rasp until Cicero appeared at the door dressed in grease-stained chinos, a wrinkled Hawaiian shirt, and slippers that were a couple of sizes too large. He clutched a soiled handkerchief in one hand and looked as though he had been on a week-long binge rather than asleep. The whites of his eyes were bloodshot, and although it looked as if he had made a hasty attempt to brush his hair, the sides were matted down and the remaining tufts on top were standing on end. Cicero stood a little under six feet, and to the untrained eye he might have looked solid, but the pendulous flesh beneath his upper arms and the washboard rolls of skin looping beneath his chin announced to the more than casual onlooker that here was a man who hadn't lifted anything heavier than a bottle in years.

Cicero frowned and squinted into the dim porchlight, straining to bring CJ and Bobby Two-Shirts into focus. "I'll be damned," he said when he realized CJ had recovered his $15,000 worth of human flesh. He undid the two deadbolt locks on the screen door and swung the door back. "Where'd you find him?" he said, hastily ushering them in.

"Damn near in Utah."

"Give you a rough time?"

"Not until we were halfway home." CJ rubbed his swollen ear. "He tried to bite my ear off outside Glenwood Springs. Jabbed me in the hand with a penknife, too." CJ held out his wounded palm toward Cicero. "Other than that, things went okay."

"I've gotta piss," said Bobby, rocking from side to side, a look of pure agony on his face.

Ignoring him, Cicero squinted through his bifocals at CJ's injured ear. "You got a knot the size of a walnut on that ear. Ain't bleeding, but it's one ugly mess."

"Thanks for the good news," said CJ, examining the stab wound in his palm in good light for the first time. Although it looked superficial, it hurt like hell and when he pushed around the edges, ropy pink mucus bubbled up from the wound. He was about to massage his palm again when Bobby Two-Shirts yanked his shackled arm away, grasping at his crotch. "I need to pee!"

"Let this jackass pee before he floods the place." CJ looked toward Cicero, then reached into his pocket, pulled out a key, unlocked the handcuffs, and freed his prisoner.

"Down that hallway," said Cicero, motioning Bobby in the direction of a doorless bathroom at the end of the hall. His directions were given with the aid of the .25 caliber Raven he had pulled from his pants pocket. "And don't fuck with me," he hollered to Bobby, who was already halfway down the hallway. "As sleepy as I may look, I can still pop a cap in your ass if you do anything in there but piss."

After fumbling with his zipper and bouncing from toe to toe, Bobby Two-Shirts let out a stream of urine that lasted for the better part of two minutes. When he turned to head back through the open doorway he found Cicero there to greet him.

"Wash your goddamn hands, you filthy son of a bitch."

Bobby turned back to the sink and did as he was told. When he finished and began looking around for something to wipe his hands on, Cicero burst out laughing. "Towels are for law-abiding citizens, my friend. Try the front of your pants."

"Screw you, old man."

Cicero let out a defiant snort and waved Bobby back down the hallway. "Meet you in my office," he called out to CJ as he tracked Bobby Two-Shirts down the hall.

CJ stepped into Cicero's car barn of an office off the entryway just as Cicero flipped on the room's lights. Cicero nudged Bobby Two-Shirts inside, the nose of his

Raven a few inches away from the small of Bobby's back. The spartan room smelled like sour summer sausage and contained nothing but a couple of drab green army surplus metal desks that were bolted to the floor and four equally unattractive file cabinets. Except for a row of dime-store photographs of Pikes Peak and a pen-and-ink drawing of a six-point elk facing them, the walls were bare.

The pine floors creaked as Cicero moved across the room. He walked Bobby Two-Shirts slowly over to a straight-backed chair in front of one of the desks and pushed him down into it. Then he backed over to the other desk and leaned back against its edge, never letting the Raven's barrel stray from Bobby's chest. Leaning across the desk, he pulled out the middle drawer, retrieved a pair of handcuffs, and tossed the cuffs across the room to Bobby. "Slap these babies on and cuff yourself to the U-bolt in the desk." As soon as the handcuffs clicked shut, Cicero put his gun away.

CJ watched Cicero pocket the Raven and tried not to inhale too deeply. Although he had never seen a grill or even a hotplate in Cicero's front office, the room's offensive smell told him that somewhere deep in the bowels of the building Cicero must have had a place where he stuffed sausage casings with tainted meat.

Satisfied that Bobby was securely locked down, Cicero turned the 1950s-vintage rotary-dial phone on the desk toward him and dialed the Denver City Jail. "I need someone to come over to my place to pick up a prisoner; this is Cicero Vickers at Superior Bonding across the street," he said to the gruff-sounding sergeant who answered.

"Name of your prisoner?"

"Robert Deepstream. His friends call him Bobby Two-Shirts."

"Got a warrant?"

"Sure do."

"I'll patch you through to somebody who can help."

"Thanks," said Cicero, adjusting his butt on the desk's edge, preparing for what he knew would be a lengthy wait.

Although the entrance to the Denver City Jail is less than forty yards from Cicero's front door, it took the better part of an hour for someone to show up to take custody of Bobby Two-Shirts. For most of that time Bobby sat stoically in the chair where Cicero had planted him, staring toward the room's bay window and peering between the dusty slats of metal plantation-style venetian blinds out into the darkness. CJ and Cicero sat across from him, discussing what kind of team they thought the Broncos would have during the coming NFL season, trying to remain awake. The first light of sunrise had worked its way up to the second slat of the window blinds when Bobby Two-Shirts broke his silence. "You're a dead man, Vickers. You too, boy." He grinned and nodded as if it were mandatory that he reinforce his statement with the gesture.

"Name's Floyd," said CJ, ignoring Bobby's insult.

"Floyd, Lloyd, shit, it don't matter. My sister'll kill you both."

CJ had to admit that Bobby's continued references to the woman he now knew was Bobby's sister had him making a few mental notes. "Maybe your queen bee'll take pity on us. It's summer, and love is in the air."

"Funny. Won't be no joke, though, when you're begging for your life. You interrupted her business schedule, and she don't like that. You fucked with me. She likes that even less."

"I'll take my chances," said CJ, glancing over at Cicero for his reaction. Any other time, Cicero might have called someone to drop by, paid them $200, and watched them beat Bobby Two-Shirts senseless. But at the moment he was too tired to do much more than match Bobby's threats. "Listen, you fuckin' snaggletoothed beanpole. Your little war dance to the Western Slope cost me three thousand dollars." He glanced over at CJ. "You're lucky I put a man like Floyd on your ass and not one of the meat grinders I know who would've brought you back here in the trunk of their car beat to shit."

Bobby Two-Shirts mustered a defiant grin that blossomed into the Cheshire smile of someone with insider knowledge. "Dead meat, both of you," he said softly, before resting back in his chair and once again staring out the window.

The policeman who came to take Bobby Two-Shirts into custody was a young uniformed patrolman unfamiliar with prisoner transfer procedures. It took Cicero fifteen minutes to get him to understand that he needed a prisoner receipt to "get off his bond" and that he wasn't about to let Bobby Two-Shirts leave until he got one. The unschooled cop had to run back across the street to the jail and get an official transfer receipt book in order to comply with departmental rules and Cicero's request. That trip took another fifteen minutes and by the time he returned, Cicero had raised the venetian blinds in his office, something he did only a few times a year.

The sun streamed through the dirt-caked bay window, giving the room a freshness it hadn't had in months. The officer hastily completed the transfer papers, Cicero signed the document, and all four men made their way out onto the front porch as a cream-colored city street sweeper badly in need of a wash brushed its way past and moved slowly up Delaware Street toward downtown. The grumbling noise from the street sweeper's engine was the only sound on the strangely quiet Denver morning.

Prisoner receipt in hand, Cicero broke into a broad smile, satisfied that he had cut a potential $15,000 loss by eighty percent without having to risk life or limb. The cop, now fully schooled in prisoner transfer detail, nudged Bobby Two-Shirts down the front steps of the building and across the sidewalk. CJ and Cicero watched as the two men crossed Delaware Street and disappeared into the shadows of the jail.

"I'll have your three grand for you by noon," said Cicero. "Cash, check, any way you want."

"Cash'll do just fine," said CJ, rubbing his ear, trying to decide if it hurt more than his hand.

"Think that little weasel's really got a trigger woman backing him?"

"Hope not. I don't want my other ear to end up matching this one."

"You can never tell about Indians," said Cicero. "Their faces never tell you what's going on inside."

Realizing that Cicero was fully capable of substituting the word *niggers* for the word *Indians* if the situation had warranted it, CJ cut his eyes, but ignored the remark and started down the steps. "I'll be back for my money before noon."

"Fine," said Cicero, surprised at the agitated look on CJ's face as he headed across the grass toward home. He watched CJ a second longer, then, shrugging his shoulders, he turned and went back inside the house.

As the street sweeper disappeared in the distance, the first automobile of the morning cruised its way slowly down Delaware Street, a noisy old clunker of a Dodge with temporary tags taped to the back window. The car stopped directly in front of the jail. CJ could see that all of the car's occupants were women. He watched as one woman exited the car and headed toward the jail's entrance. She was large, round-faced, rumpled, and very obviously Indian. CJ stared at her until she disappeared, wondering whether he would have stopped and watched the woman with the same intensity if it hadn't been for Bobby Two-Shirts's stream of threats.

Chapter 7

CJ hadn't been asleep an hour when the noise of someone pounding on his back door jarred him out of the sweetest dream he'd had in months. In the dream he and the sweet wrinkle of femininity in his life, Mavis Sundee, were luxuriating in a hot tub in the Sangre de Cristo Mountains overlooking Santa Fe, New Mexico. Mavis had just wiggled up bare-breasted to his chest, and a sensual warm rush had started to circulate through his body when the pounding began.

Bolting up in the bed, he felt a sharp pain in his ear, and the dream floated away. The clock on the nightstand next to him read seven-forty A.M. Since his secretary, Julie Madrid, wouldn't report for work until eight-thirty, he knew she wasn't pounding at the door. The only way anyone could have reached the back entrance to his apartment would have been to scale a locked gate and fence and climb the back stairway. He normally used that route only in emergencies, if he was working in his garage, or if he was hosing down his mint-condition '57 Chevy Bel Air convertible. Reluctantly, he decided to leave the comfort of his bed. On the way to the back door he slipped into a pair of jogging sweats and grabbed the ball-peen hammer he kept by the bedroom door. He had taken two steps into the hall when a vise-grip of pain shot through his right ear. He reached up and felt a knot that seemed twice the size it had been when he went to bed.

Before retiring he had soaked his ear and his injured palm under a hot shower, coated them liberally with Neosporin, and popped a couple of Tylenols. Suddenly questioning whether Bobby Two-Shirts's bite might end up giving him some kind of infection, he muttered, "Fucking little thief," as he made his way through the kitchen and to the back door. A couple of steps from the door he called out, "Who is it?"

"Drop the hammer, CJ. I know you're probably carryin' it. No need, it's just me and Dittier."

CJ immediately recognized Morgan Williams's gravelly voice. Laying the hammer aside, he flipped back the deadbolt and opened the door. Dittier Atkins rushed in, holding a battered twenty-four-ounce 7-Eleven plastic coffee mug in his left hand, cradling a cantaloupe in the opposite arm, and swinging a quart of orange juice from two fingers. Morgan followed, carrying a similar mug and clutching a box of day-old doughnuts to his chest. CJ knew they had been to the Greeley

Stampede the previous day, and he suspected from the way they were each loaded down with a sugar-high breakfast that Morgan's niece, Lisa Darley, had given Morgan some mad money.

Dittier set his mug and orange juice down on a nearby countertop. Then, rolling the cantaloupe down his arm and into the palm of his hand, he let CJ know he needed a knife by quickly running his finger around the melon's skin. CJ could barely sign, but he had been around Dittier so long that when it came to simple things, they rarely miscommunicated.

Accustomed to Dittier reading his lips, CJ said, "Second drawer to your left, over by the wall." Dittier put the cantaloupe down and headed for the drawer.

Morgan set the doughnuts down on the antique pine table in the middle of the room and took a healthy swig of coffee. Because CJ was turned sideways, Morgan failed to see the angry-looking knot on his ear. "You must've been dead to the world. I bet you Dittier was bangin' on your door for close to five minutes. Shit, I was beginnin' to think Mavis slept over. But knowin' you, I figured you'd rather be enjoyin' those fancy digs of hers than your own, and since the Jeep was in the driveway and the Bel Air was in the garage, I said to Dittier, 'He's in there all right, keep on poundin'.'"

"I got the message," said CJ, taking a seat at the table.

As Dittier headed back for the table, steak knife in hand, he caught a glimpse of CJ's ear. He stopped and pointed the knife.

Morgan craned his head to see what Dittier found

so interesting. "Ugly," he said, frowning. "How'd you get that?"

"Long story, but I can tell you it wasn't from dancing at the ballet."

"Better soak it in camphor oil before it gets infected." Camphor oil was Morgan's standard cure for every human affliction. During Denver's often gruesome winters he splashed it on liberally to ward off colds, the flu, foot rot, and rheumatism. CJ knew better than to argue the pros and cons of folk medicine with a man who had been known to set his own fractured bones, sew up ten-inch-long skin lacerations with a needle and thread, and even extract teeth.

"I'll do that." CJ hoped his response would put a lid on any further recommendations from Morgan. He leaned back in his chair and turned his attention to Dittier, who had now cut the cantaloupe in half. A trail of cantaloupe seeds swimming in sticky juice oozed out as Dittier reached across the table, grabbed a linen place mat from a stack of four Mavis had given CJ for his forty-sixth birthday, and mopped up the mess. Sensing that a second place mat would soon become a blotter, CJ slid the other three mats out of harm's way. Then, turning to Morgan, he said, "What brings you two out so early?"

Morgan's face turned stern. "Business," he said authoritatively. CJ had encountered Morgan's mood swings before, but he knew something was irreparably wrong when he looked at Dittier and noticed a hint of fear in the aging rodeo clown's eyes.

"I ever mention Hambone Dolbey to you?" asked Morgan, his voice almost cracking.

"No."

"Well, if I didn't, I should've. Hambone's the one who taught me to ride a bull, and he helped me get a pro rodeo card when I was just a pissant teenager tryin' to prove I could be a man." Morgan shot a quick glance at Dittier. "Above all, he taught me about bein' loyal."

CJ knew a lot more about Morgan's life before he was a champion bull rider than Morgan realized, courtesy of Lisa. He knew Morgan had never fitted into the churchgoing, good-colored-folks, pull-yourself-up-by-your-bootstraps world he had grown up in. He knew Morgan had parted ways with his family when he was sixteen and lost himself in a bottle for the next three years. He had always suspected that somewhere along the line someone had given Morgan a leg up, but this was the first time he had heard of Hambone Dolbey.

Morgan inched up straight in his chair, announcing proudly, "Hambone was a contemporary of Myrtis Dhightman, the first black cowboy to ever qualify for the national rodeo finals." Then, in a voice full of sorrow, he added, "Yesterday up at the Greeley Stampede somebody killed him." Morgan lowered his head to hide his emotion. It was a side of the stocky, hard-as-nails bull rider CJ had never seen.

"You sure it was murder?"

Morgan looped his thumbs over his belt and slid them up against the edges of his ever-present Greeley Stampede championship belt buckle. Shoving the buckle out at CJ, he said, "As sure as I am that somebody'd have to kill me to get this belt from around my waist. As sure as I heard the Weld County coroner say so himself."

Dittier, who had been busy reading lips and quarter-sectioning the cantaloupe, nodded in support.

"How do I fit in?" asked CJ, recalling that Morgan had started the conversation by saying he and Dittier were there on business.

Morgan hesitated before responding. "Me and Dittier agreed on this," he said, looking at Dittier for support before blurting out, "We want you to find out who killed Hambone."

"Come on, Morgan, you know I leave that kind of stuff to the cops."

CJ inched his chair up to the table. Before Morgan could answer, Dittier smiled and slid a section of cantaloupe toward CJ as if he expected the offering to help convince CJ to take the job.

"Come off it, CJ. We both know better." A couple of winters earlier Morgan and Dittier had helped CJ track down another killer, and in the process they had ended up saving CJ's life. Morgan wasn't about to accept a *no* response to his request so quickly. He pulled a knife out of his pocket and cut off a bite-sized square of cantaloupe, which he chewed only once before washing it down with a long swig of coffee. "Besides, it ain't like Dittier and I won't be there to help you out."

CJ ran his tongue around the back of his front teeth, a lingering habit that always seemed to surface when he was caught short for an answer. Searching for a way to couch his response, he suddenly remembered one of his drunken uncle's sayings: *You ain't never even in this world, long as you owe a friend.* It was all he could do to keep from saying *damn* out loud.

In a few hours, he'd be $3,000 richer and he had a trip to Santa Fe with Mavis planned for the first of the week. He also had a junk-shop dealer in Albuquerque

primed to hook him up with a couple of mint-condition
antique license plates at a price he could afford, and he
was even planning to pull his fly-fishing gear out of
mothballs and sneak off on a side trip to the Rio Grande.
In a nutshell, he had cash, his lady, free time, and a plan.
And now he had two sad-sack ex-cowboy street bums
who had once saved his life begging him to do them a
favor. To complicate things, Julie Madrid, his longtime
secretary, had just graduated from the University of Denver's law school after six years of going to night classes.
She was busy trying to get the next phase of her life in
order and studying for the bar, and he didn't have a replacement. To net it all out, things were suddenly in flux.

He watched Morgan cut off another square of cantaloupe and pop it into his mouth, then pull a dingy
handkerchief from his pocket and begin to wipe up after
Dittier. Morgan made one last swipe of the tabletop before he looked up at CJ pleadingly. All that goes around
comes around, thought CJ. "Where the hell would I start
looking for your friend's killer?" he said, trying his best
to sound noncommittal.

"Back at the Stampede, where else?" Morgan
tossed two cantaloupe rinds into the trash can under-
neath the table, shaking his head as he did to protest the
fact that Dittier had begun licking his sticky fingers one
by one. "Lighten up, Dittier. The Safeway's got more
cantaloupes."

Dittier smiled sheepishly and sat back in his chair.

"Just so you don't think we're freeloadin', Dittier
and me brought you a down payment on the job," said
Morgan, turning his attention back to CJ. He pulled a
wad of crumpled tissue paper from his pants pocket and

laid it on the table. When he realized that Dittier hadn't done the same, he shot his friend an icy stare, and Dittier reluctantly pulled a second wad of paper from his pocket and set it on the table. CJ couldn't help but notice Dittier's obvious reticence. "Open 'em up," said Morgan.

CJ began unwrapping Dittier's wad first, knowing the skinny rodeo clown's feelings would have been hurt if he were second. He stripped back the layers of tissue until he uncovered a gleaming silver belt buckle that was still as pristine as the day Dittier had received it twenty years earlier as top all-around PRCA rodeo clown of the year at the Calgary Stampede. A rodeo clown tugging at his protective barrel was set in high relief on the buckle's face. The words *PRCA Rodeo Clown of the Year* rimmed the bottom margin.

"Have a look at mine," said Morgan, ignoring the fact that Dittier immediately retrieved his buckle and stuck it back in his pocket. CJ laid back the tissue paper until he found an even more elaborate silver buckle that was nearly twice as large as Dittier's. Engraved in the upper right corner was a rider on a bull, one arm straining at the bull's rope, the other splayed high above his head. A cluster of three rubies dotted each of the buckle's other corners, and a banner that read *Champion Bull Rider, 85th Annual Cheyenne Frontier Days, The Daddy of 'Em All*, dominated most of the rest of the buckle. The name *Morgan Williams* had been scripted beneath the banner. "They're valuable pieces," said Morgan, brimming with pride. "And they're pretty much all me an' Dittier got that's worth a damn. Count 'em up as a down payment for findin' out who killed Hambone."

CJ swallowed hard. He knew what the buckles meant to Morgan and Dittier, but as a collector of Western memorabilia he also knew that even though the buckles were mint and designed in the rare pre-'80s style of the Professional Rodeo Cowboy Association, their street value was no more than one hundred dollars. CJ had heard Morgan's tale of how he had won the Cheyenne Frontier Days buckle after completing a record-setting ride on a bull named Twister, a stubborn Brahma that no rider had ever been able to stay on for a full eight seconds. He knew the story of how Morgan's hand had gotten hung up in the bull rope after his dismount, and he had heard more than once from Morgan how Dittier had teased the two-thousand-pound bull into charging his barrel instead of stomping in Morgan's head just as Morgan freed his hand. Dittier had ended up with a broken collarbone and Morgan had walked away with a championship buckle and his life. But their glory days were behind them, and CJ knew that the two shiny belt buckles they had placed in front of him represented the very essence of Morgan's and Dittier's lives. He eased the buckle back across the table. "These babies are worth a lot more than my services. Why don't you tuck them back away for safekeeping."

Still unsure of whether he had convinced CJ to investigate Hambone Dolbey's murder, Morgan tried one final maneuver. "Take your fee out of what Lisa sends you for me every month."

CJ wondered how Morgan knew about Lisa's catastrophic account. The money she sent was intended to be used in case either Morgan or Dittier had a major medical emergency. The last time CJ had checked the account, it held $3,200, barely enough to cover a serious emergency room visit. "Can't. The money's locked up in a trust," he said, bending the truth.

"Then we'll figure somethin' else," said Morgan.

Realizing that Morgan wasn't going to take no for an answer, CJ sat back in his chair and thought for a moment before responding. "You know that firewood yard you keep an eye on for that good-old-boy friend of yours from Texas?"

"Yeah," Morgan said, unsure of where CJ was headed. During the past two years Morgan and Dittier had moved up from sleeping in the back doorways of downtown high-rises to living in an abandoned flat-topped building in the Platte River Valley. A fast-talking Texan Morgan and Dittier knew from their days on the rodeo circuit had turned the two acres surrounding the building into a self-service firewood business. In exchange for their keeping an eye on the place, collecting money, and helping people load their pickups with cherry wood, piñon, and pine, the Texan let Morgan and Dittier call the building home.

"How about asking the Texan to let you have a cord of his best cherry wood? That'll be payment enough. Mavis likes the smell of cherry wood. Even better, she loves the fact that it overpowers the aroma of my cheroots."

"Deal," said Morgan, looking toward Dittier for his okay.

When Dittier didn't respond with a nod, Morgan said, "Dittier."

Eyes to the floor, the skinny rodeo clown reluctantly nodded his approval.

It was obvious that Dittier didn't have the same enthusiasm as Morgan for finding Hambone Dolbey's killer. And since the two rarely disagreed, CJ had the uneasy feeling that he was missing something very important about the case he was about to jump into headfirst. Unwilling to fan any underlying friction between two best friends, he decided to push past the apparent difference of opinion and save it for discussion later.

"Now, when do we start looking for whoever killed Hambone?" asked Morgan.

"As soon as I collect three grand someone owes me and run by and tell Mavis that our vacation plans are on the back burner for a while. She'll love that," said CJ, shaking his head and thinking of how he was going to deliver the bad news.

"She'll understand," said Morgan.

"If she doesn't, I'll let you explain."

Dittier broke into a wheezy half snicker that Morgan silenced with a raised-eyebrow stare. Sensing an undercurrent of tension once again, CJ said, "How'd your friend Hambone die?"

"Bled to death from gettin' clubbed in the head with a brandin' iron."

"Serious." CJ fished around in an old cookie tin on the tabletop and pulled out a cheroot.

"Yeah. But that ain't the strange part. What's strange is, they found him floatin' face up in a horse trough, and decked out in one of them diver's wet suits. Hell of a thing too, because Hambone had a death fear of water."

"Any reason why he'd be outfitted like that?"

Morgan scratched his head. "None I can figure, unless . . ." Morgan's eyes widened.

"Unless what?"

"Unless wearin' that wet suit was somehow connected to him playin' games with a lady friend he'd been livin' with. From what Hambone told me, she was the high-rollin' type. You know, the kind that likes flashin' money. I think he said she was from Texas."

"You got a name?"

Morgan's forehead muscles knotted up as he tried to recall the name. "Nadine. That's it," he said finally. "And she lives in Greeley. Got her address back home."

"Then Greeley's where we'll start. The Stampede grounds first, and this Nadine woman after that."

"Sorry about screwin' up your vacation with Mavis," said Morgan apologetically.

CJ shrugged. "We'll get around to it later. For right now, why don't you and Dittier think about who else might've wanted to kill Hambone? Meet me back here at one and we'll take the Bel Air to Greeley." CJ looked in Dittier's direction, wondering if he might be reluctant to go. "By the way, Dittier, how's Geronimo?"

Geronimo was the two-hundred-pound Red River hog that Dittier had won a year and a half earlier in a New Year's Eve raffle. The housebroken pig was Dittier's pride and joy, and CJ swore he had an IQ higher than some of the street thugs for whom he posted bail. Mentioning his name always got a proud-owner kind of rise out of Dittier. When Dittier mouthed only a reluctant *okay*, CJ knew the Hambone Dolbey case would bring problems. In an obvious attempt to cover the rift, Morgan said, "Geronimo's spendin' the summer at Lisa's. Pig's in hog heaven."

CJ smiled at his two old friends, but it was a restrained, cautious smile, tempered in part because he knew he was starting after a murderer who had enough explosive violence to have smashed a man's skull.

Chapter 8

Mavis Sundee had spent the last twelve months rebuilding the Five Points community soul food restaurant it had taken her father a lifetime to build. A woman with a bomb and a vendetta against one of CJ's clients had blown most of Mae's Louisiana Kitchen into Welton Street. Since then, Mavis had spent so much time sparring with architects, trade unions, building inspectors, and contractors that she could spout half of Denver's building codes by memory.

Mae's had reopened on Memorial Day weekend to a flurry of *Rocky Mountain News* and *Denver Post* articles that reiterated at length the details of the restaurant's destruction the previous year while spending less than four lines each describing the reopening festivities.

Willis Sundee, Mavis's seventy-eight-year-old father, had demanded that the rebuilding be as faithful as
possible to Mae's original design. So except for building
code mandates that required handicapped-accessible rest
rooms and wheelchair-negotiable hallways, the new
Mae's had returned as a clone; an understated, plain
brown wrapper of a place squeezed between the Rossonian Club and Prillerman's Trophy and Badge.

In true Louisiana tradition, the restaurant was still
nothing more than a long, narrow box, reminiscent of a
New Orleans shotgun house. The entryway was tunnel-
like and narrow, with barely enough room for three people to stand. Mavis once again greeted people at the
mahogany pulpit that had belonged to her circuit-riding
preacher grandfather and had long ago been modified for
more pedestrian use. The pulpit had miraculously es-
caped being blown to bits in the bombing, and half of
the neighborhood customers claimed that the sparing of
the pulpit was a sign from God to rebuild.

Twenty tables covered with checkerboard wax
cloths hugged the restaurant's walls. Most tables seated
only two people, but a few jutted out to accommodate as
many as six, so the center aisle undulated in and out, increasing and decreasing in size. The barely damaged
modern kitchen had survived the blast, requiring only
minor repairs, and after a year of restoration the restaurant's only concession to extravagance remained its Colorado marble floors and ceilings of ornate tin.

The sixty-year-old restaurant sat squarely in the
middle of Denver's Five Points community, which in
terms of history, place, attitude, and race remained the
only truly predominantly black neighborhood in the city.

Five Points was in fact only a landmark, the intersection of 27th Avenue, Welton and Washington Streets, and 26th Avenue. A brisk twelve-minute walk from Denver's bustling high-rises downtown, Five Points had been the core of Denver's black community since early in the twentieth century. In addition to its homes, churches, shops, and schools, Five Points had one historically famous nightclub, the Rossonian. During the 1930s, '40s, and '50s, the Rossonian was to Denver what the Cotton Club was to Harlem. Since the 1950s the club had fallen into decline and was now a boarded-up relic of the past. But Mae's, its next-door neighbor, had endured as a restaurant and neighborhood gathering place since 1937.

After the restaurant was destroyed, Mavis had had to hire Morgan Williams and Dittier Atkins as security guards for a month in order to keep vandals from stealing what remained of the building's copper pipes and antique ceiling tiles. She did hand-to-hand combat with her insurance company to get it to cover all the damages. And she had been able to convince only two of the six employees who had worked at Mae's for years to return to their jobs. The ordeal had taken its physical and psychological toll on her, and it showed. Since Mae's had reopened she had been told more than once that she was acting jittery. In the past week she had taken the comments to heart and convinced CJ, the only man she had ever seriously let into her life, that they both needed a vacation.

CJ arrived at Mae's a few minutes after the breakfast rush. Mavis greeted him at the pulpit, somber-faced, looking as though she had just totaled an uninsured car. She was anything but her animated self, and her usual old-fashioned, down-to-earth kind of friendliness was absent. Her naturally curly, coal-black hair was uncharacteristically out of place, and her flawless deep, rich, cocoa-brown skin was as washed out as CJ had ever seen it. A large gravy stain just beneath the pocket of her blouse accentuated the fact that Mavis was out of sync.

CJ removed his straw Stetson, slipped it on Mavis's head, and leaning across the pulpit, lifted her chin and planted a quick kiss on her lips. Normally he would have gotten a more lingering kiss in return. But this time, Mavis just continued checking the addition on the ticket she had been working on when he walked in. "After working here for ten years, you'd think Thelma would at least know the price of a scrambled egg special with biscuits and grits." Mavis scratched out the $3.95 on the ticket, inserting $4.95 in its place, recomputed the tax, and jotted the new total across the bottom of the ticket.

CJ took back his Stetson and cleared his throat. "Edgy, aren't we?"

Mavis frowned, but even in her perturbed state she remained a strikingly attractive woman. There was hardly a wrinkle on her face, and she looked much younger than forty-one. When she finally turned her full attention to CJ, the first thing she noticed was the purple knot on his ear. She knew that CJ's work sometimes involved violence, but she was never prepared when it came to seeing him hurt.

"How'd you get that?" she said, staring at his ear, restraining herself from reaching out and caressing the wound.

"Tell you later."

"Another bounty-hunting tale? Hope it's good."

Realizing that he needed to change the subject or get bogged down in another argument over how he earned his living, CJ turned the conversation back to the errant ticket. "Guess I'm gonna have to teach Thelma how to count." Then he walked around behind the pulpit and pulled Mavis toward him with a reassuring hug. Mavis resisted briefly before slipping into the familiar curve of CJ's arm. "Things are rough, CJ, or haven't you noticed we've got competition? There's a Wendy's down the street that wasn't there a year ago, and a Pizza Hut on the way. Every day it seems like another downtown business is creeping in. The next thing you know, Five Points will be nothing more than fast-food joints, computer stores, and a new haven of condos for Generation X."

CJ knew that Mavis's response was an overreaction to the stress of watching the restaurant business, which her family had worked so hard to build and sustain, struggle for survival. He also knew that unfortunately Five Points *was* changing. The cohesive black inner-city island that he and Mavis had grown up in and called home all their lives was gasping for life. The struggle reminded him of a story he had been forced to read in high school for a book report. It was a simple tale set in the West, and it turned out to be the catalyst that moved his reading interest beyond the world of comic books, car magazines, and *Jet*. He had never understood why the story had been such a spark other than the fact that perhaps he was tired of being forced to read about white people in the East, and here at least was a tale of white people in the West. He always had difficulty remembering the author's name, but the message of "A Bride

Comes to Yellow Sky" had been abundantly clear to him even at fifteen: nothing stands in the way of progress.

Mae's Louisiana Kitchen had at least one thing going for it that held the real estate speculators and fast-food operators at bay: a unique market niche. The restaurant's spicy, mouth-watering soul food and Louisiana Creole cooking couldn't be matched any-where else in the state. There was little doubt that Mae's would survive, but the survival of Five Points, at least as CJ and Mavis had always known it, was a different matter.

CJ dropped his arm from around Mavis and read-justed his Stetson just as a burly black man in coveralls brushed by the pulpit. A four-by-four-inch patch on the bib of the man's overalls read *Morton's Plumbing & Heating.* "Servin' catfish yet?" he said to Mavis, ac-knowledging CJ with a nod.

Mavis checked her watch. "In about twenty min-utes."

"Guess I'll nurse me some coffee till then."

Mavis smiled and cast CJ one of her patented be-back-in-a-second glances as she walked from behind the pulpit and ushered the man inside the restaurant.

CJ fumbled around in the pocket of his worn calico vest for a cheroot until he remembered the promise he had made to Mavis at the Memorial Day reopening to work on giving up smoking. Mavis returned just in time to catch the look of frustration on his face. She knew the look well. "Try this instead." Reaching over the pulpit she pulled an hour-glass-shaped toothpick holder from a hidden shelf and offered CJ his choice of brightly col-ored substitutes.

CJ picked out a yellow toothpick and slipped it into his mouth with a frown.

Mavis smiled at her small victory. "Why don't you go on inside? I'll be in in a minute."

CJ had taken a couple of steps toward the restaurant's main room when he felt a hand on his shoulder and looked back to find his best friend, Roosevelt Weaks, smiling at him.

A large, boxy-looking black man who stood an even six feet four, Rosie had an enormous head, virtually no neck, and broad, bulky shoulders squared off like football pads. Unlike CJ, he was even-tempered and slow to anger. His size intimidated most people who didn't know him, and he had been known to freeze people in their tracks if for some reason they provoked one of his legendary ice-dagger stares. Rosie, as he was known in Five Points, had owned Rosie's Garage and Car Emporium, a 1950s-style gas station and auto repair shop at the corner of 26th and Welton, for close to twenty-five years.

"Damn, CJ, that's one hell of a bee sting you got on your ear. Queen bee got you, I take it."

CJ reached for his ear self-consciously as they continued into the main dining room. "It's a bite, not a sting, courtesy of a beanpole-looking little bond skipper named Bobby Two-Shirts."

Rosie, who loved hearing CJ's bounty-hunting war stories, rubbed his hands together, anticipating a spellbinder. "Sing your song, my man. And don't leave nothin' out."

Reaching the table they almost always sat at, they pulled out chairs and sat down. Rosie had finished off

four scrambled eggs, close to half a slab of bacon, and
two orders of home fries by the time CJ finished his
Bobby Two-Shirts tale. Just as CJ had begun his story,
Monroe Garrett, Rosie's chief mechanic, had joined
them. Monroe had worked his way through a stack of
buckwheat pancakes, and he was eyeing his empty plate
as if he expected another stack to miraculously appear,
while CJ nursed a third cup of coffee and eyed the bill
Thelma had just laid down in front of him.

"Sounds to me like your skinny firecracker man's
sister don't like the fact that you brought her brother
back to jail." Monroe let out a rumbling, satisfied belch.
"I'd watch my testicles if I was you, CJ." He eased his
chair away from the table and loosened his belt. Then,
slipping a toothpick out of his shirt pocket, he began
sucking on it.

"Appreciate the advice," said CJ, who had been
waiting to ask Monroe a question ever since his arrival.
"By the way, Monroe. Didn't you keep Morgan Williams
and Dittier Atkins's vehicles running during their rodeo
days?" He tried his best to make the statement sound
like an accolade rather than a question.

Monroe had been a successful back-alley mechanic
when he was younger, but he had no business sense, and
paying taxes always seemed to slip his mind. Ten years
earlier Uncle Sam had helped him make the transition
from small businessman to employee when the IRS had
demanded that he pay six years of back taxes or face ten
years in jail. Somehow Monroe found the money, and
since that time he had been accepting a monthly tax-
encumbered paycheck as an employee of Rosie's
Garage. Monroe removed his toothpick from his mouth

and sucked a stream of air in through the gap in his teeth. "Yeah, I kept Morgan and Dittier rollin' back then. Maintained their drop-top deuce and a quarter, one of them long-ass extended-cab one-ton duallies, a piece-of-shit ATV, and a couple of fancy Steidman horse trailers they had."

"Did you get to know any of the rodeo people they hung around with?"

Monroe smiled at the question. He prided himself on knowing everyone in Five Points business. "Sure did, especially the ladies. And I'll tell you one thing, when it comes to women that Dittier's not as deaf and dumb as he makes out. Brother's got a hose on him that—"

"Save it for the tabloids, Monroe. I'm looking for information about a bull rider named Hambone Dolbey. Name ring a bell?"

Monroe snatched his toothpick out of his mouth. "Now, ain't that a blast from the past. Damn sure does. Hambone's the one that taught Morgan to ride them bulls. Real fastidious SOB. Sort of pranced when he walked, like a fancy show horse. I think he was one of the first brothers on the planet to ever win one of them pro rodeo belt buckles. Yeah, I knew him all right. Ain't heard from him in years. What's he up to now?"

"Not much these days. Somebody killed him."

"Damn," said Rosie, who hated violence and who until then had been enjoying a final honey-drenched biscuit and only halfheartedly listening to the conversation. The news about Hambone Dolbey didn't seem to faze Monroe. The look on his face was one of acceptance rather than surprise. Noting Monroe's response, CJ said, "Know anybody who might have wanted to hammer Dolbey?"

Monroe leaned back in his chair and thought for a moment. "Hell, I ain't thought about the man in years. I only knew him—how do the white folks say it—peripherally. But I can tell you this. Back when he was rodeoin' he pissed off a shitpot of them redneck cowboys. Struttin' around all the time like he was John Wayne and humpin' the snot out of them tight-jeaned groupie white girls that was always hangin' around. Ask Morgan; better still, try Dittier. He'll know what I mean. Like I was tryin' to say earlier, Dittier did his own fair share of humpin'."

It was hard to picture Dittier as a ladies' man, and it showed on CJ's face.

"Don't look so surprised, CJ. When it comes to women, defenseless pups like Dittier have a special kind of luck," said Rosie, who had been drinking in the conversation in silence.

"So I've been told," said CJ, responding to Rosie's observation by pulling his wallet out of his back pocket and teasing out a twenty. He examined the $17.36 tab and then laid the twenty down. "My treat," he said, looking directly at Monroe, hoping that by springing for breakfast he was leaving the door open to ask Monroe a few more questions about Hambone Dolbey later.

Rosie patted his stomach. "Hell, if I'd known you were buying, I would've ordered more biscuits. But since I didn't, here's some advice for treating that ear of yours. Soak the sucker in Crisco every night. It'll heal up before the week's out, I guarantee it."

"Think I'll pass," said CJ, amazed at how quickly all his friends were willing to give out medical advice.

"Then suffer the consequences," said Rosie.

"You got any advice?" asked CJ, looking at Monroe.

Monroe eyed CJ's twenty and grunted, "No," as he moved to get up from the table.

Rosie followed, stretching up from the table to his full intimidating height. "Catch you later. Some folks have to earn an honest day's work," he said with a smile.

They walked away quickly, leaving CJ staring into his coffee and wondering whether there was something about Hambone Dolbey and his interactions with women that had gotten him killed and had Dittier Atkins spooked. He was deep in thought, still staring into his coffee, when Mavis walked up to the table and pulled out a chair. She rubbed her left calf purposefully against his and winked as she sat down and scooted her chair up to the table. "When did you start reading coffee grounds?" she said, noting the intensity of CJ's stare.

CJ didn't respond until Mavis stopped rubbing her leg against his. "Just thinking about a job," he said finally.

Mavis fidgeted uncomfortably in her chair, knowing that in CJ's world a job could mean anything from bonding a drunken teenager out of jail to hand-to-hand combat. She stared at the soiled tablecloth and brushed a cluster of biscuit crumbs away from her. A year earlier, in order to reduce the tension that always surfaced between them when CJ took on what he liked to call a job, they had developed a method for gauging the assignment's risk by giving the job a risk factor number of two through ten. A two usually meant the job probably involved no more than a simple bond posting, arraignment, or maybe an appearance in court; a ten meant that CJ would be putting his life at risk. The problem with the system was that CJ never told Mavis about the tens, and if she somehow found out on her own it usually sent their relationship into a temporary tailspin. So there was a tendency for them both to label everything a two. "Hope it's no more than a two," said Mavis, trying her best not to sound judgmental.

"It's something for Morgan and Dittier. A friend of theirs was murdered yesterday up in Greeley."

"Can't the police handle it?" said Mavis, noting that CJ hadn't responded with a number and already thinking ten.

"I'm just giving Morgan and Dittier a hand. I owe them that."

"What about our trip?"

CJ fidgeted uneasily in his chair. "We'll have to put it off until I'm done."

Mavis's face went expressionless. The problems she was having with the restaurant already had her stomach in knots. Now their Santa Fe vacation was about to be scrapped. She wanted to lash out at CJ, but she knew that if she did, he would roll himself up into a protective ball like some wounded animal or turn the conversation into a self-defensive rationalization about why a college-educated woman and someone like him couldn't maintain a relationship. So she reluctantly decided to back off. "Guess the vacation can wait," she said. "Now how about telling me what happened to your ear," she added, wondering why she always had to be the one to acquiesce.

CJ reached over and squeezed her hand, realizing how hard it was for her to accept his world. "A little runt of a bond skipper tried to bite off more than he could chew."

Chapter 9

When he got back to his office, Julie Madrid, CJ's petite, curvaceous, green-eyed, thirty-one-year-old Puerto Rican secretary, was standing in the middle of her converted entry alcove of an office talking to a large black woman he had never seen before. The woman was wearing two-inch-diameter copper earring hoops, a sea-mist-green rayon blouse that glimmered as if it had been ironed a thousand times, and a knee-length skirt that was tugging at the seams. As she towered over Julie, her six-foot height accentuated by two-inch platform heels, CJ had the sudden sinking feeling that the woman's presence had something to do with Julie leaving.

In the eight and a half years that she had worked for CJ, Julie had succeeded in transforming his previously disorganized mess of an operation into an efficiently running business. She had turned CJ's Dark Ages filing system, which before her arrival had consisted of stuffing each client's paperwork into a folder and wrapping it with a rubber band, into an index-based chronological system that actually worked. She had also computerized the office, softened his often hostile interactions with the Denver police, and brought him business from Denver's Hispanic community. When CJ had once asked her how a New Jersey transplant had invested herself so quickly in Denver's Chicano community, she had answered, "It's my *West Side Story* charm," and meant every word of it.

For the past year CJ had been dreading the day Julie would finish law school. They had discussed the possibility of her staying on, but Julie had a nine-year-old asthmatic son, and she wanted him to have the chance to become more than, as she put it, just another Jersey City wharf rat. The law degree for which she had struggled so hard would now afford her the chance to make sure he did.

When the woman with Julie stopped talking long enough to smile at CJ, he recognized the smile immediately. He had seen it hundreds of times before Julie entered his life. It was the insecure half-smile of an office temporary.

"Come on in." Julie motioned for CJ to join them in the cramped alcove. "I want you to meet Flora Jean Benson. She's going to temp for a while."

CJ almost said, "I knew it," but extended his arm to shake hands with Flora Jean instead.

"What's happenin', brother?" Flora Jean's gravelly torch-singer voice reminded CJ of Ma Rainey's. Her right hand shot out to meet his and CJ noticed that her arm was encircled wrist to elbow with intricately designed, brightly colored African bracelets. Flora Jean pumped his hand a couple of times before he looked at Julie with a pleading expression that said, *You can't leave me stranded like this!*

"What's happening yourself?" he said finally.

"Not much now, child," said Flora Jean. "But I'm expectin' better. Especially since I hear you track down all kinds of bad people and stuff. When the agency called this morning I said to myself, 'Flora Jean, you got a chance to go to work for a man who wants to make the world better, take it.'"

It was all CJ could do to keep from shaking his head and saying, *Why me?*

Flora Jean gazed around the alcove, eyeing the pleasant, tastefully decorated, but confining space. "Cramped in here, ain't it, child?" she said, looking at Julie.

Trying to put a positive spin on things, Julie responded, "Everything you'll need is right here at your fingertips."

"Space don't matter anyway. Long as I got a place for my box. Can't work without my music." She surveyed the room again. "Top of that file cabinet over there'll do just fine. You got a plug nearby, don't you?"

CJ ran his tongue around his teeth and looked at Julie, trying to hide his discontent. "Why don't you run through a few procedural things with Ms. Benson? When you're finished, step into my office." He was proud of the fact that he didn't add, *And then maybe you can explain what the hell's going on!* "Nice meeting you," he said to Flora Jean before heading toward his office.

"Pleasure," said Flora Jean, who then said to Julie,

"See you got yourself one of those IBM setups. Don't know much about 'em. Prefer Macs myself."

CJ cringed as he pulled the door tightly shut behind him.

Ten minutes later CJ was still seated in his office beneath his portrait gallery of the more than ninety bond skippers he had brought to justice. Moments earlier the nicotine monkey had grabbed him, and he had broken down and lit up a cheroot. The pungent, semisweet smell of cigar smoke filled the room. He ran his hands up and down the thighs of the new pair of slightly too large Wrangler jeans he was wearing, thinking that once they were washed he'd have a near perfect fit. Trying his best to relax, he slipped both feet up on the edge of his desk. A small clump of dirt broke loose from the heel of one of his boots and he watched it fall, thinking that the half-dollar-sized mound of dirt on the floor represented a kind of earthly permanence that would be around long after Julie was gone, Bobby Two-Shirts was doing two to five, and Hambone Dolbey's killer was rotting in jail.

He tried to gauge how upset Mavis really was about him canceling their New Mexico trip and decided that although the disappointment she had displayed was no more than a two, deep down the postponement had hurt like a ten. He didn't know how he could continue to keep an educated woman like Mavis in his corner. It seemed as though all of a sudden the ivory towers of higher education were about to swallow him. Law degree in hand, Julie was leaving for a better life. One of his oldest friends, Dr. Henry Bales, a Vietnam shipmate, had become chief of pathology at the University of Colorado Medical School, and with the new job pressures he barely had time for CJ. And of course there was Mavis. CJ had the haunted feeling that if Mae's did somehow fail, Mavis might end up, MBA and all, in some downtown corporate tower, leaving him behind. He had pondered the question of what life would be like without Mavis many times, and no matter the time, place, or circumstances, the answer was always the same: not much.

As he sat in the glow of the morning sunshine streaming through the bay window in his office, blowing smoke rings and thinking about Mavis, he couldn't help but wonder if his decision to pay back a debt to two old friends and find out who had killed Hambone Dolbey hadn't been a mistake.

Julie interrupted CJ's examination of his guilty conscience with a knock on his door.

"Come in."

Julie rushed in, looking exasperated. "Houston, I think we have a problem."

"Ms. Benson?"

"In the flesh."

"She quit already?" asked CJ, hoping Julie's response would be yes.

"Not on your life. She's getting her boom box out of her car." Julie shook her head in disgust. "The woman can barely type, and she hardly knows the front end of the computer from the back."

"Then get somebody else."

"Are you kidding? I've tried three temp agencies already. Flora Jean's was the only one that would send someone down here to Bondsman's Row. Seems as though in the past month each of them has had a female employee harassed or molested in offices in the six-square-block area surrounding us. No one wants to come down here to work."

"You mean Ms. Benson is as good as it gets?"

"Afraid so," said Julie apologetically. "But if it's any consolation, she does have one good point. She's an ex-marine. Did a tour in Desert Storm."

CJ rolled his eyes. "Great."

There was a brief moment of silence before the hip-hop gangsta rap sounds of Tupac Shakur began rebounding off the walls of Julie's outer office, sounds that seemed to intensify when CJ jumped up from his desk as if someone had just run their fingernails down a blackboard. Although music was one of the great passions of his life, his tastes didn't include any form of rap. The gut-wrenching guttural Mississippi Delta sounds of the blues were his chosen form of intoxication. Rap was something he just couldn't stomach. The drum-thumping background and staccato lyrics reminded him of machine-gun fire careening off the hull of the navy swiftboat he had served aboard during Vietnam, and the rappers' voices reminded him of the sounds of wounded men dying.

He walked over to the door and opened it to find Flora Jean adjusting a plastic case overflowing with tapes next to a huge black boom box that now occupied the top of Julie's lateral-drawer file. When Flora Jean looked back to see both CJ and Julie staring, she broke into a broad, excited smile. "Ain't that music to the bone? Makes you want to cry."

In a final fit of frustration, CJ bit down on the nub of his cheroot, catching the edge of his tongue with his teeth. Stunned and in acute pain, he looked over at Julie helplessly and said, "It sure as hell does."

Chapter 10

The rusting pea-green Chrysler was a junker, a candidate for cinderblocks. No one knew for sure when the car had first appeared in the northern New Mexico desert west of Shiprock. But it had been sitting there baking in the sun, without windows or tires, its body riddled with bullet holes, for as long as Celeste Deepstream could remember. Celeste was crouched down on one knee thirty yards away from the long-dead relic from Detroit, rifle aimed at the window, baking in the sizzling northern New Mexico sun. Exhausted from having driven nearly the entire length of Colorado the previous night, she was having difficulty concentrating on her target. But even haggard and rumpled and dressed in clothes that had soaked up two days of cross-country sweat, Celeste's exotic beauty and leggy chorus-line-dancer's body would have been hard to miss.

For much of her life she had been an athletic, Madison Avenue poster child dream. She had earned a Phi Beta Kappa key from the University of New Mexico, where for three years she had also competed as a world-class swimmer. Her impressive athletic and classroom credentials had helped her win a Rhodes Scholarship to study anthropology in England, which she had turned down in favor of spending almost a year detoxifying her brother, Bobby, who at the time had been strung out on Ritalin, Darvocet, alcohol, and model-airplane glue. Celeste had helped Bobby win the drug war, but not without paying a price. Her painstaking nine-month sisterly intervention turned the twin-sibling dependence between them into Bobby's crutch, and a bond that had always been tenacious into an unhealthy codependent union fueled by Bobby's instability and Celeste's guilt.

An unruly lock of hair dropped across her face as Celeste steadied her aim. Sighting the Remington, she inhaled quickly and squeezed the trigger. A split second later the thumb button on the Chrysler's door handle disintegrated into fragments of flying metal. She squeezed off six more rounds into a six-inch square of rusting metal beneath the door handle. Satisfied with the results, she got up slowly, swept her hair off her shoulder, and adjusted the Remington's sling over her left arm.

All the while a man had been watching her, partially hidden from view by the jutting bank of a nearby dried-up creek bed. Now that Celeste was finished with her target practice, the man came jogging out of the shadow of the creek bed into view. A short, pudgy man whose entire body seemed to sag, distressed from the burden of carrying sixty pounds of extra weight, he was sunburned and had a thick head of coarse, unruly hair. His expensive gabardine slacks and open-necked custom-tailored shirt were glaringly out of place, and they clashed dramatically with the run-over logger's boots he was wearing. Holding her ground so the man would have to come to her, Celeste suspected that Leon Archuletta probably had a couple of changes of clothes and several pairs of ungodly expensive Italian loafers tucked away somewhere in the Range Rover he had parked next to her truck and trailer earlier. Archuletta jogged up to Celeste, totally winded. "You're wasting ammo," he gasped, trying to catch his breath.

"Practice makes perfect," said Celeste, heading toward the Chrysler to check her handiwork as Archuletta followed like a loyal puppy. When she reached the car she eyed the new bullet holes, ran her hand across what remained of the door handle, and smiled. Then, probing each hole with her pinky, she looked up at Archuletta. "Ever wonder if the metal plates they use to repair fractured skulls are as thick as this?" She rapped the door with her knuckles. Her question and the impressive target practice demonstration were meant to keep Archuletta, whose eyes were now undressing her, from saying or doing something that might force her to blow a hole in his skull.

Archuletta, one of Celeste's longtime contacts in the shadowy underground world of fencing stolen Indian artifacts and rare antiques, shook his head and shrugged his shoulders, recognizing that the target practice demo and the skull plate comment were warnings. "You planning to open up somebody's head?" he said with a grin.

Looking Archuletta up and down, Celeste swung the Remington off her shoulder. Then, resting the rifle butt in the sand, she leaned on it and said, "Only if I have to."

Archuletta kicked at a beer bottle near his foot, wondering how it had gotten to the middle of nowhere. "Now, Celeste, both of us know you didn't come out here for either target practice or brain surgery. I've checked out your trailer. Damn good stuff." He smiled, trying to imagine what Celeste might look like without her rumpled clothes. "I'll give you twenty thousand for everything."

Celeste responded with a snort. "Get real. These aren't just fireworks for topping off some redneck's Fourth. And I'm not my brother. Did you look at the front half of the trailer or just stop at the back? I've got artifacts and weapons in there you'll never get a chance to buy again. Thirty grand or I'm packing."

Archuletta pulled a handkerchief out of his pocket and wiped his brow. He didn't like haggling in the heat of day, but he decided to string the conversation out in an effort to get his price. He also knew what buttons to push to get Celeste thinking about something other than a mere $10,000. "Speaking of fireworks, where's Bobby?" He leaned against the Chrysler's fender, and his entire midsection jiggled.

Celeste watched Archuletta nervously shift his weight on the Chrysler's fender and smiled at his discomfort as she thought about some of the things she had done for her twin brother. She had once nearly killed a hooker who had stolen Bobby's wallet after making three quick minutes of love to him in an Albuquerque motel. She had bailed Bobby out of jails across Colorado, New Mexico, and Wyoming. And two years earlier, when a judge in Gallup, New Mexico, who had seen Bobby in his courtroom one too many times, asked Celeste why she continued to coddle Bobby as if he were a child, she had answered as honestly as she could, "Bobby's really nobody but me, Your Honor. He's just wearing a different suit of clothes." When the judge gave Bobby three months of jail time, Celeste had a friend torch his car.

Celeste watched Archuletta's eyes follow the outline of her cleavage, realizing that he was playing the same game he always played, waiting for her to blink. This time she didn't. She swung the Remington up from her side and aimed the barrel squarely at Archuletta's Adam's apple. "You know, Leon, one day your reckless eyeballing is going to get you killed." She teased the fleshy throat bulge, bumping it with the barrel several times. "Thirty thousand is as low as I go."

Archuletta backed away from the rifle's muzzle, his heart rhythm suddenly gyrating. He was used to Celeste skirting his innuendos and sidestepping his lewd comments and advances, and since he had closed five big deals with her in the past twenty-four months, he thought he knew her. The rifle barrel that had just tickled his throat told him he was wrong. Realizing that it had been a mistake to meet Celeste in such a remote area carrying $30,000 in cash, he promised himself that in the future he wouldn't let his hormones get the best of him. "Twenty-five thousand," he said, smiling nervously, backing farther downwind from the rifle.

Celeste ran her finger around the curve of the rifle's

trigger and watched ribbons of sweat stream down Archuletta's face. "Maybe I should just kill your lecherous ass and leave you out here with the coyotes. Twenty-seven five. I'd say yes if I were you."

Archuletta thought about testing Celeste's nerve but decided against it when he realized that in the past minute her trigger finger hadn't moved even a fraction of an inch. "Deal," he finally said, realizing only then that while Celeste was tickling his Adam's apple, he had urinated in his pants.

Celeste glanced down at the crescent of wetness on the front of his trousers and smiled. "Hook up the horse trailer and cart your toys away, my friend. I've got a long drive staring me in the face."

Embarrassed, Archuletta turned back toward the partially hidden dry wash he had jogged out of earlier and started to walk away.

Celeste quickly stepped into his path. "Not until I see the color of your money."

Archuletta reached into his pocket and pulled out a wad of urine-stained bills. He counted off several and handed them to Celeste.

"That's only twenty-five hundred," said Celeste, placing the money on the trunk of the Chrysler.

Archuletta undid his belt buckle and slipped off his belt. "I've got the rest of it here," he said, teasing off the money pouch Velcroed to the back of his belt. "There's twenty-five thousand here," he said, watching as Celeste aimed her rifle back at his head.

"You wouldn't lie to me?"

"No." Archuletta tightened his rectum, hoping to hold back any new flow of urine.

"Then just dump it all over with the rest of the bills on the truck."

"Not my belt!"

"It's the least you can do. I'm giving you temporary use of a perfectly good horse trailer in exchange."

Archuletta eyed the rifle again, then did as he was told.

"Come on, I'll walk you to the trailer and unhook my vehicle," said Celeste.

As they walked toward the gully, Archuletta's pants slowly started dropping, and before they reached the trailer he had hitched them up a half-dozen times.

Ten minutes later Celeste spun Bobby's big-block 457 Ford dually out of the dry wash, kicking a fantail of sand and gravel up in her wake. Archuletta, still red-faced with embarrassment, was checking the trailer's hitch to make certain it would fit the towing ball on the back of his Range Rover.

As she powered her way back toward the disabled Chrysler, Celeste couldn't help but wonder if Archuletta had enough sense to negotiate the heavy trailer out of the dry wash without getting stuck in the sand. When she reached the Chrysler the sun was three o'clock high, and a flock of crows was circling overhead. An old Acoma storyteller had once told her that crows were drawn to the scent of urine. She got out of the pickup, grabbed the money belt off the truck, and tossed it through the open window of her truck. Then she reached back for the wad of urine-stained bills and waved them up at the crows before tossing them through the window and onto the truck's floor.

As she got back into the truck to head for Denver to

try to find Bobby and deal with Cicero Vickers, she realized that she was now sweating as badly as Archuletta. She wiped the sweat from her brow and gazed up at the crows before taking off. She had no real idea why half a mile down the road the crows were still following, cawing as if she had robbed all of their nests. She stopped the truck, stripped off the gamey blouse that was plastered to her with sweat, and dropped it beside her on the seat. Her bare breasts jiggled as she sped across the sandy soil, dodging massive clusters of prickly pear and stubby knots of sagebrush. The warm rush of air streaming through the truck's windows began to cool her down. Feeling relaxed for the first time all day, she glanced at the wad of bills and the money belt on the floor. Then with her free hand she rubbed the salty sweat from between her breasts and wiped it on the seat, as if she were marking her territory. When she looked back into her side mirror to see if the crows were following, she wasn't surprised to see that they had disappeared, melting into the blinding glare of the desert sun.

Chapter 11

In 1872 Colorado implemented what became known as the Board of Immigration period, a self-serving adventure in hucksterism that would eventually become the forerunner of the modern-day Chamber of Commerce. The board's principal goal was to promote the Centennial State at all costs. The marketing experiment worked so well that a string of kibbutz-like cooperatives, where work profits and decisions were shared in a communal spirit, immediately sprang up along the Rocky Mountain Front Range. These experiments in agrarian socialism ultimately produced a series of farming utopias, the most famous one being the town of Greeley.

The fastest route from Denver to Greeley is a straight shot north up I25, with a final fifteen-mile dog-leg to the east, out onto Colorado's barren, windswept eastern plains and into the arms of the former farming utopia. The trip normally takes just over an hour. But CJ had never liked the monotonous drive on the interstate, so when he headed north he usually took back roads through the towns of Lafayette, Longmont, Berthoud, and Loveland, ultimately picking up U.S. 34 just east of Rocky Mountain National Park's gateway, the Big Thompson Canyon, for an easy last leg into Greeley. The drive took about twice as long, but the ride through the lush green landscape of the former immigration colonies was refreshing and relaxing. The sight of hundred-year-old cottonwoods swaying rhythmically along creekbeds thick with willows and the aromatic smell of burning thatch being cleared from irrigation ditches always made him wonder if he and Mavis couldn't one day escape Denver and move to a five-acre plot of former commune land.

Cruising along rolling hills dotted with cattle, CJ had the speedometer of his restored drop-top '57 Bel Air pegged at fifty-five. Dittier was lounging in the back seat, and Morgan was riding shotgun. CJ drove the Bel Air only during the summer and early fall, so the tires had never suffered the indignity of plowing through snow. CJ had longed for a '57 Bel Air since he was six years old, when his uncle had brought one home as collateral on a bond. Back then he would sometimes sit in the driver's seat for hours, pretending to drive, his eyes barely level with the dash, his hands firmly gripping the wheel. He was in his mid-thirties when he finally acquired his own Bel Air, a long-forgotten wreck that had been stashed away in a rancher's barn. Rosie Weaks had resuscitated the car's deteriorated power plant, drive train, and transmission, a process that took the better part of a year. CJ had reluctantly contracted the body work out to a California shop, and he had been on pins and needles for the entire time that the car was out of his sight. Since then CJ had pampered the car as if it were the only one in existence.

The only non-stock modification CJ had ever made to the Bel Air was to add a tape deck to a dash intended to house only a radio. Reaching across Morgan, he pulled a John Lee Hooker tape out of the glove box and popped it into the tape deck. He cued up the last song, and seconds later John Lee was belting out his powerful rendition of "Wednesday Evenin' Blues." Morgan set aside the *Jet* magazine he had been reading and began humming and snapping his fingers to the refrain. When the song ended, Morgan and CJ looked at one another and smiled. CJ ejected the tape and glanced back over the seat, hoping Dittier would now be willing to answer a question he had refused to answer when they began the trip.

"Had enough time to think about what we were discussing back in Denver? You know, the thing about who else might've wanted to kill Hambone," said CJ, turning far enough for Dittier to read his lips. When Dittier didn't respond with even so much as a grunt, CJ accelerated around a semitrailer full of cattle, thinking about what Morgan had had to say about his friend Hambone as they were leaving the office for Greeley. "Hambone always did have problems with women. Maybe one of 'em got him killed," had been Morgan's exact words.

Morgan glanced back at Dittier in frustration. "If

you don't tell CJ what he needs to know, Dittier, I will."
When Dittier still didn't respond, Morgan said, "Okay,
here goes. Woman's name Dittier's holdin' back on is
Rebecca Baptiste. Fine as wine. Shit, she'd make any
man pop his gizzard. Longest legs I ever seen, like the
legs you see on them Vegas showgirls. And shaped like
the kind of woman you'd squeeze out of your dreams.
She was one of them rodeo groupies I'm always talkin'
about, and wouldn't you know it, she took a fancy to
Hambone's struttin' and Dittier's clownin' right off.
Didn't care too much for me." Morgan looked across the
seat back at Dittier. "Sorry, champ, this here's murder.
Everything's gotta come out in the wash."

Looking sad-faced, Dittier remained slouched in his
seat.

Morgan continued, "She latched on to us at a
Fourth of July rodeo up in Helena, Montana, and stuck
with Dittier and Hambone pretty much the rest of the
year. One other thing you should know right off, CJ, she
was white."

Morgan's comment finally triggered a response
from Dittier, who sat up straight and shook his head
back and forth as he tapped Morgan's forearm. CJ
looked at Morgan for an explanation.

Morgan grinned. "Dittier's sayin' color don't matter
to him. Hell, it don't matter to me or CJ neither," said
Morgan, glancing back at Dittier. "But it sure as hell
stuck in the craw of that gun-totin' father of hers. Or has
your memory suddenly gone south?"

Dittier grimaced. Then, slouching back down in his
seat, he stared straight ahead into the dead space between CJ and Morgan. Morgan cleared his throat.

"Woman's entire family was nuts. Never met her mama, mind you, but her zonked-out, pot-smokin' brother and Jesus-freak, Bible-totin' father were enough to let me know the whole kaboodle were missin' a few marbles."

Morgan looked back to gauge Dittier's reaction to find that Dittier hadn't budged and his eyes were still locked straight ahead. "The father and brother didn't show up until about a month after Rebecca hooked up with us in Helena. We'd hit a few rodeos in between, and by the time they materialized, Hambone had Rebecca thinkin' he was God. He could've told her to crawl over the Rockies on all fours and she would've done it. Anyway, the day her old man and the brother appear, me and Dittier had just finished helpin' Hambone and an old saddle-bronc rider we ran with back in those days water half a dozen head of horses. Rebecca's doper of a brother walks up on us as silent as a bullet and out of the blue pops Hambone in the head with the business end of a shovel. Hambone drops to the ground like a wounded duck and starts floppin' around in the mud like he's got the DTs. Next thing we know Rebecca's old man steps out from behind one of the horse trailers. He's decked out in black except for the dingy white preacher's collar he's wearin', and he's got a Bible in one hand and a .45 in the other. He looks down at Hambone wallerin' in the mud and starts quotin' the Good Book like he's some TV evangelist.

"I don't remember much of what he said other than he kept screamin' at Hambone about bein' a woolly-headed heathen and the son of Ham. Then he starts wavin' his .45 in the air, firing into the sky. When all the bullets were spent, the brother kicks Hambone in the ribs, spits on him, and screams, 'Keep your black bull-ridin' ass away from my sister,' and the two of 'em walk away like nothin' happened. It all went down so fast that I couldn't do anything. Me and the bronc rider helped Hambone to his feet, and I remember checkin' his head for blood. The whole time things was goin' down, I don't think Dittier moved a muscle. He just stood out of the way, eyes big as saucers, lookin' scared to death. I'd never seen Dittier afraid of much of nothin', so it surprised me the way he acted. I didn't think much about it until we were comin' back from havin' a doctor take a look at Hambone's head. Hambone was leanin' all his weight on me like I was his damn staff of life. Except for a knot on his noggin the size of a pregnant plum, he was all right, but I figured he was delirious when he jammed his elbow into my neck to keep from fallin' and said, 'Dittier's been pokin' Rebecca too.' It sure explained why Dittier was actin' so scared."

CJ adjusted his grip on the steering wheel, thinking, *I'll be damned.* "That true?" he said, looking back at Dittier, hoping for some kind of response.

Dittier remained silent.

"Come on, Dittier, if I'm gonna find out who killed your friend, I'll need some help." When Dittier still wouldn't respond, CJ decided it was time to prove he was serious. He pulled the Bel Air over onto the shoulder and eased to a stop. Then, turning around fully in his seat, he looked squarely at Dittier, refusing to blink until Dittier's stare met his. "We're talking murder here, Dittier. Think about it." Then, not wanting to push his confused friend any further, CJ turned around, popped the

Bel Air back into gear, and nosed the car back onto the highway.

No one said another word until they pulled up to the parking lot ticket booth across from the Greeley Stampede rodeo grounds. A squeaky-voiced teenaged boy greeted them, smiled courteously, tipped his Stetson, and said, "Three dollars."

CJ pulled a five-dollar bill out of his vest pocket and gave it to the boy. When the kid bent down to hand CJ his change he spotted Dittier still moping in the back seat. He did a double take as he gave CJ two limp one-dollar bills. "That Dittier Atkins you got in the back seat, mister?"

"Sure is," said Morgan before CJ could answer.

The boy reached for his back pocket, pulled out a small leather-bound autograph book with a couple of rubber bands wrapped around it, and shoved it at CJ. "Could you get him to stick his name in this here book for me? He's one I don't have."

CJ passed the book back to Dittier, who bent forward and stared at the boy.

"You got my signature?" asked Morgan, smiling up at the kid.

The boy bent down and studied Morgan's face for a moment. "You a clown?" he asked, his high-pitched voice full of suspicion.

"No, a bull rider."

"I only collect signatures from clowns. Sorry."

Morgan swallowed hard, sat back in his seat, and mumbled, "I see."

Dittier had the rubber bands off the book and was flipping through the pages, looking for a place to write his name. Signatures of famous clowns in every size and shape filled the book. Jerry Olson, George Doak, Luke Coffee, and Willie "Smokey" Lornes were just a few. When Dittier finally found a space for his signature, he had thumbed past more than fifty famous names. Boldly adding his own name to the book, he thought about all the bull fighting and barrel rolling he had done during his career. He remembered being taunted, called *nigger* to his face, and laughed at because he was mute. But more than anything, he remembered the vibrations of the cheers. He blew on the signature, wrapped the rubber bands around the book, and handed it back to CJ, thinking that for most of his life the pro rodeo circuit had been his home and family.

"Thanks," said the boy, still crouched down, staring at Dittier. Out of habit he readjusted the rubber bands, then slipped the book into his back pocket and waved CJ into the lot.

CJ eased past the ticket booth, looking for a spot to park the Bel Air out of harm's way. He was busy dodging potholes and surveying the lot when Dittier tapped Morgan on the shoulder and signed, "I'm ready to talk about it now."

"Good," said Morgan.

"What's up?" asked CJ, noting the exchange as he headed for a space in the shade of the cottonwood-lined far west edge of the lot.

"Dittier's ready to talk."

CJ shot Dittier a supportive wink before angling the Bel Air directly under the gnarled branches of a huge cottonwood. He shut down the engine and got out of the car with a series of grunts and groans, joint-aggravated testimony to a two-hour ride in a vintage automobile that hadn't been designed to comfortably accommodate someone his size. Morgan and Dittier followed, stretching their arms and legs. On their way back across the parking lot, CJ caught a glimpse of the boy who had collected their money. The boy was now directing traffic twenty yards down the road from the booth. From the look on his face CJ could tell he was disappointed at having to vacate the perfect autograph hound's perch.

CJ didn't know exactly what had made Dittier decide to change his mind and open up, but he knew it had something to do with the young autograph seeker. As his uncle used to say, *Sometimes being in the right place at the right time's more important than all the preparation in the world,* CJ thought. As they crossed the VIP parking lot next to the Stampede grounds and started their trek down the asphalt rodeo midway, Dittier began signing to Morgan, telling him the Rebecca Baptiste story in detail. Morgan passed the information on to CJ, his voice full of surprise. "Dittier says that after Hambone's encounter with Rebecca's father and brother, Rebecca flat-out disappeared for over two months. Says when she resurfaced, it was in the back seat of our brand-new drop-top electric 225 at a rodeo outside of Clovis, New Mexico. She was drunk and butt naked except for a straw Stetson and an old army blanket. Dittier says all he could think of when he saw a white girl in the back seat of our car with her boobs floppin' out from beneath a blanket was that he was gonna end up in jail. Not knowin' what to do, he ended up stashin' Rebecca in a hotel room."

Morgan stopped in his tracks as Dittier signed what

he had to say next. "Dittier says he knew Hambone was behind Rebecca's reappearance, and he expected Hambone would come get her by our next rodeo stop in Gallup." Morgan hesitated as Dittier continued signing, then said, "Shit! Hambone came and got her all right, but seems like after that one thing led to another, and Rebecca ended up bouncin' back and forth between Hambone and Dittier's beds for the rest of the year."

Morgan stared Dittier down. "Why the hell didn't you tell me what was goin' on?"

Dittier shrugged his shoulders as if to say, *You wouldn't have understood,* and continued signing until Morgan bellowed, "What the fuck?"

"Don't keep it to yourself, Morgan," said CJ, now on pins and needles.

Morgan slammed his fist into his forehead. "We got problems here, CJ. Problems I didn't see comin'. Dittier says Hambone was down in Denver about a week ago scared to the point of havin' runny stools. Must've had something to do with Rebecca's father or brother, or he wouldn't't've come lookin' for Dittier."

"Maybe," said CJ, unwilling to rush to the same conclusion. Then, turning to Dittier, he said, "How long since you last saw Rebecca?" making certain that Dittier could read his lips.

"Six years," mouthed Dittier, holding up six fingers.

"How about Hambone? How long since he'd seen her?" asked CJ.

Dittier grinned sheepishly as his nimble fingers shot back a response to Morgan.

Morgan shook his head in disgust and looked at CJ. "Dittier says last week."

Dittier placed an index finger across his lips, then signed, "Hambone said not to tell," as a couple of ATVs carrying cowboys with official Stampede entry bibs pinned to their shirt backs beeped and skirted around Morgan.

"What about Rebecca's shovel-toting brother?" asked CJ, ushering Dittier onto a grassy shoulder and out of the midway traffic. "Did you or Hambone actually hear from him?"

Dittier shook his head back and forth, refusing to respond.

A group of teenaged boys, all in roper boots, hundred-dollar Stetsons, and colorful yoke-shouldered rodeo shirts, veered around CJ. They were ten yards down the midway when one of the boys turned back and pointed at Dittier. It was the boy from the parking lot booth. The rest of the boys turned to gawk. When they turned away to continue, CJ caught a glimpse of the look of vulnerability plastered on Dittier's face, and he suddenly had an inkling of why Dittier kept some secrets to himself, realizing that Dittier could never really be certain whether the finger-pointing directed at him was because he was a famous rodeo clown or some sideshow deaf mute.

Deciding that Dittier needed a break from finger-pointing, CJ patted him reassuringly on the shoulder and then ran the investigative plan he had hastily pieced together before they left Denver back through his head.

He planned to check out the Stampede crime scene, talk to anyone who might have seen what happened, and then drop by and question Hambone Dolbey's latest flame, Nadine. Morgan had assured him before they left Denver that not only was the Greeley address he had for her correct but her last name was Kemp. The question of why Hambone had been found dressed in a diver's wet suit had been gnawing at CJ ever since Morgan and Dittier had rousted him that morning. He was hoping that Nadine Kemp would be able to shed some light on Hambone's strange getup. Considering Hambone's sorry history with women, the Kemp woman had been CJ's number one suspect. But the Rebecca Baptiste story had thrown him a curve. Now he had a Bible-wielding old man, his daughter, and a drugged-out son to contend with. He looked over at Morgan and Dittier, wondering as he did just how much longer the list of Hambone's enemies could grow. Adjusting his Stetson, CJ shaded his eyes and frowned up into the sun before looking back at Morgan. "Why don't you show me where they found Hambone?"

Morgan pivoted in the direction of the horse barns where Hambone's body had been found. "This way."

CJ followed, but Dittier didn't budge, remaining stoop-shouldered along the edge of the midway, looking like a lost puppy in need of its master. Realizing that Dittier wasn't coming, Morgan did an about-face. "Come on, Dittier. Won't be no bodies floatin' in no water troughs today."

The look in Dittier's eyes told CJ that Dittier was afraid of something more than a floating corpse.

"Okay," said Morgan, nodding toward a cast-iron park bench ten yards away. "Why don't you just park yourself on that bench over there. We'll pick you up on our way back."

CJ watched Dittier head toward the park bench, knowing something was eating away at him inside.

Chapter 12

They moved it!" screamed Morgan, pointing to where the water trough Hambone Dolbey's body had been found floating in had been. In its place was a wide circle of iridescent orange dots. Morgan walked the full three-hundred-sixty-degree circle of paint dabs suspiciously. "It was right here," he said after a complete turn.

CJ slipped off his Stetson and wiped his sweat-peppered brow. It was 95 degrees, and the midway asphalt had started to release the unpleasant locked-in aroma of tar and livestock. CJ knelt down to inspect the paint dots, trying to estimate the size of the trough and wondering how long a body in a wet suit could remain afloat. Suddenly a voice behind him boomed, "Looking for something, Mr. Floyd?"

CJ spun around to find himself at eye level with Weld County Sheriff Carlton Pritchard's crotch.

Pritchard and CJ had crossed paths a couple of years earlier when CJ had been searching for a bond-skipping ecoterrorist. But Pritchard, who had been sheriff of another county at the time, had found the terrorist strangled with a strand of barbed wire wrapped around her neck. He had no real love for bounty hunters like CJ, but he was pragmatic enough to understand that everybody has to earn a living some way.

"I'll be," said CJ, standing up slowly, extending his hand toward Pritchard's. They were in a firm hand clasp before CJ noticed the man at Pritchard's side.

Pritchard acknowledged the slump-faced man with a nod. "Whitaker Rodgers, meet CJ Floyd. Floyd's a bail bondsman out of Denver. Suspect you already know the man with him, Morgan Williams."

CJ wasn't surprised that Pritchard had recognized Morgan. Morgan was, after all, a pro rodeo Hall-of-Famer, and Pritchard was the kind of man who did his homework.

"I know Williams," said Rodgers matter-of-factly, extending his hand to shake CJ's. Quickly slipping his nubby fingers out of CJ's grasp, he announced authoritatively, "Whitaker Rodgers."

"When Whit here said that two of the cowboys who found the dead man were black and proceeded to describe them, I had a suspicion they might be the same two involved in that case we bumped heads on a couple of years ago. Guessed that sooner or later you'd be showing up. Small world," said Pritchard, stringing his words out in a slow drawl as he shot Rodgers a told-you-so kind of look.

CJ ignored Pritchard's analysis, more concerned with what he was doing in Greeley. "Thought your beat was on the other side of the mountains."

Pritchard hiked up his sagging pants. "Was, till a year ago when I got the itch to try out a bigger pond."

Pleasantries and job descriptions exchanged, CJ decided to get back to the issue at hand. "What happened to the water trough?" he said, pointing toward the iridescent circle on the ground.

"Evidence." Pritchard's response was curt.

"And the water?"

"Evidence too," Whitaker Rodgers chimed in.

The sheriff shot Rodgers a butt-out kind of stare and turned his attention to Morgan. "Understand you and Dolbey went back a long way."

"Over twenty years."

"Did he go back that many years with your sidekick Atkins too?"

Morgan looked at CJ before answering.

"It's okay, go on and answer," said CJ.

"Dittier knew him just as long as me."

Whitaker Rodgers butted in. "The three of you ever have any serious differences?"

Pritchard turned salmon pink. He considered one Rodgers interruption a nuisance. A second was just plain ill-mannered. The ice-cold stare he shot Rodgers would have made anyone but Rodgers clam up for the rest of the day. "I know you're Stampede chairman, Whit, and president of a big oil company to boot. And I'm aware you're a home-grown boy with roots deeper than I'll ever have a chance to grow around here. But I don't remember deputizing you. And when I checked this morning, I was still the Weld County sheriff. So I'm asking you to let me do the talking here, or I'm gonna have to ask you to leave."

Rodgers rolled his eyes. "Just trying to help."

"I can appreciate that. But I'm sure Morgan here can speak for himself."

CJ decided to test Pritchard's true frustration level by sliding in a question of his own. "What about the wet suit Hambone was wearing—any special reason for the getup?" When Pritchard didn't respond, CJ added, "Strange costume for a rodeo bull rider to be wearing."

"Maybe he was practicing up on becoming a clown," said Pritchard, stone-faced.

"Come on, Sheriff, you know sooner or later the answer's gonna surface."

"I expect it might, but not from me," said Pritchard with a smile. "And for the record, there're a couple of things you need to know about doing business in Weld County. Whitaker here might be pushy, but he's a constituent of mine." He glanced at Morgan, then back at CJ. "You and your friends aren't. If you start sniffing too hard around the edges of my investigation, I won't give you the kind of warning I just gave him."

CJ watched as a smug, self-satisfied grin spread across Whitaker Rodgers's face. "Any more rules I need to know about?"

"No. But I would like to speak to Williams and Atkins without you chiming in."

"Now?" asked Morgan.

"The sooner the better."

Morgan pulled off his Stetson and scratched his head. "Dittier's back up the midway."

"Then let's go finish up our business there."

Morgan looked at CJ for support.

"It can't take but a few minutes," said CJ. "Go ahead, get it over with."

Morgan quickly weighed his options and then said, "Catch you back here when we're done?"

"Yeah," said CJ, back to eyeing the outline where the water trough had been.

"You sign?" Morgan asked as he and the sheriff turned to leave, smiling to himself and hoping the sheriff's answer would be no.

"With the best of 'em," said Pritchard, signing the words as he spoke.

CJ and Whitaker Rodgers were left facing one another uncomfortably.

"They keep anything in that barn over there besides horses?" asked CJ, wondering whether or not the nearby barn could have served as a quick-change room for a man in a wet suit.

"Hay," said Rodgers.

CJ ignored the flip remark. "Think I'll check it out," he said, turning toward the barn.

Rodgers had already started his trek back to his Stampede headquarters office and didn't respond.

On his way to the horse barn CJ thought about why the president of an oil company would want to spend his spare time honchoing a rodeo. He also wondered just how well Rodgers had known Hambone Dolbey. He wasn't sure whether Morgan or Dittier would be able to fill in the blanks, but he did know that he had an even better source. Morgan's niece, Lisa Darley, a former Stampede rodeo queen, was bound to have inside dope on Rodgers.

He stepped onto a sliver of a dirt trail that led to the barn. Thick pockets of thistle hugged the edge of the trail. As he entered the subdued light of the barn, something shiny just to the left of one of the horse stalls caught his eye. As he continued down the barn's alleyway toward the source of the glint, he realized that a painter's dropcloth had been draped over something circular. A few feet from the covering, he recognized the source of the reflection. The shiny galvanized lip of the missing water trough was smiling up at him.

Chapter 13

The decaying Greeley neighborhood CJ was cruising through could have been a campaign billboard for some populist politician's cry for urban renewal. Broken whiskey bottles, fast-food wrappers, and feces-stained disposable diapers littered the streets. The doleful sound of whining dogs chained to backyard cottonwood stumps and the nauseating aroma from a nearby potash plant filled the noonday air. The T-square-straight rows of post–World War II cookie-cutter crackerboxes lining both sides of the street had been thrown up without the benefit of proper soil testing, so the forlorn starter homes now sagged on crumbling concrete foundations that had been poured in expansive bentonite soil.

As CJ shaded his eyes, staring into the sun through the Bel Air's windshield, looking for Nadine Kemp's address, he noticed a gaggle of unwashed preteens playing baseball in the street. When the boy standing at bat, crowding the torn lawn-chair cushion serving as home plate, caught sight of the Bel Air, he dropped his bat and whistled so loudly that everyone in the game turned to take a look. "Slick," said the batter, "slick as shit."

"Fifty-six," barked a lanky, saucer-eyed boy standing at first base.

"Bullshit," shot back the boy at home plate. "Fifty-seven."

The entire ragtag brood of seven moved to let the Bel Air pass before closing in behind the car and following it. They coalesced into a flying wedge at the car's rear bumper when CJ turned the motor off. While the boys played grab ass, CJ checked the faded address stenciled above the front door of the house he had pulled in front of.

"This is it," said CJ, turning to Dittier, who was riding shotgun.

Dittier nodded, glancing back toward the boys in puzzlement.

Morgan leaned forward from his slouched position in the back seat. "Let's get it over with."

The disassembled baseball team now rotated around the Bel Air, gawking. When CJ and Dittier opened their doors to get out, the boy who had been batting got a good look at CJ's size. With his hands stretched apart as if he were measuring CJ's girth, he looked at one of the other boys and rolled his eyes. "Big MF, ain't he?"

Ignoring the remark, CJ waited until Morgan was out of the car. Then he shot the boy who had made the comment an ice-dagger stare. "Touch this car and your little hoodlum ass is mine." The boy seemed unfazed. "Does Nadine Kemp live here?" asked CJ, in a quick guilty afterthought remembering how the chance to view a classic car would have attracted him as a preteen.

"Sure does," said the prepubescent voice of a boy who was running his hand across the Bel Air's front fender.

He's not hurting it, thought CJ, gritting his teeth as he watched the boy move to caress the car's hood.

"She at home?" said Morgan, directing his question to the boy who had been standing at home plate.

"She got a doorbell, check it out for yourself."

"We'll do that," said Morgan, biting his tongue as he turned and headed for the house.

Dittier followed, with CJ bringing up the rear. Halfway up the sidewalk to the house, CJ glanced back over his shoulder toward the Bel Air, hoping the warning he had given the fledgling gang-bangers had been enough to let them know he was the kind of man they shouldn't cross.

The front porch of the house was listing badly to the right, and the uneven planking, once a bright fire-en-gine red, was peeling and rotting at the seams. A rickety banister supported by a few snaggletoothed spindles rimmed the porch's perimeter. The planking creaked as CJ moved across it and punched the rusty doorbell. The doorbell's irritating death-rattle buzz caused Morgan to freeze in his tracks.

While they waited for someone to answer the door,

CJ fumbled in his pocket with the four raisin-sized pieces of rock he had found in the bottom of the water trough at the Stampede. The rocks weren't much of a lead, but he couldn't help but wonder if they might not have had something to do with Hambone Dolbey's death. When he had pulled back the canvas covering the tilted trough, he had noticed that several gallons of turbid water had collected into a triangle along one side. There were a series of scuff marks and a recent three-foot-long gouge in the galvanized metal that he thought must have been the result of someone moving the water-filled trough with a piece of heavy equipment. Staring down into the water, he had noticed what looked like a cluster of small rocks hugging the water's deepest point. He gathered that whoever had drained the trough had missed the rocks because they had been more interested in the water. Rolling up his right sleeve, he had fished around in the water and pulled out four rocks.

He had just slipped the rocks into his pocket and started to reposition the canvas over the trough when Sheriff Pritchard eased up behind him without so much as a light heel thud, tapped him on the shoulder, and said in a voice meant to intimidate, "You're pushing your luck, Floyd. Out of here." Pritchard had motioned him toward the barn door with a quick flip of his thumb, and it wasn't until he reached the light of the doorway that CJ realized Pritchard's other thumb was resting on the butt of his holstered .38. "Just looking," CJ had said, leaving the barn. Pritchard hadn't responded. He had remained straddling the doorway no-trespassing style, hand above his gun butt, until CJ disappeared into the midway crowd.

CJ stopped rolling the rocks around between his fingers and punched Nadine Kemp's doorbell again.

"Maybe she ain't here," said Morgan.

Before CJ could respond, a high-pitched female voice screeched, "What do you cow turds want?"

CJ turned to find a petite, dark-skinned black woman with a round butterball face, pockmarked skin, and stringy shoulder-length hair staring up at him from a thin strip of grass that separated the house from its next-door neighbor. The woman looked to be in her late fifties, but she had the youthful figure of a seventeen-year-old. She was dressed in tight-fitting jeans, a ruby-red silk blouse, threadbare at the sleeves, and handmade cowboy boots with steep riding heels. Expensive, one-of-a-kind silver and turquoise Indian jewelry hugged both of her wrists, and three toothpicks all jutting in different directions poked from one corner of the woman's mouth. When she realized that CJ was staring directly at the toothpicks, she teasingly rolled them inside her mouth with her tongue. CJ didn't notice the pearl-handled derringer sticking out from beneath the woman's belt until Dittier nudged him in the side and pointed at the gun.

"If you're Nadine Kemp, I'd like to ask you a few things about Hambone Dolbey," said CJ, his eyes still glued to the derringer.

"Get the hell off my porch and take your two friends with you."

Dittier's lip-reading skills had him already moving toward the steps. Morgan bristled, but he held back on responding because of the derringer. CJ held his ground. "Hambone was a buddy of my two friends here, Morgan

Williams and Dittier Atkins. They rodeoed together for a lot of years."

"Never heard of 'em," said the woman. But the look on her face told CJ that she recognized the names.

"I've heard of you," said Morgan.

CJ shot Morgan a look that said, *Button your lip.* "Like I said before, we're looking for Nadine Kemp. If you're not her, we're sorry for the bother."

The woman broke into a self-congratulatory smile that told CJ he had just been put through a test. "I'm her, so my mother told me. She also told me to watch out for strange people I find trespassing on my property, especially if they're men."

"Good rule, but I'd prefer to think we're visiting, not trespassing. By the way, I'm CJ Floyd, and I'm trying to find out what happened to Hambone."

Looking away from CJ and off into the distance, Nadine said, "I can tell you right now what happened. Somebody brained Hambone with a branding iron." Her eyes moistened as she batted at them nervously. Nadine's body language told CJ that she wasn't quite as tough as she appeared, or she was putting on a show. He glanced out toward the Bel Air to make sure it still had its tires. Most of the boys had dispersed, but a couple were standing on tiptoe, leaning across the door to survey the dashboard. When he looked back Nadine had regained her composure. "Sure would be nice if we could talk without having to shout back and forth over this banister."

Nadine hesitated before reluctantly heading across the grassy strip toward the porch, dodging broken glass and ruts. "Come to think of it, Hambone did mention somebody named Morgan a few times, but never no Dittier. Which one's which?" she said, looking at CJ for help.

Before CJ could answer, Morgan eased across the porch toward Nadine. "I'm Morgan."

Nadine shook Morgan's hand briefly before glancing over at a very reticent Dittier. "You're awfully shy, my friend. I don't bite."

"Dittier's mute," said Morgan.

"Oh," said Nadine matter-of-factly, as if she dealt with deaf mutes every day. She looked toward a couple of ratty wicker chairs in one corner of the porch. "Two seats are all I got—pick your poison." She walked over to the corner and took one chair for herself. Morgan grabbed the remaining chair, leaving CJ and Dittier standing.

As Nadine cocked her chair toward him, CJ noticed a fine three-inch scar just below her left eye. "When did you hear about Hambone?" he said, trying to imagine how Nadine had gotten the scar.

"Yesterday, late. The county sheriff came over and told me about it, then asked me a bunch of stupid questions."

CJ stepped back and leaned against the banister. "Like?"

"Like how long had I known Hambone, did we live together, and were we having any problems? When I told him it was none of his fucking business, it didn't seem to faze him in the least. Next thing he wanted to know was did I know anybody that might've wanted to kill Hambone. I told him no to that too!"

Nadine's response made CJ recall something his

uncle used to say about people who were avoiding telling the truth. *Liars tend to cap what they say with an exclamation point. People that's tellin' the truth don't need no punctuation.* "Were you telling the sheriff the truth?" said CJ.

Nadine slipped her toothpicks from one corner of her mouth to the other. "Mostly."

"Meaning?"

The look on Nadine Kemp's face told CJ she didn't like having to explain herself.

"You ever rodeoed?" she said, her tone of voice condescending.

"No."

"Then you wouldn't get my drift." She shot Morgan and Dittier each a quick glance. "But I bet your two friends here would. Ain't a champion ever been made that didn't pick up a few enemies along the way. Bull riding's no different. Hambone rubbed a few good old boys' noses in it on his way to the top. White boys on top of it, that makes it worse. From what he told me, most of 'em let it pass. Guess they figured life's too short, but a few let things fester inside 'em over the years and ended up carrying around sacks of hate."

"Any names in particular?" CJ asked.

Ignoring CJ, Nadine turned toward Morgan. "You ever heard of a bull rider named Percy Lewis?"

Morgan forced back a frown. "Yeah," he said, as if the mention of the name somehow left a bad taste in his mouth.

Nadine turned back to CJ. "Lewis supposedly lost his rodeoing career because of Hambone. Ain't that about right?" she said, looking to Morgan for confirmation.

"Close enough."

"Want to tell me about it?" asked CJ.

"Later," said Morgan in a tone of voice that told CJ he didn't feel like sifting back through the past right then. Knowing that sooner or later he'd get the full Percy Lewis story, CJ turned his attention back to Nadine. "Anybody else I need to know about?"

"No."

"How long were you and Hambone together?" asked CJ, expecting Nadine to give him the same fuck-off response she had given the sheriff.

It surprised him when she said, "A couple of years."

"All harmony and bliss?"

Nadine bit down on one of her toothpicks, cracking it in half. "Blissful enough."

CJ smiled and filed Nadine's toothpick-cracking response away in the back of his head. "Had Hambone been acting strange lately—anyhow different than normal?"

Nadine tugged at her belt loops and spit out the broken toothpick. "You looking for the same answer I gave the sheriff?"

"No, just the truth."

"Then why don't you try talking to a man named Whitaker Rodgers? He's chairman of the Greeley Stampede. Maybe he'll have that truth serum you're hunting for."

"Were he and Hambone having problems?"

Nadine leaned forward in her chair. "Nothing I can prove. But Hambone and Rodgers spent enough time kissing up to one another over the last six months to convince me that their dealings were more than just everyday rodeo business."

"You sure Rodgers and Hambone hadn't just become friends?"

"Not hardly. Until recently the two of them were more like fire and ice. I'd say their newfound relationship had to do with the easement Hambone had given Rodgers across a worthless patch of land he owned up near the Devil's Backbone."

CJ had Rodgers pegged as a rich, rude, and condescending drugstore cowboy wanna-be. But it sounded as if Rodgers also enjoyed conducting a little business when he was out riding the range. CJ didn't know much about the Devil's Backbone except that it was a well-known northern Colorado landmark and the country surrounding it was as rocky and pig ugly as Colorado could get. "Any idea why Rodgers needed that easement?" asked CJ, making a mental note to explore the link more thoroughly regardless of Nadine's answer.

"No!" said Nadine, punctuating her response so forcefully that according to CJ's uncle's rule, she had to be lying.

Her answer made CJ decide that while he was investigating the link between Hambone and Rodgers, he needed to also find out a whole lot more about Nadine Kemp.

"Any other reason Rodgers would have had to hook up with Hambone?"

"Just one, his pushy girlfriend, Evelyn Coleman. A real first-class witch. If you ask me, she's the one who convinced Hambone to give Rodgers that easement. I wouldn't be a bit surprised to find out that she promised Hambone a roll in the hay to agree to it."

"Sounds like a real sweet lady," said CJ. "Where do I find her?"

"Find Rodgers and you'll find her. He's never too far away from sniffing up her butt."

"I take it you don't like Ms. Coleman."

"You could say that," said Nadine, patting her derringer.

CJ eyed the derringer, wondering how good a shot Nadine was and whether she could wield a branding iron with enough force to fracture a man's face. Deciding that the answer was yes, he turned to Nadine with a final question. "Did Hambone ever mention a woman named Rebecca Baptiste?"

Dittier jumped at the mention of Rebecca's name.

"No," said Nadine, surprised at Dittier's reaction.

"What about her father or her brother?"

"Hambone never mentioned any of them," said Nadine, still staring at Dittier.

Morgan patted Dittier reassuringly on the shoulder.

Nadine turned her attention back to CJ. "You finished with your questions?"

"For now," said CJ.

Ignoring the inference, Nadine stood up and glanced out toward the Bel Air. "Nice ride."

"Thanks." CJ fished one of his business cards from his vest pocket and handed it to Nadine. "Call me if anything new crops up," he said, moving to leave.

Nadine slipped the card into her pocket without so much as a glance.

Before heading down the sidewalk, CJ said, "By the way, how do I get to that land of Hambone's?"

"The turnoff's seven miles to the penny west of where 34 crosses I25."

"Thanks," said CJ, hoping to find the Bel Air the same way he had left it. When he reached the car, he found two boys in the front seat. One boy, the talkative batter, had his hands draped nonchalantly over the top of the steering wheel. The other boy was smoking a cigarette, lounging back in the seat, looking as though he were prepared for a cross-country trip. The batter was staring straight ahead, his eyes locked on a superhighway dream.

"You got a driver's license?" asked CJ, walking around to open the Bel Air's front door.

"Don't need one," said the subdued batter. "Ain't goin' nowhere."

CJ glanced around the decaying neighborhood, surveying the blight. Looking back into the boy's eyes, he recognized the same trapped anger and sense of hopelessness he had known as a teen. As he motioned the boy out of the seat, he couldn't help but hope that the boy's words would turn out to be off the mark.

Chapter 14

There was a simple explanation for why Morgan didn't have to do his usual arm-twisting to get CJ to stop by his niece's horse ranch and veterinary practice on their way back to Denver. In everyday rural parlance, Lisa knew the lay of the land. And since Nadine Kemp had given him a reason to suspect a sinister link between Rodgers and Dolbey's murder, CJ was hoping Lisa might be able to flesh the relationship out further.

Knock off an old rodeo legend and all sorts of people come out of the woodwork, thought CJ as he nosed the Bel Air down U.S. 34 toward Lisa's, his speedometer pegged at sixty-five. In addition to Whitaker Rodgers, he had the whole Baptiste clan to investigate: father, daughter, and brother. Add to that the fact that Hambone had also made an enemy of some disgruntled fellow bull rider named Percy Lewis, and he had a whole gaggle of folks who might have enjoyed sending Hambone to the other side.

He couldn't quite decide where the derringer-toting Nadine Kemp fit in, but since she hadn't seemed very candid during their visit, she was on his list for further consideration. Ferreting out what kind of relationship Hambone and Nadine had had was a job he usually would have reserved for Julie. He frowned as he thought about the hole Julie's new law degree was going to leave in his operation, and caught himself laughing out loud when, for a second, he considered assigning the project to Flora Jean. He accelerated around a minivan and pondered the one thing about Hambone Dolbey's murder that made the least sense. If someone harboring a long-term grudge against Hambone had killed him, like one of the Baptistes or Percy Lewis, why had they decided to surface after so many years? He glanced in the rearview mirror at Dittier, knowing that that was where he would have to start to find the answer.

Slowing to forty-five, he eased the Bel Air into a curve, and slipped a brand-new B. B. King tape that Mavis had given him the week before into the tape deck. For the next three minutes he listened to B. B. complain about the sorrows of being a second-string lover and watched Dittier enjoy the wind blowing across his face in the rearview mirror. He had the feeling that Dittier was prepared to assume that position forever before he startled him by reaching over the seat back, tapping him on the leg, and mouthing slowly, "Need some answers, Dittier. About you, Hambone, and Rebecca Baptiste."

Dittier immediately looked to Morgan for help.

"I wasn't there, champ," Morgan signed, turning briefly back to Dittier. "You're on your own."

Dittier swallowed hard, staring up at a bank of thin, wispy clouds. After a few moments he tapped Morgan on the shoulder and signed very deliberately.

Morgan shrugged his shoulders. "Fine by me." Facing so that Dittier could read his lips, Morgan leaned back against the car door until the back of his fully shaved head was almost peeking beyond the open window. "Dittier says for me to tell you about Percy Lewis first."

"Shoot," said CJ.

"First off, Lewis was a loudmouth show-off. Hambone didn't do a thing to him he didn't deserve." When Morgan cleared his throat and adjusted his rear in the seat, CJ knew that he was about to get an earful of one of Morgan's rodeo war stories.

"The whole Hambone-Lewis thing started in a little backwater rodeo outside of Clovis, New Mexico. It was near the end of the season, and Hambone and Lewis were pretty much even in their point totals toward the championship that year. It had been rainin' all over the state for the better part of a week—so hard in fact that my bad ankle joints were startin' to pain me. Clovis had turned from a bone-dry desert pimple into a sloppy mudhole, and the whole town smelled to high heaven. Me and Dittier didn't get into town until late the night before the rodeo, nine-thirty, ten. I was drivin' our drop-top deuce and a quarter, and I remember real well when we got there, it was cold. Cold enough in fact to have the deuce's heater turned on high. We picked up Hambone at the motel we were all booked into, tossed our bags in our room, and headed uptown for a drink to lubricate our bones." Morgan flexed his bicep to punctuate the point.

"We'd had a couple of drinks at a little bar that sold to rodeo contestants at a discount, and we was all three startin' to feel a little warmer inside when Percy Lewis strolls in with a pack of his groupies. He spots Hambone right off and walks over to our table with his lapdogs in tow. He had to have been drinkin' or feelin' some special kind of country white-boy oats or else he never would've said what he did to Hambone. Called Hambone a suck-up coon right to his face. Said Hambone was gettin' high-pointed during his rides and drawin' rockin'-chair bulls because he'd been kissin' up to the judges all season and slippin' 'em money under the table.

"Hambone sat still for a bit, starin' down into his drink like he was expectin' the liquor to tell him what to do. Then he jumps up out of the little horseshoe-shaped booth we was sharin' like somebody had lit a torch to his ass and cold-cocked Lewis with a right cross to the temple that dropped him like he was a sack of shit. Hambone watched Lewis wiggle around on the floor for a few seconds, then sat back down, cool as a mint julep, and went back to nursin' his drink. Me and Dittier didn't move the whole time, figurin' that if anybody was gonna get hassled and dumped in the can for startin' a brawl, it would be three liquored-up, out-of-town brothers.

"But the law never showed, and to this day I don't know why none of Lewis's suck-ass groupies didn't come to his aid instead of standin' there lookin' down at him like he'd just had a stroke. Lewis didn't move for the better part of a minute, not even a twitch. When he finally did come around a ribbon of blood was dribblin' from his right ear. He got up on his feet real wobbly like, dusted off his ass, spit on the floor and mumbled that he'd settle up with Hambone later. Then he nodded for his group of leeches to follow him, and with two of 'em bracin' him by the arms, the whole pack headed out the door. Hambone never once looked up."

Morgan glanced straight back at Dittier. "Did I leave anything out?"

Dittier shook his head.

"Word about what had happened was all over the town by the next morning. But nobody said a damn thing to me or Dittier about it. Don't know what folks said to Hambone. He pretty much stayed out of sight for most of the day, and I only saw Lewis once before he was scheduled to ride that afternoon. He was talkin' to a bunch of people outside one of the livestock corrals, all hunched over in a muddied-up rain slicker. I was close enough to him to see that most of the right side of his face was one big purple bruise and that he had a cotton wad stuffed in his ear. Later I heard he drew a nasty shit of a bull named Thunder for his first go-around. Hambone told me later that when he heard Lewis had pulled Thunder, he had a feelin' somethin' terrible was gonna happen.

"An hour later I caught a glimpse of Lewis sittin' on top of that bull seconds before he left the chute. The wind was cuttin' up somethin' fierce, and the drizzle that had been pissin' at us all day long had turned into a steady rain. Lewis looked new-daddy nervous when Thunder bolted out of the chute, head to the ground, snortin' like a locomotive with Lewis floppin' back and forth on his back like a rag doll. The ride lasted for four, maybe five seconds at the most. Lewis came off the animal at one of them weird angles, his arms straight up in the air and out of position for breakin' his fall. When his head hit the arena muck, I heard his neck snap. After that the only thing I ever seen Percy Lewis ridin' was a wheelchair." Morgan sat back in his seat, out of breath.

"So Lewis blamed Hambone for what happened?" said CJ, suddenly reaching up and rubbing the back of his own neck.

"Sure did. In the space of a few hours his groupies had the local sheriff and a couple of finger-pointin' doctors involved, sayin' Hambone's right cross to Lewis's head the night before had contributed to him breakin' his neck. The sheriff wouldn't let Hambone leave town and the name-callin' and finger-pointin' went on for over a week. The whole mess didn't go away till the country doctor who first examined Lewis after his fall wrote up a report sayin' there wasn't no—how do you say it—extenuatin' circumstances involved. Said Lewis just got thrown off a bull and plain and simple broke his neck."

CJ throttled back, wondering why Percy Lewis would have waited so long to go after Hambone, and how a wheelchair-bound man could have wielded a branding iron with such murderous force. Deep in thought, he found himself staring at two miles of open road. Flooring the accelerator, he watched as the speedometer inched past seventy, eighty, and finally ninety. And he didn't ease off the gas until he had clocked ninety-five for a solid minute. The throaty sound of the engine backing off and the feel of the dry high-plains air rushing past his face had CJ wondering what it felt like to ride a bull. "Didn't see any cops, did you?" he called out to Morgan as they dropped back down to the speed limit. Morgan shook his head.

"Then I guess it's back to business," said CJ. "What happened to Lewis after that?"

Morgan, who hated speed, heights, tunnels, and hospitals, adjusted his muscular body in the seat, trying to recover from CJ's drag-racing exhibition. "He dogged Hambone for the next two years, followin' him around the circuit. Badmouthin' him every chance he got. Even tried to get Hambone's pro card yanked. When he couldn't, the SOB disappeared. Didn't see him again for years. Then last year at the Bill Pickett Rodeo in Denver, I caught a glimpse of his pitiful-lookin' peanut head peekin' out from behind one of the concession stands. He was feastin' on a short stack of spareribs, lookin' sloppy as usual, with a trail of barbeque sauce runnin' down the front of his shirt.

"I wondered what a sourpuss, wrinkled-up old white man like him was doin' at an all-black rodeo event until it hit me that he was probably tryin' to beam in on Hambone. Dittier and me watched him slither around in his wheelchair for a while, sucking on rib bones, and then went on inside the arena. I told Hambone about seein' him, thinkin' that it was real strange that Lewis would start doggin' his ass again after so many years. Hambone shrugged the whole thing off, sayin' Lewis had been followin' him for weeks because some Albuquerque reporter had dug his Great White Hope story back out of the grave."

Morgan wiped away a ribbon of sweat that had

started working its way down the side of his face.
"That's all Hambone ever said about Lewis. Never another word. Me and Dittier spotted him at a couple of
local rodeos outside Denver in Adams County this past
season, but we kept our distance and I didn't say nothin'
to Hambone. I'd lay odds that Lewis was as likely as
anybody to have sent Hambone on to an early grave."

"Got any idea where Lewis is now?" asked CJ,
whipping the Bel Air around a VW bus and taking his
place in a conga line of traffic approaching the outskirts
of Loveland.

"Can't tell you that, but I do know he once had a business outside of Denver in Parker peddlin' farm equipment.
Used to be listed in the yellow pages big as day under farm
machinery and equipment. Seems like he called his operation Lewis's Farm Implements and Repair."

Parker was a bedroom and ranching community fifteen miles south of Denver. CJ made a mental note to ask
Julie to check out Lewis's Farm Implements and Repair
when she did her background search on Nadine Kemp.
"We'll find him," said CJ, hoping that Julie would accommodate him. He accelerated around a Winnebago and
slipped back into line behind a flatbed tractor-trailer wobbling from side to side. He checked his watch, hoping he
could get by Lisa's and back to the office before Julie left.
Worried that he might not meet his timetable, he reached
back over the seat and tapped Dittier on the knee. Then,
glancing back to make certain Dittier could read his lips,
he said, "Story time, Dittier. You're up."

When Dittier remained unflinchingly silent in his
seat, CJ turned to Morgan for help. "Get through to him,
Morgan; we're talking murder here."

Morgan turned and faced Dittier squarely. "Spit it out, champ. Hog's rump's in the skillet now." Morgan only called Dittier *champ* when he was deadly serious.

Dittier swallowed hard and nervously began gnawing his lower lip. "It's bad," he signed to Morgan.

"Can't be no worse than bein' dead," Morgan signed back.

"Close."

"Try us. Me and CJ ain't here to judge."

Dittier thought hard for a moment; then, deciding to release something that had been festering inside him for the past fifteen years, he signed, "It started out real simple with me, Rebecca, and Hambone just being friends, sharing good times on the road. Mostly it was just drinking till all hours of the night." He looked at Morgan sheepishly. "You were just hitting your championship stride back then. There was no way you had time to look after everything I did."

Dittier's words bit into Morgan's conscience. He didn't like to be reminded that during the time he was playing rodeo king, he hadn't always been there for Dittier. Maybe if he had been, neither of them would've succumbed to alcohol and he wouldn't have frittered away all the money they had made. But it was water under the bridge now.

"Dittier say anything important so far?" asked CJ, eyes glued to the wobbling flatbed behemoth in front of them.

"No," said Morgan, nodding for Dittier to finish his story.

Dittier continued, his signing rhythm back to normal. "The first time Hambone told me that Rebecca wanted me to, uh—make love to her, I thought he was joking. It was in Laramie in a hotel room, and all of us were tipsy. She'd been teasing me all night and giggling. When we all ended up on the long side of drunk, I found out she was serious. She had stripped down to nothing but her cowboy boots and panties and I was stretched out on the floor, barely able to sit up. She kept circling me, saying, 'Come on Dittier, give yourself a break.' And I kept looking up at those long, God-awful beautiful legs of hers, thinking, might as well. The next thing I knew we were rolling on the floor. I was pretty groggy, and so was Rebecca, but I remember Hambone in the background egging Rebecca on."

Dittier cleared his sinuses with a quick snort. "After that first time, the three of us had ourselves one real bad habit." He looked at Morgan apologetically and dropped his hands to his sides.

The look on Morgan's face told CJ that Dittier had just told Morgan something that shocked him.

"So the two of you was screwin' the same woman," said Morgan, looking back at Dittier but aiming his words at CJ. "Big deal."

"It went on for almost a year before—" Dittier stopped signing in midsentence.

"Before what?"

"Before I found out Rebecca was only fifteen!"

When Morgan didn't follow up his question, CJ looked back at Dittier to catch the glimpse of torment on his face. "What's Dittier holding back?"

Morgan frowned and shook his head. "That Baptiste woman I was tellin' you about earlier, the one with the Bible-thumpin' father and the brother on edge. Seems like she, Hambone, and Dittier got involved in a three-way kind of thing while she was underage."

Suddenly Dittier's reluctance to have him go after Hambone's killer made sense to CJ. He now also knew the real reason that Rebecca's brother had tried to take Hambone Dolbey's head off with a shovel and why Dittier had been so reluctant to talk about the brother's and father's motive. CJ didn't like the idea of asking Morgan to probe Dittier's psyche much further, but he needed a few concrete answers about the Baptistes. "Ask Dittier if he knows where Rebecca is now, and whether he thinks she might be carrying around enough of a grudge to have killed Hambone after all these years."

Morgan signed the question back to Dittier.

"Last I heard she was living with her father and brother on a ranch outside of Laramie, Wyoming," Dittier signed. "As for killing Hambone, no way."

Dittier's answer surprised Morgan. Turning to CJ, he said, "She's livin' on a ranch outside Laramie, and Dittier says ain't no way she would've murdered Hambone."

"Why not?" asked CJ, glancing in the rearview mirror to catch Dittier's rapid-fire response to Morgan.

Morgan's eyes widened in surprise. "Dittier says it's because she had a baby by Hambone."

CJ floored the accelerator and shot around the flatbed, thinking about Dittier's declaration and the fact that it gave Hambone Dolbey's murder another new twist. As they passed the Loveland city limits marker, CJ checked to make sure he wasn't speeding into a town known for its strict traffic-law enforcement. With his speedometer pegged just under twenty-five, he looked over at Morgan. "How old would the baby be now?"

"Late teens would be my guess. Right, Dittier?" said Morgan.

Dittier nodded yes.

"Boy or girl?" said CJ.

Morgan relayed the question to Dittier. "Boy," he said, turning back to CJ.

CJ let out a sigh as he ran a growing list of murder suspects through his head. One that already included Whitaker Rodgers, the three Baptistes, Percy Lewis, and Nadine Kemp. Cruising slowly through Loveland with one eye out for cops, he added Hambone Dolbey's nameless son.

Chapter 15

There are places that define the Colorado high country as uniquely as a genetically engineered DNA fingerprint. The face of the Rockies west of Loveland is no exception. A few miles before the mouth of the Big Thompson Canyon just east of the Rockies' spine, a mass of Dakota sandstone sweeps up into a prominent gunmetal-gray rocky hogback. The resulting outcropping piggybacks its way for nearly two miles as a jagged, exposed vertical fold of stone. This ominous-looking expanse of bedrock, which mimics the jagged spines of a prehistoric stegosaurus as it briefly parallels the Big Thompson River before petering out into rolling ranchlands to the north, is known as the Devil's Backbone. Cruising past the outcropping on his way to Lisa

Darley's, CJ remembered his uncle once telling him that the Devil's Backbone was a modern-day gargoyle, strategically placed at the mouth of the canyon to warn all who entered to beware. Lisa's large-animal veterinary practice and horse farm occupied a twenty-acre high-country meadow just off the highway a mile west of the Devil's Backbone. A rambling metal horse barn and Lisa's log home dominated a two-acre terraced mesa in the middle of the property, where both had unobstructed views of the mouth of the canyon to the west and the Devil's Backbone to the east.

A gentle downslope breeze had kicked up out of the west when CJ turned onto the gravel lane that led up to Lisa's office to the sounds of speckled toads croaking in the alpine-meadow ferns along the edge of the lane.

"She ain't expectin' us," said Morgan as CJ pulled in front of the house. Morgan dusted off his pants, hoping he didn't look too rumpled and street-weary and praying that he wouldn't have to endure another of Lisa's lectures about him moving from Denver to live with her.

"She's here, she's here," mouthed Dittier, pointing to Lisa's Cherokee. As soon as the car stopped he bolted out of the back seat over the door and straight toward the barn, where Lisa kept his Red River hog, Geronimo.

Morgan shook his head as he watched Dittier streak for the barn. "God forbid anything should ever happen to that pig."

CJ got out of the Bel Air to catch a glimpse of Lisa stepping out of the early evening shadows of the barn. She was drinking a Diet Coke and leading Dictator, her Swedish Warmblood gelding. During her college years she and Dictator had collected enough jumping ribbons to cover one entire wall of her office. Now that Dictator was an aging arthritic, Lisa pampered him like a baby. As a result of spills taken during her jumping days, Lisa had suffered two separated shoulders and had her left knee reconstructed twice. An aggressive rider, willing to lay everything on the line, she had learned her riding and jumping skills under the tutelage of Morgan, who understood that as a black woman attempting to forge her way into a lily-white sport, she had to be able to separate herself from the crowd. Five foot seven and athletic, Lisa had blossomed over the years CJ had known her from a chubby, wide-eyed college student to a strikingly attractive woman.

Lisa stopped a few feet short of CJ. "Good boy," she said, reaching back to scratch Dictator between the eyes. Then, reins looped over her wrist, she stepped forward and hugged CJ. "If I'd known I was having company, I would've dressed for it." Handing the reins to CJ, she stepped over and gave Morgan a kiss on the cheek and then a lingering hug. "Dictator's bad knee's been giving him fits," she said, taking the reins back from CJ. "I just finished rubbing him down and taking off his heat wrap." She looked at Morgan. "What did you think of his gait?"

"Horse was limping," said Morgan, never one to hold back on the truth. "Should be—he's old. Next thing I know you're gonna buy him a whirlpool." Morgan began gently stroking the aging gelding's withers, unable to hide how he really felt.

Lisa smiled. "I've been thinking about it, but I haven't been able to get my rich uncle to spot me the money."

"Maybe you should try that boyfriend of yours, the banker."

Lisa forced a halfhearted smile, afraid the friendly banter was about to take a turn for the worse. Her long-time boyfriend, Brian Eggers, vice-president of one of Denver's largest banks, was a fast-track, hard-driving executive type who hadn't quite figured out that being black in a white-dominated profession didn't mean he had to continue proving himself every second of every day. Morgan didn't dislike the man, even though he suspected he probably starched and ironed his shorts. It was just that he was like a doting father when it came to Lisa, and he had never been willing to cut Brian any slack.

"Don't start with Brian," said Lisa.

Morgan shrugged and held out his palms hands-off style.

Happy that they weren't going to revisit the Brian Eggers saga, Lisa turned to CJ. "What brings the three musketeers out my way?" she said, knowing the visit was somehow related to Hambone Dolbey's death.

"We're looking for a little inside dope on your local Weld County rodeo kingpin, Whitaker Rodgers."

Dictator nudged Lisa's shoulder, shoving her aside. Regaining her balance, she ran her fingers through his mane. "Let me get Mr. Old Bones here bedded down, and I'll tell you what I know." Then, giving Morgan an I've-got-a-secret kind of smile, she added, "But the person you should really be talking to is Brian." She slapped Dictator on the rump, urging him into a wide U-turn. "Be back in a minute. Go on inside and make yourself at home," she said, leaving CJ and Morgan wondering what kind of information Brian Eggers had on Rodgers.

When Lisa returned, Morgan was in the kitchen feasting on a giant bag of tortilla chips and some bean dip he had found in one of the cupboards and gazing out the kitchen's sliding glass patio doors into the backyard meadow of wildflowers and timothy. CJ had declined Morgan's offer to share in the feast and headed for Lisa's private office, where he stood surveying her wall of diplomas, plaques, and ribbons. He was happy that it was after six and all the staff had left. He had learned over the years that talking to anyone about a murder with big ears around could sometimes come back to bite you.

Lisa came through the patio door to catch Morgan devouring a handful of chips. "Lay off the chips, Uncle M, I don't want you spoiling dinner. One of my clients just picked up his mare and dropped off six world-class steaks."

Morgan clipped the bag shut and pushed it aside. Then he watched as Lisa walked over to the refrigerator, opened the door, and pulled out four mammoth T-bones.

"Where's CJ?" said Lisa, setting the steaks aside.

"In your office, I think," said Morgan, shaking his head at the size of the cuts of meat.

"How about going outside and firing up the patio grill?" Lisa reached back into the refrigerator and pulled out a head of lettuce and two nearly grapefruit-sized-farm-fresh tomatoes. "Hope steak, fries, and a salad'll be enough." She bumped the refrigerator door closed with her hip without waiting for a response and said, "Think I'll go talk to CJ while you get the charcoal started."

Morgan ignored her request and had started to follow her out of the kitchen when Lisa spun around and pointed her finger directly in his face. "I don't want you in this loop, Uncle M. CJ's investigating a murder. He's used to it. You're not. I want you and Dittier to stay out of the way."

Morgan had the urge to remind Lisa that he had helped CJ out on cases before and even saved CJ's bacon once or twice. But he knew that if he did they'd end up arguing, so he backed off, figuring that once they were back in Denver he'd get to do things his way. Retreating, he headed for the patio to fire up the grill without one word of protest.

CJ was admiring a photograph of Lisa and Mavis that he had taken several years earlier in front of the Colorado State University Veterinary Hospital when Lisa quietly walked into her office. In the photograph Lisa was dressed in powder-blue hospital scrubs, looking tired and overwhelmed from a recent six-week surgery rotation. Mavis, who had just come from guest lecturing to a group of minority student business majors at the CSU business school, was dressed in an expensive silk blouse and a gray tweed power suit. She looked every bit the Wall Street power broker, and every time CJ saw the picture he asked himself what a woman with an MBA from Boston University was doing operating her father's soul food restaurant when she could have been a successful banker or stockbroker. The question was always followed by a second, more personal one. What in hell was Mavis doing hanging out with him?

"Awfully good-looking woman, isn't she?" said Lisa, approaching CJ from behind.

Startled, CJ pivoted toward her. "You or Mavis?"

"You know who I mean. By the way, how's Mavis doing?"

"Besides struggling to keep Mae's afloat and disappointed at having to postpone a trip we had planned to Santa Fe, she's fine."

"Give her my best."

"I'll do that." CJ backed away from the photograph and took a seat in an overstuffed leather chair in the corner of the room. Lisa sat down across from him in an old pressed-back chair that she had refinished herself. CJ was getting comfortable and patting his vest pocket for his box of cheroots, when he remembered that Lisa forbade smoking in the house. "Tell me what you know about Whitaker Rodgers," he said, dropping his hands.

"First tell me about your ear," said Lisa, getting her first good look at the swollen ear she hadn't noticed before.

"It's screaming at me less and less."

"Want me to take a look?"

"After you fill me in on Rodgers."

"Okay," said Lisa, trying not to stare. She leaned forward in the chair, chin cupped in her hands, hoping CJ's ear wasn't already infected. "Here's my take on Rodgers. He's a rich oil man who hangs around rodeos dreaming he's in charge and barking orders at the people he wishes he could be. Concise enough?"

"To the point. What other dreams do you think he's missed out on in life?"

"Running the family ranch north of Greeley is the scuttlebutt I get from my office staff. The way I hear it, Rodgers wanted to be a rancher all his life, like his mother's side of the clan. Instead he got stuck peddling gas and oil."

CJ stroked his chin, thinking about how best to explore the Dolbey-Rodgers relationship. Having to plod through life as a frustrated cowboy and unhappy oil company exec certainly wouldn't have been reason enough for Rodgers to kill Hambone Dolbey. "Do you know of any other ties between Rodgers and Dolbey besides their interest in the rodeoing?"

Lisa sat back in her chair and thought for a moment. "None that I'm aware of, but I can tell you what one of my animal techs who's lived around here all his life said about Rodgers recently." She paused as if to punctuate her words. "Man's got financial problems dripping from both ears, is the way he phrased it. I didn't ask him to elaborate."

"Have you seen any of his oil or gas rigs making the rounds?"

"No, but I have seen a few pieces of his heavy equipment, earth graders, caterpillars, things like that, on the roads around here. You can't miss them. They're all plastered with the Pandeco Oil corporate logo."

Lisa's answer came as a surprise. Although it wasn't unheard of for someone in the oil and gas exploration business to have the kind of big dirt equipment she had described, CJ knew it was excess baggage as far as lean and mean Colorado high country oil drilling was concerned. He tucked the information away in the back of his head. "Maybe he's branching out."

Lisa shrugged. "Anything's possible up here in the boonies. There's one sure way to find out. Give Brian a call. He's had a few business transactions with Rodgers over the years."

The look on CJ's face told Lisa that he didn't think Brian Eggers would be the least bit willing to pass along anything confidential about Whitaker Rodgers.

"I'll ask for you," said Lisa defensively. "You never know. It might turn out that Brian's not as pompous as you and Uncle Morgan think."

"Anything's worth a try," said CJ. He was about to remind Lisa not to mention anything about Hambone Dolbey's murder to Brian when Morgan walked in, T-bone steaks piled eight inches high on a platter in one hand and a bowl of barbecue sauce in the other.

"Let's get this show on the road. My stomach's bitchin'," said Morgan, nearly dropping the steaks.

"One last thing," said CJ, as Lisa made a beeline for Morgan to rescue their dinner.

"Shoot," said Lisa, taking the platter from Morgan.

"Know anything about Dolbey's girlfriend, a woman named Nadine Kemp?"

"Never heard of her."

"What about a woman named Rebecca Baptiste?" said CJ, cutting his eyes at Morgan.

Lisa thought for a moment before answering, "No." She hadn't missed the glance CJ had flashed at Morgan. "I hope Morgan and Dittier aren't tied into this any deeper than asking for your help."

"They aren't."

"Good." Lisa eased the bowl of barbecue sauce out of Morgan's hand. "Why don't you go down to the barn and get Dittier? CJ, you're in charge of the salad," she added with a wink. CJ started toward the kitchen, thrilled that Lisa had wrestled the steaks away from Morgan, who had a knack for turning prime meat into shoe leather.

Morgan headed off to get Dittier, unaware that he had just been eased through a revolving culinary door.

During the half hour it took to prepare the meal, the sun set and an evening chill filled the air. Lisa donned a sweater, and CJ and Dittier slipped on gray laboratory coats that Lisa retrieved from one of the examination rooms. Morgan remained coatless, his arms peppered with goose bumps.

CJ, who had been staring toward the Big Thompson Canyon narrows, turned his gaze in the opposite direction toward the foothills to the east. "Ever wonder what's up in that rimrock?" he said, extending a nearly empty beer mug toward the shadowy spine of the Devil's Backbone.

Morgan shook his head and poached a handful of french fries off the sizzling cookie sheet Lisa had just set down on the redwood tabletop. Lisa slapped the back of his hand. "Wait," she said, before heading back into the house to get the salad dressing she had forgotten.

Dittier's adrenaline rush over seeing Geronimo had subsided. He walked over to the patio's edge and stared out toward the rock outcroppings, now almost invisible in the darkness. After a few seconds he turned to Morgan, signing so rapidly that CJ missed what he said.

"What's Dittier's opinion?" said CJ.

Morgan chuckled. "Says that if anything's livin' up there it must be mean as hell or crawlin' on its belly."

"Makes sense to me," said CJ, smiling at Dittier and taking a final swallow of beer before placing his mug on the table to watch the Devil's Backbone fade into darkness.

Chapter 16

CJ dropped Morgan and Dittier off in front of the abandoned Platte River Valley building they called home, just west of Denver's lower downtown district. The building always reminded CJ of a gigantic chicken coop, and the cluttered yard of junk behind it, overflowing with firewood, commodes, sinks, pipes, electrical wiring, and mammoth wooden cable spools, triggered old-time movie images of graveyards and the walking dead for him.

"I'll be in touch," said CJ, watching Morgan and Dittier head for the building's doorway. Morgan fumbled with a hefty lock that held the makeshift plywood door in place, then, nudging Dittier ahead of him, he nodded back at CJ and disappeared inside.

CJ pulled away in the Bel Air, hoping he'd be able to finish the job of finding Hambone Dolbey's killer without having to dig too deeply into the money he had earned for delivering Bobby Two-Shirts to Cicero Vickers. Stuffed from too much steak and one too many beers, he reached down and loosened his belt a notch. Then, sucking in his gut, he patted his stomach in an attempt to convince himself that he was slapping a midsection that was on the youthful side of forty-seven. He thought briefly about lighting up a cheroot, but he remembered his promise to Mavis. Frowning and shaking his head, he adjusted himself in his seat and zigzagged his way out of the Platte River Valley warehouse district.

He eased along the southern edge of downtown past the tourist glitz of Larimer Square, caught a rare green light at the intersection of Larimer and Speer Boulevard, and sped south on the tree-lined boulevard toward home. On the way he ran an investigative game plan through his head. He put Whitaker Rodgers and Percy Lewis at the top of his agenda for the next few days. With a little luck, maybe he'd be able to convince Julie to run down what she could on the Baptistes in between studying for the bar exam. He had a fleeting thought of just how difficult things were going to be without Julie and swallowed hard as he pictured a future with an endless string of office temps like Flora Jean Benson.

He exited Speer onto 14th, made the short jog past the *Rocky Mountain News* building, and turned onto Delaware Street to be greeted by the amber and red flashing lights of an ambulance halfway up the block. Easing off the accelerator, he tapped his brakes, realizing that the ambulance was parked directly in front of Cicero

Vickers's driveway. He was about to swing around the ambulance and into his own driveway next door when he saw two men wheeling a stretcher down Cicero's front walk. In the glow of his headlights he could see that the man at the stretcher's rear was holding an IV bottle just above the occupant's head with the IV line wiggling its way down into a limp arm resting along the edge of the stretcher.

CJ slipped the Bel Air into reverse and parked behind the ambulance. When the two Denver General Hospital paramedics eased the stretcher over the curb and into the street, CJ realized that the man being attended to was Cicero Vickers. He jumped out of the Bel Air, leaving the motor running as the paramedics rolled Cicero directly into the path of his headlights. The feisty old bail bondsman's face was a mass of blood. His left eye was bulging from its socket, his right eye closed. Teaspoon-sized divots of flesh were missing from his forehead, and a spongy-looking ruby-red clot mushroomed from one nostril. The paramedic at the front of the stretcher waved CJ back.

"Give us some space, buddy. This ain't show and tell." As the paramedics struggled to maneuver the stretcher between the back of the ambulance and the Bel Air, CJ realized he was so close to the ambulance that he hadn't left room for the men to angle the stretcher in.

"Move your goddamn car, CJ," boomed a raspy voice that seemed to come out of nowhere.

CJ looked toward the house to see Herman Currothers, the lecherous little bug-eyed weasel of a man who owned AAA Bonding Services two doors down from Cicero, rushing toward him. Herman, the only person CJ had ever heard Julie say she hated, looked ready to pee in his pants.

Since Herman had a strong disdain for humanity, especially minorities, cops, and gays, CJ had never fully understood how he had managed to stay in the bail bonding business for as many years as he had without getting his skull cracked by someone he had either bad-mouthed or crossed. CJ jumped into the Bel Air and backed up, giving the paramedics the room they needed to maneuver Cicero into the ambulance.

Herman was now standing curbside, shaking his head, gripping the topless Coke can he usually carried. Eyeing CJ nervously, he spat a foul-looking brown glob of saliva and chewing tobacco into the can. "Somebody beat the shit out of Cicero," he said, in an authoritarian I-told-you-so kind of tone. "Probably one of your brothers from the Points looking to separate Cicero from his last quarter. Or maybe one of his faggy clients who finally got pissed off enough to tenderize his face."

CJ gave Herman a raised-eyebrow stare that screamed, *Shut the fuck up.* Herman had seen the stare before, and since he had also once seen CJ grab a Five Points gang-banger who had threatened Mavis and nearly rip his Adam's apple out, he knew it was time to put a damper on his name-calling. He decided to allevi-ate the situation by telling CJ what had happened. "I found Cicero lying on the kitchen floor about fifteen minutes ago. We were supposed to go to a poker game tonight. Walked right into his place when I found the front door unlocked. Now you know that wasn't like Ci-cero. When I found him, he was bleeding from damn near every opening in his head." Herman looked toward the ambulance, where one of the paramedics now had Cicero's stretcher stabilized in place in the back. The paramedic made an adjustment to Cicero's IV, then eased his way out the back of the ambulance, slamming the door.

CJ stared at the man inquisitively. "How's he doing?"

"Iffy," said the paramedic, flipping his hand back and forth touch-and-go style before heading toward the cab.

CJ turned back to Herman. "Did you call the cops?"

"They're inside." Herman pointed toward a nearby patrol car that CJ had missed in the excitement. The high-pitched whine of a siren pierced the Delaware Street quiet as the ambulance pulled away from the curb, kicking up gutter trash in its wake. CJ watched the ambulance gain speed, rounding the corner at 14th, before he turned and headed toward Cicero's building to see what was going on inside. Herman drifted behind him up the walkway.

A young patrolman was kneeling in the entryway when they reached the house. A matchstick protruded from his mouth, and his eyes were glued to the floor. He looked up briefly at Herman, then cast a suspicious look at CJ. "Who's your sidekick?"

"Another bondsman. He lives in the building next door."

The patrolman eyed CJ for a few more seconds before moving aside. "Sergeant Corker's in the kitchen. He'll have some questions for you. I've already taped the place. Don't touch anything on your way in."

CJ knew Corker as well as any man in blue and

considered him innocuous enough for a cop. As he and
Herman headed down the wide, semidark hallway toward the kitchen, CJ noticed that the living room, dining
room, and business office had been taped off with yellow
crime-scene tape. In contrast to the hallway darkness,
the kitchen, where the ever frugal Cicero spent much of
his time watching sports on a small, fourteen-inch black-
and-white TV, was lit up like a television studio. The
screen of Cicero's cherished black-and-white had been
smashed and milk, canned goods, flour, cereal, and silverware had been tossed helter-skelter across the room.
The refrigerator door was wide open and someone had
taken the time to smash its contents against the walls.
Chicken parts, frozen peas, and meatball-sized knots of
ground round were floating in a kitchen sink half full of
murky water. Two empty half-gallon milk cartons occupied the center of Cicero's century-old claw-footed walnut kitchen table, spouts puckered open, kissing one
another. CJ's eyes narrowed into a squint of disbelief as
he surveyed the tabletop. Scores of thumbprint-sized
gouges peppered what had been a mirror-gloss walnut
finish. Dumbfounded, CJ started into the kitchen, still
ahead of Herman.

"Hold it right there," said a lanky police sergeant,
greeting him from a kneeling position ten feet away. He
held up his hand traffic-cop style for them to stop as he
stood up. It wasn't until the sergeant was a couple of feet
away that CJ noticed the starburst-shaped swatch of
dried blood in the spot where he had been kneeling.

"See you rounded up Floyd," said the sergeant to
Herman. Acknowledging CJ with a nod, he dusted off
his hands, then reached into his pocket and pulled out a

tab of yellow Post-it notes. He stuck the top note on the kitchen countertop next to a shiny U-shaped piece of metal and drew an arrow on the tab. When he noticed CJ staring intently at the sticky note, he spoke up. "Somebody beat the dog crap out of Vickers. I'm guessing they used a chain of some sort." He nodded at the metal fragment on the countertop. "Looks like they tried to beat the table to death too. Know anybody P.O.'d enough at Vickers to want to send this kind of message?" He looked around the room, spreading his arms out for dramatic effect.

Herman shrugged his shoulders and looked at CJ.

CJ's mind was racing. Ever since they had rolled Cicero into the ambulance, he had been thinking about Bobby Two-Shirts's threat. The skinny beanpole of a bond skipper's image danced in front of him as he began counting the blood spots on the floor. "I brought back a bond skipper for Cicero the other day—a little fence named Bobby Two-Shirts. Right now he's bunking across the street." CJ nodded toward the jail. "He claimed to have someone backing him up who would settle up with me and Vickers."

Sergeant Corker shook his head. "He must be one hell of a friend."

"She," said CJ, still tallying the blood spots.

"Tough mama." The sergeant's words reverberated in CJ's head as he scanned the floor one last time and noticed a saucer-sized pool of blood he had missed. *Tough mama indeed,* he thought, ending his count at an even dozen.

Chapter 17

Celeste Deepstream's legs felt crampy, knotted up from sitting in the front seat of her pickup, where she had been watching CJ's house for the past hour. The deep muscle achiness reminded her of the kind of pain she used to experience near the end of the two-hundred-meter butterfly. She had never heard of CJ Floyd until Cicero Vickers had moaned his name through a mouthful of frothy blood and broken teeth a few seconds before he slipped into a semiconscious lump at her feet. During his beating, Vickers had admitted that it was CJ who had tracked Bobby down, dragged him back to Denver, and humiliated him, threatening to make him urinate on himself before handing him over to the Denver police. An unsympathetic arraigning judge had set

Bobby's bond at $50,000 when a list of Bobby's prior criminal transgressions surfaced and he found out that the prisoner's prior brushes with the law included child molestation and five other outstanding warrants. The bond was $20,000 more than Celeste could ante up so she had had to let Bobby remain in jail. She blamed Vickers and CJ equally for Bobby's predicament, and she had retaliated against Cicero by trashing his place and beating him nearly to death with a three-foot length of snow-tire chain she kept in the bed of her truck.

Now she was thinking of how she would settle up with CJ Floyd. Before Vickers had slipped into unconsciousness she had learned two all-important things about Floyd. He was black, and he ran a bail bonding operation out of the building next door to Vickers. Her pickup was parked on the diagonal, next to a telephone pole in a brightly lit, all but empty parking lot at the corner of 13th Avenue and Delaware Street, half a block south of CJ's office, giving her an unobstructed view of CJ's building.

Clutching a pair of binoculars, she was hoping to get another look at the two men she had seen rush up the sidewalk and disappear into Vickers's building ten minutes earlier. Agitated, sweating, and fidgeting in her seat, she wasn't sure whether she had killed Vickers. She had casually driven away from the scene of the beating, returning to the parking lot later to watch for Floyd and to find an ambulance already on the scene. The thought of killing Vickers made her briefly uneasy until she remembered that Bobby was in jail because of him. She understood things about Bobby that people like Vickers and Floyd couldn't possibly appreciate, things that had her feeling edgy and desperate. Like the fact that the last two times Bobby had been jailed, he had tried to kill himself. And the fact that Bobby was so homophobic that once during a jail stint in Arizona, he had fashioned a couple of rusty pop-bottle caps into a knife and tried to castrate the gay queen he was sharing a cell with because the man had touched him on the shoulder as he welcomed Bobby to the cell. The assault had earned him an additional four months on what turned out to be a two-year sentence.

She adjusted her binoculars, focusing on the streetlight in front of Vickers's building. A ring of miller moths circled the flickering light, trapped in its glow. She was about to lower her binoculars when the two men she had seen earlier emerged from the house. After leaving the front porch they stopped halfway down the walkway. The white man said something to the much taller black man, and they split up.

She focused on the black man, hoping she had found CJ Floyd. She watched him get into a Chevy convertible that earlier had been blocked from view by the ambulance. As she watched the man slip behind the wheel of the car she had the sinking feeling that he might pull off and she would end up having to tail him, still uncertain whether he was Floyd. But when he swung the convertible in a wide arch into the middle of the street and pulled into the driveway next door to Vickers's, she knew she had found her man. She smiled as she watched him step back out of the convertible, run the top up, and then fish into his vest pocket for a smoke and light up.

Earlier she had thought about breaking into the building just north of Vickers's and taking a chance that it would be Floyd's, but she had decided that a stakeout would be a better course of action. It had turned out to be a wise decision because the man with Floyd had gone into the house she had originally considered breaking into.

As she watched CJ enjoy his smoke, she thought about Vickers flopping around on the kitchen floor, blubbering and gasping for air. She broke into a half-mast smile and, suddenly calm and pensive, surveyed her new adversary, memorizing his features as she watched a plume of smoke curl up in front of his face. Puzzled at why Floyd seemed to be taking things so leisurely, she shot a quick glance toward the butt of the hunting rifle resting in the passenger-side footwell and thought about dropping him on the spot. She ran her free hand down the stock and glanced toward the jail, wondering how Bobby was doing, knowing that he still struggled with night terrors that had haunted him since he was a child. When she looked back, CJ was entering the front door of the house.

She made a mental note of how quickly he moved for a man his size, as she watched a series of first-floor lights come on inside the house, followed a few minutes later by a battery of second-floor lights. Now she knew where Floyd lived and worked. She glanced back down at her rifle, knowing that she would have another chance at Floyd as she thought about the fact that because of Vickers she was now on the run. She started the truck and thought back to her college days as a swimmer, remembering what it was like to feel an adrenaline rush of power as she made a final turn toward the finish, chasing or being chased as she broke for home.

As she pulled away, crisscrossing the lot's glow-in-the-dark yellow-striped spaces, she couldn't help but wonder whether Floyd would be a tough frontrunner she would have to struggle to catch up with or a loser like Vickers.

Chapter 18

Whitaker Rodgers was pretending to enjoy the tasteless continental breakfast he had just been served in the sterile paneled Pandeco Oil and Gas corporate boardroom. A rancid-tasting almond croissant with one bite out of it, a glass of orange juice as tart as a persimmon, and a cup of artificially flavored coffee rested on a crisp white paper place mat before him. A five-foot-wide teakwood table separated Whitaker from Evelyn Coleman and his mother. Rolling his eyes let's-get-this-show-on-the-road style, Whitaker paused, took a sip of coffee, and then glanced across the table at his mother, hoping she hadn't noticed the gesture.

Whitaker's reckless eyeballing and juvenile gestures were not lost on Virginia Rodgers. She dabbed the corner of her mouth with an overstarched linen napkin as a look of disappointment crossed her face. It was a look Whitaker had seen since childhood, a look that told him he didn't have what it took to make it in either the cowboy or the corporate world.

He looked down at the croissant and then over to Evelyn. Unlike him, Evelyn was an expert at ingratiating herself to his mother. Plain-Jane looking, willowy, and superbly fit from rock climbing and white-water rafting, Evelyn had played hatchet woman for his mother when it came to downsizing Pandeco, and because of it she had moved up the corporate ladder from junior engineer to chief of engineering operations as rapidly as if her last name were Rodgers. She was the type of woman he could have learned to hate, but instead she had become a kind of alter ego who fulfilled both his corporate and sexual fantasies. He often wondered whether his passion for Evelyn was the result of grasping something forbidden, harboring something from his mother, or just plain lust.

Whitaker glanced back at his mother, preparing himself for the recitation Evelyn had warned him Virginia would give. Fidgeting in his seat, he prepared himself for the worst.

Looking pensive and every bit the oil company CEO, Virginia Rodgers stared into her coffee. She was a sixty-two-year-old, extremely fit, ruggedly handsome woman who looked barely more than fifty and still spoke with the distinctive Western dry-land rancher's drawl that she had been trying to shake for most of her adult life.

She cleared her throat three quick times, a ritualistic preamble to dressing down her son. "Why you would do something so stupid as to become partners with that man

Dolbey is beyond my comprehension, Whit. And all over a tract of worthless land."

For the past two days Whitaker had been asking himself the very same thing. Dolbey certainly wasn't the kind of person he normally did business with, and he had yet to come up with a single valid reason for why he had entered into a written agreement with Dolbey except perhaps that the stakes in the game he was playing required something tangible, something he could see. Maybe it was just greed. It didn't matter now; he had struck the deal. Everything had made the situation look like a masterful, well-orchestrated win-win. Dolbey's forty acres of worthless land would offer Pandeco an ingress and egress easement to the three thousand acres he needed to access just south of it. It had seemed like such a simple right-of-way deal. He looked at Evelyn, sitting across from him poker-faced, and sighed, knowing she had never favored any of the methods he had employed in dealing with Dolbey. But she had also never understood the importance of Dolbey's water rights, something any geologist worth his salt knew had immense value in a mining venture, and something Dolbey had tossed in to cap the deal for the promise of five thousand more dollars.

Whitaker's stomach rumbled nervously as he contemplated how to answer his mother. "Dolbey wouldn't take any money once he realized what I was looking for wasn't oil but diamonds. He demanded a piece of the action."

"And you gave it to him just like you were handing over a bone to a dog?"

"I didn't have much choice unless you think I could have accessed the top of a mountain and developed an open-pit diamond mine without going through his land.

Since he wouldn't take money, I had to offer him something. Besides, the agreement we had was worthless, nothing but scribblings on a piece of paper. Ask Evelyn." He glanced at Evelyn for support, but she remained uncommonly silent.

Virginia Rodgers shook her head in disgust. "Whitaker, the man turned up murdered."

"I tore up our agreement."

"Tore, shmore—that piece of paper gives you a motive for killing him." She glanced at Evelyn, one eyebrow cocked disconcertingly as if to say, *He's done it again,* then turned to Whitaker. "If the police don't show up on our doorstep asking you questions, I hear some black bail bondsman will. I hope you've got a reasonable story prepared."

Whitaker sat up straight and craned his neck at Evelyn. He had told her about his encounter with CJ Floyd, but he had expected her to keep the information to herself. He was ready to scream, *Can't you keep your fucking mouth shut!* but he knew she'd just ignore him and that in a few hours she'd be nudging up against him, purring like a kitten, rubbing his inner thigh, licking his ear, asking him if he wanted to go to bed. "I wouldn't worry. Even if someone connects me to Dolbey, who's to say he didn't give me permission to cross his land?"

Evelyn surprised him by suddenly speaking up. "Can we forget about Dolbey for the moment? What about the mining?"

Whitaker shrugged his shoulders. "What about it?"

"Is everything moving along okay? This thing isn't going to turn into another Colorado diamond hoax, is it?"

Whitaker smiled self-assuredly, secure in the knowledge that for once he was in the driver's seat; because neither Evelyn, with all her manipulative skills and engineering expertise, nor his skeptical mother knew anything about diamonds.

"It's no hoax." He sat back and stroked his chin, recalling the story of Colorado's great diamond hoax of 1872. The hoax began on the Western Slope in Moffat County when two prospecting cousins from Kentucky brought a canvas bag containing what they claimed to be diamonds and rubies from a Moffat County mining strike to a San Francisco investment banker named William Ralston. Ralston offered to back the cousins in what he saw as a get-rich-quick mining opportunity. To make certain the mine was a reality and not a myth, he had the two miners take a mining engineer and several of his trusted associates back to Colorado to explore the gemstone site. They were allowed to sweep the wilderness site for several hours and collected a sampling of precious stones which were sent to Charles L. Tiffany, America's most renowned gemologist, who declared them genuine and appraised the stones at $150,000.

Ralston hastily founded the San Francisco and New York Mining and Commercial Company and set about raising the funds he needed to back the gemstone exploration. He ultimately raised four million dollars from a group of elite investors and began mining the fields in earnest. The two Kentuckians were eventually bought out, and as soon as they received their cash they promptly disappeared.

Before mining operations could begin in earnest, a U.S. geologist who knew the region well became suspicious of the great diamond claim. He tracked down and questioned the engineer who had originally accompanied the two Kentucky prospectors to survey the land. When he inspected the claim site and found diamonds everywhere, especially in rocky crevices, their artificial placement told him that the area had been salted.

The diamonds turned out to be low-quality African diamond mine rejects that the two Kentuckians who perpetrated the hoax had bought in England and Holland for next to nothing. As the story of the scam unfolded, nearly everyone involved ended up either broke or saddled with a tarnished reputation. The ingenious scheme drove the Bank of California, a heavy investor, into short-term insolvency. William Ralston killed himself, and only one of the Kentucky prospectors was quickly located. After returning $150,000 to the state of California in return for immunity from prosecution, he was never extradited. The second prospector became a mortician and died in 1896.

Whitaker leaned forward in his seat and took a sip of coffee, knowing that Colorado's latest diamond mining exploration had cost a man his life because it was anything but a hoax. Defending himself against Evelyn's accusation, he countered, "You know I've been excavating the Devil's Backbone site for months. We're finally into serious kimberlite pipes. It's only a matter of time before we find something big."

Virginia Rodgers had enough geological smarts to know that kimberlite was the volcanic rock in which diamonds are embedded. She also knew that most North American kimberlite contained no stones or too few stones to make any mining operation commercially viable. She looked Whitaker up and down and gave him a penetrating arched-eyebrow stare. "I don't know why I don't cut this fiasco off this second." What she didn't say was, *You've stuck Pandeco with another one of your failures, and any other CEO but a mother would have cut their losses long ago and booted you out the door.*

Whitaker eyed his croissant, knowing full well what his mother was thinking. "Anything else up for discussion?"

"We should probably get our stories together for the police or that Floyd character in case they come nosing around," said Evelyn.

Whitaker thought for a moment. "I've got a message-machine tape from Dolbey saying it's okay to cross his land. That could help."

Evelyn laughed. "Not good enough. That was before he knew about the diamonds and withdrew the offer."

Whitaker wrapped his hands around his coffee mug and took a final sip. "I know that, but he's not here to dispute it." Setting his mug aside, he reached into his pocket and pulled out a jagged piece of kimberlite and a small diamond, which he laid on the table. The kimberlite fragment was nearly identical to the rock CJ had found in the water trough at the Greeley Stampede. The three-carat diamond had been cut from an eight-carat stone Whitaker had found during one of his rockhounding expeditions near the Devil's Backbone. He eyed the kimberlite and the gemstone and smiled, knowing that this time around the great diamond fields of Colorado were for real. Then, looking up at Evelyn and his mother, he said, "I think it is time we get our stories together."

Chapter 19

The pulsating sounds of Snoop Doggy Dogg rapping about the white man's injustice greeted CJ as he headed down the stairway from his apartment to his office to start the day. All he could think about as the music became louder was the legwork facing him as he tried to solve a murder case with too many suspects. Luckily, the night before, he had reduced the number of suspects by one when he had sweet-talked Julie into checking on the whereabouts of Percy Lewis, the Hambone Dolbey–hating ex–bull rider.

Restless and unable to sleep, he had called Julie just past midnight to tell her what had happened to Cicero Vickers and then rolled directly into a plea for her to take a break from studying for the bar to do a background check on Lewis. Julie had grudgingly agreed only after CJ promised he would teach her ten-year-old son, Damion, to fly-fish that fall. CJ didn't mention that the person who had beaten Cicero nearly to death was probably looking to do the same to him.

Julie had awakened him with a phone call just before eight to say that according to the man who had purchased his farm implement business, Percy Lewis was now confined to a nursing home in Northern California. He wasn't ready to dismiss Lewis completely, since Lewis sounded like a troubled man at the end of his life who could very well have hired someone to kill Hambone, but he decided that for the moment Whitaker Rodgers and the Baptistes were more promising suspects.

CJ had slipped out of bed, showered, and then called Denver General Hospital to check on Cicero's status, only to learn that the miserly bondsman was in ICU and listed in grave condition. After hanging up he remembered that Cicero had a married sister who lived twenty miles south of Denver in the town of Castle Rock—a mousy, unkempt slip of a woman with an alcoholic's spidery complexion and Dumbo-sized ears. He thought about calling her to make certain she knew about Cicero but couldn't remember her name. He could only hope that the police or the staff at Denver General would follow through.

The stairway from CJ's apartment stubbed into a short center hallway with towering twelve-foot-high Victorian ceilings. Since there was no access to his office from the hall, he had to enter the office by passing through the cramped alcove just inside the front door that had served as Julie's office for the past eight years. He had often thought about knocking a hole in the wall to make a private entrance to his office, but something always told him that if he did he would be violating the old painted lady, so he never acted on the idea.

The thought of tunneling through the eight-inch-thick plaster and lath surfaced once again as he stepped into the alcove to the ear-splitting sound of nearly unintelligible rap coming from Flora Jean's boom box. Wondering why he had let Julie palm Flora Jean off on him, he stopped in his tracks as he found himself suddenly staring at what could easily have been a scene from a fashionable, upscale restaurant.

Julie's desk was draped with a white linen tablecloth. Her books, telephone, desktop files, and computer had all been stacked neatly in a corner of the room. A bowl of raisin bran topped with fresh strawberries and a chilled pitcher of milk occupied the middle of the desk. A bowl overflowing with the plumpest blackberries he had ever seen flanked the pitcher, and a huge platter stacked with cinnamon rolls, apple and lemon twists, and half a dozen cracklin' cakes occupied the leading edge of the desktop. Flora Jean stood with her back to him, humming to the music's beat, arranging a carafe of orange juice and coffee cups. The culinary arrangement caught CJ so off guard that for a moment he completely forgot about the rap music blasting from the boom box just to the left of his head.

When Flora Jean turned to catch the astonished look on CJ's face, she broke into a rumbling laugh that escalated until it eclipsed the voice of Snoop Doggy Dogg. "I was wonderin' if you planned to do any work today. If not, I sure wasn't gonna be shy about diggin' in all by myself." She waved her arm magic-wand style at the expansive spread.

Speechless, CJ looked squarely at Flora Jean, realizing for the first time how large a woman she was. He estimated her height at five foot eleven and suspected that she weighed somewhere in the neighborhood of 180 pounds. Her squared-off face, deep-set eyes, and closely cropped hair gave her a look of perpetual seriousness. She was wearing a purple jogging suit, sleeves puffed up to the elbow, and the kind of inexpensive mass-market perfume that could make your eyes water. The silver jewelry she had been wearing the first time they met was now accentuated with colorful plastic bracelets and a necklace of buffalo nickels.

"Everything's healthy. That's the only way I cook. Pull up a chair. Ain't nothin' gonna snap at you here."

CJ stepped over to retrieve one of the folding metal chairs he kept behind Julie's lateral files and found himself eyeball to eyeball with one of the speakers of Flora Jean's boom box. "Mind if I turn the music down?" he said, teasing the chair from behind the file cabinet.

"Suit yourself."

CJ gave the volume knob a quarter turn. Then, chair in hand, he took two quick steps toward Flora Jean.

"Ain't into rap, huh?" said Flora Jean, her voice dripping with disappointment.

"Nope. Always preferred the blues." CJ took a seat, banging his knees into the side of the desk.

"Blues, no sir, never been my thing. Too many sad-sounding lyrics and down-in-the-dumps people for me." Flora Jean slid a bowl of raisin bran toward CJ. "Cover your cereal up with some of them blackberries over there, sprinkle on a little powdered sugar and a splash of milk, and I guarantee when you're finished you'll have all the nutrition you need to make it through the day."

When CJ hesitated, she added, "Go on, honey, do yourself a favor. Dig on in."

Instead CJ reached across the desk and grabbed a huge cinnamon roll off the pastry platter.

Flora Jean smiled, showing a row of perfectly aligned white teeth. "Something sweet for the disposition first. Ain't no harm in that."

Eyeing the cinnamon roll, CJ wondered whether in Flora Jean's world of healthy eating habits anyone counted calories. "Are you gonna join me?" he asked, reaching for the bowl of blackberries.

"As soon as I give you your messages. This here's a workin' breakfast, you know, like the kind those downtown bankers have." She pulled a couple of message slips from one of the pockets of her jogging suit and handed them to CJ.

"Folks sure call here early. The first message came in at seven-thirty sharp."

The message on top was from Billy DeLong, his crusty old friend from Wyoming, whom CJ had asked to check out the Baptistes. The message, filled with misspellings, was brief and to the point. "Headed out to check on that Baptiste clan this morning. Will have the straight skinny on the whole passel for you soon."

CJ smiled, knowing that Billy, a wiry, tough-as-nails recovering alcoholic who lived in seclusion in a cabin tethered to the side of a mountain outside Baggs, Wyoming, would do exactly what the message said.

For most of his life Billy had been foreman of a forty-thousand-acre cattle spread. He was in his mid-fifties, blind in one eye from adult-onset diabetes, and as headstrong as a bull. He had helped CJ out on half a dozen bounty-hunting cases in the past couple of years, and in that time they had become fast friends.

When CJ had called Billy the previous night just after talking to Julie and told him about the Hambone Dolbey case, Billy had jumped at the chance to help him out, saying, "Just been sittin' around here counting the leaves waiting for my ass to rust off." When CJ told him about the link between Morgan and Dittier and the Baptistes and the kicker about Hambone's son, Billy sighed and said, "Sounds like one of them *As the World Turns* soap operas to me," before getting the particulars on the Baptistes possibly working a ranch outside Laramie and promising CJ that come hell or high water he'd find them.

CJ set aside the message from Billy, bit into his cinnamon roll, and savored the pastry's sweet, gooey taste for a few seconds before turning to the second message, a note from Lisa Darley asking him to return her call. An early morning message from Lisa seemed oddly out of place. He stared at the message slip for a moment before folding it in half and slipping it into his vest pocket. "Nothing else with that second message, was there?" he said, glancing at Flora Jean.

Her mouth full of bran flakes and blackberries, Flora Jean continued chewing as she shook her head back and forth.

"Strange," said CJ, diving into his bowl of cereal, certain that Lisa must have been calling about something to do with the Hambone Dolbey case. They finished their breakfast together without another word, and by the time either of them spoke again the better part of the food on the desk was gone and Heavy D was rapping in the background. CJ leaned back in his chair and patted his stomach. "Afraid I ate too much."

"Don't matter when you're eatin' healthy," said Flora Jean, who had already begun gathering the dishes.

CJ smiled, unwilling to burst Flora Jean's bubble with a lecture about the fat content of the meal. "You make the sweet rolls yourself?"

"Them and everything else on that platter." She pointed to the nearly empty pastry dish and broke into an ear-to-ear grin. "Been baking for years. Learned it from my mama. Took the edge off of being poor." Flora Jean finished clearing the desktop, folded up the linen table-cloth, and began putting the computer components back on her desk.

CJ watched, not quite knowing what to make of Flora Jean Benson. She had been on the job well before her starting time of eight, gone out of her way to please him, and seemed eager to get back to work. She was obviously intent on showing her best side. "Good having breakfast with you, Flora Jean."

"My pleasure."

"Almost forgot. Julie said to tell you she'd be in this week like she promised to give you a few skip-tracing tips," said CJ.

"Great."

"Julie's the absolute best." The words had barely left his mouth when CJ realized his error. The look of disappointment on Flora Jean's face told him that the last person on earth she wanted to be compared to right then was Julie. "I meant . . ."

Dour-faced, Flora Jean said, "I know what you meant."

CJ knew he'd just dig himself a deeper hole if he tried to smooth things over right then. "Think I'll return that second call," he said, taking the message from Lisa out of his pocket. He stood up, looking for a graceful way to exit, ready to kick himself for sticking his foot in his mouth. Flora Jean continued hooking up her computer without a response. Eyes on the floor, CJ headed around the desk for his office. Just before he closed his door, he heard the volume on Flora Jean's boom box skyrocket.

CJ's office was bright and airy, courtesy of a nearly floor-to-ceiling bay window that overlooked the driveway. His uncle had had the window, complete with a mahogany window seat, installed a few months before he died from alcoholic cirrhosis so that he could have a window on the world to keep tabs on his fire-engine-red Buick, a car he said he wanted to be buried in. His uncle never got his wish, but CJ always thought of the old man who had nudged him in the right direction in life when he looked out the bay toward the world.

CJ turned to face the photos on the back wall of his office. At one time, he could recite the name and crime of every member of what he called his rogues' gallery, but the names and crimes had all begun to run together, and lately he had started to wonder if there wasn't some less taxing way for a man to earn a living at forty-six. He pulled a cheroot out of the middle drawer of his desk and slipped off its wrapper, recalling something his uncle

used to say about the cycles of life that he called turn-
ings: *A man always feels like his feet are stuck in the
mud when he's 'bout to experience a turning.* CJ wasn't
quite certain a turning was imminent, but with Julie
leaving, his relationship with Mavis idling, and the
Hambone Dolbey case nowhere near resolution, he certainly felt as though his feet were stuck in something.

He lit the cheroot, plopped down in his well-worn
leather chair, and cocked his feet up on the desk. Then,
blowing a series of tightly bunched smoke rings into the
air, he picked up the phone and dialed Lisa's number. A
bubbly-sounding receptionist answered. "Riverside Veterinary Clinic. May I put you on hold?"

Before he could answer, CJ found himself listening
to the sounds of Fleetwood Mac. *Better than rap music,*
he thought, blowing a dozen more smoke rings before
the receptionist came back on the line.

"This is Donna, how may I be of help?"

"I'd like to speak to Dr. Darley. Tell her CJ Floyd's
returning her call."

"She's with an emergency right now. May I have
her call you back?"

"Sure. She's got my number."

"I'll have her call you as soon as possible, Mr.
Floyd," said the receptionist, hanging up.

Cradling the receiver under his chin, CJ punched
up a dial tone and dialed Mavis's number at Mae's
Louisiana Kitchen. Mavis answered, sounding out of
breath.

"It's me," said CJ. "You sound harried."

"I am. We're short a cook and a waitress. Daddy's

in the back cooking, and I'm serving and trying to handle the front."

"I was planning on heading your way in a few minutes. Can you squeeze me in?"

"You're the one who's been a shadow, CJ. I should be asking you that question."

"There's light at the end of the tunnel," he said, stretching the truth. "I'm making headway on this thing I'm working on for Morgan and Dittier. Won't be long before we have the whole state of New Mexico to ourselves."

"Promise?"

"Promise," said CJ, crossing his fingers.

"Then come on by Mae's. I'll fix you something special."

CJ was about to say he'd already eaten when he remembered the consequences of saying the wrong thing to Flora Jean. "I'll be there in fifteen minutes."

"See you then. I've got an order up, have to go."

CJ hung up, trying to decide whether to head straight for Mae's or wait for a return phone call from Lisa. He had taken a couple of short drags on his nearly spent cheroot when a shadow briefly interrupted the morning sunlight streaming through the bay window. The sudden streak of darkness startled him, jolting the depths of his consciousness as he found himself suddenly remembering Bobby Two-Shirts's threats. He walked over to the window, thinking about what had happened to Cicero, and looked up and down the driveway outside. He couldn't see a sign of anything that could have caused the shadow. But he stood in the window box for several minutes, soaking up the morning sun and wondering whether he was being stalked. If so, he knew he'd better come up with some way of flushing out the stalker if he didn't want to end up like Cicero. Deep in reflection, he thought he heard the phone in the outer office ring, but he ignored it until Flora Jean buzzed him. "Yes," he answered humbly, hoping Flora Jean had forgotten about his unintended insult.

"Lisa Darley's on line one," said Flora Jean, her tone of voice perfunctory.

"Thanks."

"Yeah," said Flora Jean, transferring the call.

"That didn't sound like Julie to me," said Lisa. "In fact, whoever it was sounded downright unpleasant."

CJ found himself defending Flora Jean. "She's Julie's replacement, and she's having a bad day—cut her some slack."

"Fine. I was just calling to tell you I don't think you'll need to talk to Brian to get up to speed on Whitaker Rodgers."

"Why not?"

"Because I talked to Brian about the man myself last night." There was a long pause. "And by the way, when you talk to Uncle Morgan, please tell him that Brian was very helpful."

"I'll do that."

"Anyway, after I beat around the bush with Brian about Rodgers for a while, trying to get him to toss me some tidbit about Rodgers's finances, he told me that if I really wanted to know about the man I should subscribe to the *Colorado Business Journal*. Seems as though Rodgers is involved in a huge mining venture. The story hit the journal this week. And guess what he's mining?"

"Got me," said CJ, stroking his chin.

"Diamonds."

"I'll be damned," said CJ, nearly losing his grip on the phone.

"You still with me, CJ?"

"Yes."

"Well, according to Brian, Rodgers's diamond mining deal's the real thing. The biggest find ever in the U.S. He's probably struck it rich."

"I thought he was already rich."

"Maybe he wants to be richer."

"Don't we all?"

Lisa laughed. "Brian faxed me a couple of clippings from the *Journal* this morning. Turns out Rodgers is excavating on three thousand acres just northwest of the Devil's Backbone."

"How about faxing me a copy of that article? Looks like you've run across a ten-carat reason for murder."

"What's your number?"

CJ recited his fax number and added, "And, Ms. Super Sleuth, you done good. I'll be sure to pass on your message about Brian to Morgan."

"You think Rodgers killed Hambone Dolbey over the diamonds?"

"It's been done for less." CJ spun his chair around and scanned the photos of several of his rogues' gallery members, finally focusing on a murderer he had hauled back to Denver chained to the back of a pickup, a man who had killed a 7-Eleven clerk during a robbery in Colorado Springs that netted him $57.

Lisa's tone turned solemn. "Promise you'll keep Morgan and Dittier out of this. It could turn ugly."

"I'll do my best."

"Do better. I'm counting on it. Right now I need to get back to a horse with its knee out of joint. If you need anything else that you think Brian can help you with, let me know. And CJ, remember your promise about Brian. He's good people."

"I'll remember."

"Bye then," said Lisa, hanging up.

CJ sat back in his chair, amazed that someone was actually mining diamonds in Colorado. After pondering the fact for a while, he remembered the fax and got up from his seat. On his way to the fax machine in Flora Jean's office he glanced toward the spot where he had seen the shadow in the bay window earlier, wondering whether the shadow represented a threat. The fax machine let out a high-pitched chirp just as CJ stepped into the outer office. "Looks like we got a fax." He smiled at Flora Jean, hoping for something other than a frown in return.

"Want me to get it?" asked Flora Jean.

CJ was about to say no when he remembered another of his uncle's sayings: *Never pays to snatch the shovel a man makes a livin' with out of his hand.* "Yes," he said, the old man's words ringing in his head. Flora Jean stepped over to the fax machine, retrieved several sheets of paper, and handed them to CJ.

Most of the page on top was filled with a poorly reproduced fax-quality photograph of Whitaker Rodgers flanked by one of the largest pieces of earth-moving equipment CJ had ever seen. Rodgers was smiling broadly. An unsmiling prudish-looking woman, described in the caption as Rodgers's mining partner, Evelyn Coleman, stood next to him. The next sheet showed a grainy impression of what looked like a lake surrounded by acres of gouged-out hillside. Somehow the scene reminded CJ of the strafed, bombed-out countryside in Vietnam. He held the second sheet of paper up to the light, straining to make out the detail. Turning the paper back and forth, he was almost certain that in the far corner of the photo he could make out the rocky spine of the Devil's Backbone.

"Looks like you got somethin' real heavy-duty there," said Flora Jean.

CJ smiled and lowered the paper. "Some people would call it a turning."

"A what?"

"A turning. It takes some explaining."

Flora Jean cocked her head to one side as the hint of a smile formed on her face. "I've got all day."

The reluctant smile told CJ the hurt feelings had passed. "So do I," he said, ready to explain the whole Hambone Dolbey case and Bobby Two-Shirts mess to Flora Jean before he headed to see Mavis, so that Flora Jean could not only appreciate what a turning meant but no longer have to be on the outside looking in.

Chapter 20

Nadine Kemp dunked the last of her sugar doughnut into a second refill of coffee and smiled. "Don't matter one way or another to me that you can't keep that son of yours in line. Only thing that matters to me is my money." She polished off the doughnut, leaving a dusting of powdered sugar rimming the corners of her mouth.

Nadine's go-screw-yourself attitude and the steady stream of semis rolling by the truck stop parking lot outside had Virginia Rodgers so on edge she was nearly shaking. Nadine was the one who had picked the spot for the meeting, which was in Denver's lower downtown warehouse district and only five minutes from the Pandeco corporate offices. Virginia, who had rushed from her breakfast meeting with Whitaker and Evelyn, had the feeling that every big rig that rolled by their window had a driver who was keeping tabs on her. "I won't keep giving you fifteen hundred a month, and that's that."

Nadine dabbed the corner of her mouth with a napkin and grinned, certain that Virginia was unaware that she was also blackmailing Whitaker and Evelyn. "Sure you will, sugar, you're rollin' in diamonds."

Virginia Rodgers's eyes narrowed in frustration. "You know we haven't found any diamonds yet."

"Sure do, honey. That's why I'm gettin' my money up front."

Virginia stared down into the cup of bitter coffee she had been nursing, then back up at Nadine. "I'll call the police."

Nadine snorted, "Hah!" and cocked her head. "You're in too deep, sweetie. That son of yours has already dug up too much of Hambone's land. Go ahead, call the cops. You'll end up doin' more time than me any day. Besides, I seen the inside of a jail cell before. I'm bettin' the closest you've ever been to a jail is when you unintentionally drive by one in that Rolls of yours on your way to Sunday brunch. Get this straight now, sugar, don't try strokin' me again with any threats."

Her voice cracking with fear, Virginia tried another tactic. "Dolbey knew we were excavating."

"And a skunk knows he stinks. Don't change the illegality of your criminal trespass on his property or the animal's scent one iota."

"Whitaker and I know people who are a lot more powerful than the police."

Nadine burst out laughing. "Powerful my ass. Hell, honey, the way I see it, Whitaker and that girlfriend of his are lookin' for the diamond promised land too. If you don't kick in the money, one of them will ante up."

A look of total frustration spread across Virginia Rodgers's face. Realizing that it was useless to continue to try to reason with Nadine, she said, "I'll come after you myself."

"In your dreams, sugar. You ain't got the heart."

Virginia shot Nadine a last-ditch, cornered-animal look. Relaxing back in her chair, Nadine said, "You got a week to get back on track with the money. That's seven days longer than I said on the phone. You'll figure out a way, sugar. I know you will." She reached over and patted Virginia's hand.

Virginia jerked her hand away and stared past Nadine out the window at a huge green and yellow Mayflower moving van that was rolling by. The words *Air Cushioned Ride* printed on the side of the van caught her attention. She looked back at Nadine and then at the van, wondering how much trouble it would be to stuff someone's body into the back of a tractor-trailer for an air-cushioned ride to oblivion, and whether she could do the prison time that would result if she were caught.

Celeste Deepstream kept telling herself that peeking into Floyd's bay window had been a childish, foolhardy mistake, the inexcusable act of someone who wasn't thinking straight. Spying on the man who was responsible for Bobby being locked up and the cause of Bobby's latest attempt to kill himself may have made her feel better momentarily, but in the competitive terms she understood best, it could have cost her the race.

After leaving her surveillance spot in the parking

lot the previous night, she had spent the early morning hours outside Denver General's intensive care unit intermittently crying and cursing CJ. Inside the unit Bobby lay comatose with a ventilator hose punched through his trachea and tubes dangling from his arms. Twice during the night he had had to be resuscitated. The amber flashing hallway light that signaled to doctors that a patient had crashed continued to blink on and off in her head.

No one knew where Bobby found the plastic bag he used to try to suffocate himself. One of Bobby's guards, who sat with her as the sun rose, a rotund Hispanic man with a high-pitched squeaky voice, had told her the bag could have come from anywhere—that Bobby could even have smuggled it in when he was booked. "Prisoners stuff things up their anus all the time," the guard had said while he sat completing paperwork.

Celeste knew Bobby was capable of something like that, especially if he had no idea how long he was going to be confined. She felt guilty and mad at herself for not being able to scrounge up Bobby's bond. She wanted to settle up with the judge who had set his bond so high, but most of all she wanted to even the score with Floyd.

After Bobby's second resuscitation, she had stared through the glass that separated them, watching the respirator breathe for him for almost an hour. When she couldn't stand watching any longer, she left the hospital determined to catch a glimpse of Floyd. On her way to his office she made up her mind to kill him.

Chapter 21

CJ left Mae's with the top down on the Bel Air, headed for what he hoped would be a meeting with Whitaker Rodgers. He was breathing heavily and stuffed to the gills from his second breakfast of the morning, and somehow he had managed to convince Mavis that their postponed trip to Santa Fe would be all the more special because of the delay. He hadn't called ahead for an appointment with Rodgers because he wanted the element of surprise working for him, and he didn't want to be subjected to the corporate runaround.

The fax from Lisa had capsulized Rodgers's entire diamond-mining venture, but what he really needed to know was how the mining project was tied to Hambone Dolbey. The obvious connection had to be Dolbey's land. The real question was whether the link was worth committing murder. CJ stopped for a light at 17th and Curtis and a delicate breeze swept through the Bel Air as gaggles of businessmen and women dressed in remarkably similar corporate attire filled the crosswalk in front of him.

The light changed, and CJ eased around the corner into one of the scores of self-service parking lots that dotted downtown. He parked, walked over to a battery of blazing yellow metal payment boxes, slipped $2 into a slot beneath the number 88, and headed for the high-rise that housed Pandeco Oil.

The late morning crowd outside the building consisted of a couple of street vendors preparing their food carts for the noon-hour rush, a tall black man in a battered top hat and tails who resembled a circus barker, and a few onlookers. The barker kept announcing to anyone within earshot that the skinny young boy twirling around on the slab of Masonite on the sidewalk in front of them was "America's New Age Black Houdini." Caught up in the boy's gyrations, CJ stopped to watch. The blindfolded, loose-jointed contortionist looked no more than twelve or thirteen. His arms were handcuffed behind his back, and his head was shaved cue-ball clean. A crowd of fifteen or twenty had gathered when the barker announced again, "Behold, America's New Age Black Houdini." He tapped a cane that seemed to appear out of nowhere on the sidewalk for effect. The kid responded to the sound of the tapping by looping his arms back and forth over his head several times and finally slamming his handcuffed wrists into his belt buckle.

"That's only a fraction of what you'll see, my friends," announced the barker, eyeing a top hat at his feet, its tattered silk lining dotted with crumpled dollar bills. The barker grunted and tapped his cane again. America's New Age Black Houdini immediately dropped to his stomach, bowed his back, reached back for his ankles, and slowly pulled his feet up toward his head until his shackled ankles looped over his head and the chains between the cuffs appeared to cut into his neck. He held the pose for effect until a middle-aged woman in the crowd let out a muffled hand-to-mouth scream and darted away. The barker smiled as a man in running shorts and University of Colorado sweatshirt dropped two dollars into the top hat and jogged away.

CJ looked back and forth from the slender, six-foot-three barker to the kid. Studying the similarity in their facial features, he decided they must be related. As he turned to walk away he reached for his wallet, pulled out two dollar bills, and tossed them into the top hat. America's New Age Black Houdini acknowledged the drop with a smile. Surprised at the gesture from someone who was supposedly blindfolded, CJ smiled back, realizing that the kid's blindfold was see-through, part of the con of a New Age father and son.

On the elevator ride up to the Pandeco offices, he ran his investigative game plan through his head. First he needed to find out if Rodgers had a reason to kill Hambone Dolbey. If Rodgers did and diamonds were the motive, he knew he might very well have to head back north and check the diamond fields out for himself. He frowned at the thought of another road trip and checked his watch. If things worked out the way he hoped, even with a drive back north to check out the mining site he'd be home in time for wine and dinner with Mavis and a night of the silky sweet lovemaking that he and Mavis hadn't enjoyed in a while.

CJ stepped out of the elevator to face a wall of imposing brass-lettered signage. Pandeco Oil and Gas, Suite 2200, was the first name on the list. An arrow above the suite number pointed down the hallway to the right.

He couldn't have missed the Pandeco offices if he had wanted to. Halfway down the hall, two massive, ten-foot-high, double-hung teak doors with the Pandeco corporate logo etched into them greeted him. He paused and ran his hand over the logo before swinging the doors open and stepping into a reception area reeking of brass and teak. A statuesque receptionist with closely cropped auburn hair was seated behind a boomerang-shaped desk that jutted out into the room. She was talking to an elegantly dressed woman of medium height with salt-and-pepper hair who CJ judged to be in her sixties.

"They just called to say your Rolls is out front," said the receptionist.

"Thanks," said the other woman, who was well tanned and, except for the areas around her eyes, had barely wrinkled skin. When the women looked up at him in unison, CJ noticed that the older woman's right arm was weighted down with a glossy black shopping bag that had the name of an exclusive Denver boutique scripted on its side. Only the receptionist seemed surprised that a black man had walked in.

"Hello," said CJ, wondering how it would feel to own a Rolls-Royce.

"Good morning," said the receptionist.

CJ cleared his throat, a habit that always surfaced when he felt he was being overly scrutinized. "I'd like to speak with Mr. Rodgers if I could."

The receptionist shot the other woman a look that was obviously that of a subordinate. "Do you have an appointment?"

"No, but it won't take more than five or ten minutes."

"And you are?"

"CJ Floyd." Reaching in his vest pocket for a business card, CJ noticed the pleasant, self-assured expression on the older woman's face fade for a fraction of a second.

"I'll take it from here," said the older woman. "You seem very intent on seeing my son, Mr. Floyd. Is it urgent?" Extending her hand to shake CJ's she added, "I'm Virginia Rodgers. Perhaps I can be of help?"

CJ remembered Virginia Rodgers's name from the fax as Pandeco's CEO. Her grip was delicate, barely perceptible. He hoped his expression wasn't telltale enough to telegraph that she had caught him off guard. Uncertain whether his next move should be to buffalo or finesse, he opted for finesse. "I really would like to speak to your son."

"If you're after a story about our Devil's Backbone excavation, you'll have to get in line. Our PR people are overwhelmed." Her tone of voice told CJ Virginia Rodgers wasn't a lady who was easily intimidated.

"I would like to know a bit more about your diamond mining project, but I'd prefer to hear the story from Whitaker if I could."

"Do you know my son?" said Virginia, surprised at the first-name reference.

"Yes."

"Well, if you do, then you're certainly aware of how busy he is. I'd suggest you talk to our people in PR." She adjusted her grip on the shopping bag and turned to the receptionist. "Doreen, why don't you help Mr. Floyd with his problem? You're in good hands," she said, smiling at the receptionist, who had already picked up the phone to dial PR. The receptionist offered CJ the same kind of on-stage show-business smile that the New Age Black Houdini had as she dialed. "I've got someone at the front desk who'd like some information about the Devil's Backbone excavation." There was a pause, then she added, "Good, I'll send him right down." She turned to CJ. "You're in luck, Mr. Floyd. Someone can help you right now."

Virginia Rodgers smiled, the instinctive, crafty smile of a bureaucrat who has just watched the system she installed run through its paces. "See how persistence pays, Mr. Floyd?"

"Yes," said CJ, realizing how efficiently he had just been given the runaround.

Virginia Rodgers adjusted the shopping bag in her hand. "Enjoy your tour, and have a good day." As she strolled toward the door, CJ couldn't help but notice the glint of self-satisfaction in her eyes.

Chapter 22

Billy DeLong had spent most of the morning driving the one hundred miles from his home in Baggs, Wyoming, to Laramie. His trip to interrogate Mitchell, Conrad, and Rebecca Baptiste about possible involvement in Hambone Dolbey's murder had started out simply enough until he hit a driving windstorm outside Saratoga. The rest of the drive had been at the mercy of the Wyoming wind. He had had to stop twice on 1-80 because of jackknifed tractor-trailers and once in order to clear dirt from the throat of his stalled pickup's carburetor.

After CJ told him about the volatile Baptiste clan in their phone conversation the night before, Billy had used his ranching contacts across the state to learn not only the names of the Baptiste men but the location of the Baptiste ranch. Expecting to find two good old boys who might be inclined to take his head off with a shovel if he didn't watch it, Billy had prepared for the worst and slipped his Winchester Magnum and his Remington 12-gauge riot gun behind the seat of his pickup before heading for Laramie.

What he found instead was a desolate, windswept, 240-acre dry-land island in the middle of a Wyoming nowhere, two poorly tended graves, and a frail, ghostly-looking woman calling herself Rebecca Baptiste. Without giving him more than a breathless death-rattle hello when she met him at the front doorstep of her adobe ranch house, she let Billy give his spiel about why he was there and then led him to the only irrigated part of the ranch, where there was a three-acre apple orchard. At the edge of the orchard she turned back to Billy, pointed to two simple white crosses rising from the weeds twenty feet away, and said, "If you want to talk to my brother and father, here they are." They had walked back to the house, threading their way through a herd of fifteen mangy-looking, underfed cattle, without saying a word.

Now he and Rebecca were sitting on a pair of rickety wooden benches facing one another in the stifling fruit orchard loft tucked into the southwest corner of the second story of the adobe. Rows of rotting apples lined pine shelves hugging the walls and a bottle of sugar water swimming with insects occupied the ledge next to the only window in the room. Intermittent gusts of wind swept through the open window, banging a set of unhinged shutters against the outside wall.

Billy studied the sad, frail features of Rebecca's face, trying to decide if she had ever been pretty. An expression that was perpetually on the cusp of a developing frown, matted dirty blond hair, and a full row of missing bottom teeth made it difficult for him to believe CJ's claim that she had. The harsh Wyoming environment seemed to have taken its toll on Rebecca Baptiste, but he suspected something else had also contributed to her decay. Although he had expected a woman in her mid-thirties, she looked closer to fifty as she sat rocking back and forth, hands nervously sliding up and down her thighs, her blue eyes filled with a kind of sinking undertow desperation.

Interrupting her rocking, she said, "They died within a year of one another. Daddy from TB. Mitch, last fall, from a broken neck."

Billy was about to ask how her brother had broken his neck, but the powerful sadness in Rebecca's voice made him skip it.

Rebecca's eyes darted around the room, finally stopping at the window. "Want an apple?"

The sweet, syrupy odor of rotting apples had Billy's stomach gurgling. He had been an alcoholic for the better part of his life, and the pungent aroma reminded him of the smell of cheap wine. "No," he said, reaching into his pants in search of the chewing gum he now used as a substitute for alcohol. He pulled out a pack of Doublemint and offered Rebecca a stick. When she refused, he slipped the wrappers off a couple of sticks and popped them into his mouth.

His act of generosity seemed to be what was needed to get Rebecca to open up. "They brought me up here to raise my baby, Aaron. He's almost nineteen now. It was hard on them, doubly hard on me and Aaron. I mean, being white with a little black baby and all. But it was the Christian thing to do, so we did it. But I can tell you for certain, it was hard leaving Texas to eke out a living up here."

Billy nodded understandingly, hoping to find out more about Aaron.

Rebecca pulled an apple off the closest shelf, polished it on her sleeve, and bit into it. "Truth is, they were always more upset about me having a baby out of wedlock than the fact that Aaron's father was black. My daddy suffered that hurt till the day he died."

Billy nodded sympathetically. Then, pausing before asking the question, he said, "Is there any chance I could speak to your son?"

Rebecca sat up ramrod straight. "I hope you're not speculating that Aaron might have killed Hambone."

"Ain't in the speculation business. I'd just like to speak to your son."

Rebecca Baptiste's voice took on a sudden defensive edge. "He's not here."

"Know where he's at?" asked Billy, trying his best not to sound too pushy.

"I don't know. He hasn't been around for over a week."

Billy stopped chewing his gum, stroked his chin, and stared pensively at Rebecca Baptiste. It was hard not to suspect that Aaron's absence and Hambone Dolbey's murder might be more than just a coincidence.

Billy's probing stare had Rebecca up from the bench, pacing the room. Her movements seemed to fan the room's fruity smell directly into Billy's face, and his stomach grumbled in protest.

"How was Hambone killed?" said Rebecca, interrupting her pacing to turn a sad-eyed expression toward Billy.

Noting how smoothly she had turned the conversation away from Aaron, Billy said, "Blow to the head with a branding iron, I was told."

Rebecca brought both hands up to her mouth as a look of pain spread across her face. "Aaron wouldn't have done that." She sat back down on the bench and stared out the window.

For the next few moments the loft was deadly quiet. "You ever been lonely, Mr. DeLong?" asked Rebecca, breaking the silence.

"Sure have."

"I mean really lonely, like a man by himself in a foxhole or a woman out in the middle of nowhere giving birth?"

Before Billy could respond, she answered the question. "Well, I have." She swept both arms around the forlorn-looking room as if it were exhibit A in her argument. "I guess maybe my loneliness rubbed off on Aaron. He did poorly in school, fighting with other kids nearly every day until they finally expelled him for good for nearly blinding a boy who called him a zebra. He tried working at a couple of jobs over in Cheyenne, but neither of them worked out. When my father and then my brother died, things just seemed to spin totally out of control for him. It was like some vacuum had sucked everything bad that had ever happened to him inside, and no matter how hard I tried, I couldn't get any good to come back out."

She gazed toward thc window and then back at Billy before continuing. "About six months ago Hambone drove in here just about like you did today. I hadn't seen him in seventeen years. If Daddy or Mitch had been alive, I suspect they might've killed him on the spot. He spent the better part of the day following me around, pleading for forgiveness, trying to get Aaron to talk to him, telling us that he was about to strike it rich. Aaron ignored him. All I could do was try. He left late that evening, but in a couple of days he was back, and like clockwork for the next two months he was here twice a week pleading his case, trying to get me and Aaron to accept him back into our lives. He even drove through a couple of God-awful snowstorms to get here when there wasn't anything moving for miles. After those two months I dropped my guard. I'm not sure Aaron ever dropped his."

She paused again as if she needed the interruption to get Billy to believe her story. "Hambone could affect you like that. Eat his way into your life, spinning whatever had happened in the past off into the distance until he had bored his way back into your soul."

"Did he say anything about how he expected to get rich?"

"No, I figured it was just another one of his boasts. And I never asked. But he and Aaron had their own conversations about it. I'm certain Aaron knew."

"And Aaron never gave you any reason to think he wanted to even the score with his father for leaving him for all those years?" said Billy, hard pressed to believe that Rebecca had no idea about how Hambone planned to strike it rich.

"No. He and Hambone seemed to be working things out."

Billy reached into his shirt pocket, popped another stick of gum into his mouth, and worked the new stick into the wad he was chewing before asking, "You wouldn't have been carrying some kind of serious Hambone grudge yourself, would you?"

"I wouldn't have killed Hambone, if that's what you mean."

For the moment Billy decided to take her at her word. "Anybody else you can think of who might've wanted to see Hambone dead?"

"No." Rebecca wrapped her arms protectively around her skinny torso in body language that told Billy she didn't plan to let their conversation go much further. The attic heat and oppressive smell of overripe apples had Billy ready to puke. He slipped off his Stetson and rubbed his sweat-peppered brow. Then, pulling up his right pants leg, he slipped one of CJ's business cards from the leather pocket sewn inside the top of his boot. A slender adjacent pocket housed an onyx-handled hunting knife. He handed the card to Rebecca. "My name and phone number's on the back of that card. If your son comes home, have him get in touch with either me or the fellow whose name's on the front, CJ Floyd."

Rebecca examined the front of the card, then the back. "He won't call either of you." She tossed the card onto a shelf of rotting apples. "It's not his way."

Billy stood up, smacking his gum and fanning himself with his Stetson as he moved to exit the stuffy room. "I'm hopin' murder ain't his way either."

Rebecca, who was back to hugging herself defensively and rocking back and forth in her seat, didn't offer a response.

"Thanks for your time," said Billy, turning back to shake her hand. When she didn't offer it, he did a quick about-face and walked out the door toward his pickup. As he drove down the winding lane and away from the lonely-looking house, he couldn't help but wonder what CJ would make of his meeting with Rebecca Baptiste and whether two pitiful, isolated creatures like her and her son, Aaron, could have been responsible for Hambone Dolbey's death.

Chapter 23

She checked the only window in the garage, making certain it was tightly latched before nervously checking the lock on the garage door for the tenth time in as many minutes. When she was certain that everything was in order, she slipped into a crouched position beneath the far end of the workbench that ran the entire length of CJ's dark, musty garage and waited for things to unfold. She had followed CJ to Five Points, watching while he wasted twenty minutes shooting the breeze and gassing up his car at Rosie's Garage. It wasn't until he stopped at a 7-Eleven eight blocks from his house that she decided to put her plan into action, certain he was now on his way home.

She had gained entry to the garage easily enough,

jimmying a locked side door. Inside she had found a battered old Jeep and enough spare auto parts lying around to tell her that Floyd was some kind of automotive nut. She would wait for ten to fifteen minutes to see if he showed. If he didn't, she'd have to come up with something else. Either way, it was worth the gamble.

Cramped and uncomfortable, she hefted the tire iron in her right hand, guessing at its weight. The sudden sound of a vehicle pulling into the driveway broke her concentration. Bracing herself on a bench leg, she laid the tire iron aside, breathing rapidly as a rivulet of sweat worked its way down her neck and between her breasts. Her right knee, injured in a college skiing accident, was throbbing. She rubbed her kneecap and held her breath as the garage door creaked open.

It was Floyd. She watched CJ slip his car keys into his vest pocket before stepping back out onto the driveway to stare at the Bel Air. Crouching down in front of the car while steadying himself by the bumper, he craned to look beneath the car. Then he slipped his hand off the bumper and patted around on the concrete beneath the engine. "Damn," he said, shaking his head disgustedly as he pulled an oil-stained palm from beneath the Bel Air. He stood up, about to wipe his hand on his pants, then turned and headed toward the garage instead.

Inside, he grabbed a soiled shop towel off the bench top and began wiping the oil from his hand. She watched the movement of his feet, and when he turned away and took two strides back toward the driveway she sprang out from beneath the bench and sent the tire iron crashing against the side of his skull. CJ dropped to his knees and reached for his head before slamming face-first into the floor.

In a rush of adrenaline she decided to make doubly certain of her kill. She stepped casually over CJ's outstretched body, laid the tire iron aside, and picked up the towel he had been holding. Then reaching beneath him, towel in hand, she slipped his car keys out of his vest pocket, hoping not to leave any fingerprints behind. She darted over to the Jeep, slipped behind the wheel, and began jamming keys into the ignition until she found one that fit. She turned the engine over, jumped back out of the Jeep, and raced over to check CJ, not wanting her plan to turn sour.

He hadn't budged, and she couldn't tell if he was breathing. *It really doesn't matter,* she thought as the Jeep's exhaust fumes waffled into her face. Satisfied that Floyd wasn't going to get up anytime soon, she sprang back up, retrieved the tire iron and grasped the frayed rope hanging from the garage door, and brought the door slamming down behind her as she left the garage. She was down the driveway, across the neighboring lawn, and away from the scene in what had taken, start to finish, no more than a couple of minutes.

Flora Jean was sitting at her desk, fuming. She had spent fifteen minutes of her lunch hour waiting for CJ to return by noon as he had promised, and she wasn't about to wait another second. Julie had told her that one of CJ's shortcomings included the fact that often he became so immersed in something he'd lose track of time. She wasn't about to try to correct the idiosyncrasies of a grown man, but she hadn't expected CJ's bad habits to surface so soon. She eyed the clock on the wall beside her, rolled her eyes in exasperation, and shut down the game she had been playing on her computer. Then she walked into CJ's office and left three messages on his desk: two from Billy DeLong and one from Julie. Except for the phone numbers, all three messages were identical: "Call back as soon as you get to the office." She hastily printed CJ a quick message of her own: "Gone to lunch. Back by 1:00," dropped it onto the pile, and headed for the door.

On the way out she turned off her boom box and grabbed her purse. She had decided to try Dozens, an egg-yolk-yellow little breakfast-and-lunch eatery just up the street that Julie had recommended. According to Julie, the restaurant served the best pumpkin muffins and Belgian waffles in Denver and, baking maven that she was, Flora Jean was dying for the chance to compare them to her own. She was halfway down the front porch steps when she heard what sounded like a car engine running. She took a couple of steps out into the grass, looking toward the sound. When she didn't see a car, she shrugged and turned to walk away. She had taken a step in the opposite direction when for some reason the still unexplained sound got the best of her, and she walked over to the driveway, thinking maybe she did need to start turning down the volume on her boom box.

She didn't see the Bel Air parked in the driveway until she had taken a couple of steps toward the garage, but by the time she reached the bay window of CJ's office, she had pegged the sound as a car motor and figured it was the idling Bel Air. Ten yards from the garage, she realized the muffled sound she heard was coming not from the Bel Air but from inside the garage. Puzzled, she stopped before approaching the garage cautiously. "Who's in there?" When no one answered, she stepped up to the door, reached down, and lifted it knee-high. The nauseating exhaust fumes sent her reeling backward, coughing. "Who the hell's in there?"

She pulled a wad of tissues out of her purse, tossed the purse aside, and, cupping the tissues over her mouth, pushed the garage door open with such force that it ricocheted on its rollers a couple of times before coming to a halt. Exhaust fumes billowed from the garage. "CJ?" Coughing and wheezing, she raced inside to turn off the engine, losing a shoe in her haste. "Shit," she said, leaning across the Jeep's steering wheel, switching off the engine.

When the engine died, she jumped away from the Jeep, suddenly feeling dizzy. Then, in a series of escalating coughs, she headed for fresh air. She was nearly outside when she heard a low moan that sounded like a cow bawling. Looking toward the sound, she spotted CJ sprawled across the floor a few feet away from the Jeep's right rear wheel. Terrified, she screamed, "Oh my God." CJ moaned again, this time louder. But there was no way his muffled groan could match Flora Jean's deafening wail.

Chapter 24

S he always carries it. A derringer with a pearl handle. She keeps it clipped to her belt. I seen the gun lots of times. Barrel's always aimed down at her crotch." The boy speaking was the pushy batter CJ had debated the day he, Morgan, and Dittier had visited Nadine Kemp.

"Then why are we breaking in to steal it if she's carrying the gun?" asked the boy with him.

" 'Cause, you own one gun, you bound to have another. I heard that from my ol' man."

The two boys inched across Nadine Kemp's backyard, crawling on their bellies, easing their way toward a basement window at the back of the house. It was just past noon.

The second boy frowned. "Hope we don't run into no dogshit slitherin' around down here in this dirt."

"She ain't got a dog."

"Wouldn't have to be hers."

The first boy gave his apprehensive friend a get-with-the-program stare. "Quit dreamin' up things, would you? You're the one wanted to come along." He dug his elbows into the dirt, smiling as he pulled himself closer to their objective. When they reached the window he stood up quickly, thinking he heard footsteps, and scanned the backyard, ready to run. Quivering in fear, his friend followed suit. The first boy placed an index finger across his lips, signaling for silence. The two boys stood rigidly still, butts against the back wall of the house, breathing rapidly, adrenaline rushing through their veins for the next couple of minutes. Satisfied that the perceived threat had passed, the first boy dropped to one knee, motioning for his friend to do the same.

"You sure she ain't home?" said the second boy, still trembling.

"Sure as my name's Curtis Johnson."

"She better not be," said the second boy. "Bitch might end up shootin' us."

"Not on your life. She ain't the type." Curtis pulled a pocketknife out of his jeans and tried to jimmy open the basement window. "Besides, I ain't seen her around here all day."

"Hope she ain't got no burglar alarm."

Curtis shook his head in disgust. "She look like the kind of person who could afford a burglar alarm?"

His friend didn't answer.

Curtis ran his knife along the seam between the

window and the casement. The grating metal-on-metal sound caused his friend to roll back on his heels, ready to run. Ignoring his friend's jitters, Curtis continued working. In a few seconds there was a loud pop. Before his friend could run, Curtis grabbed the back of his pants leg. "I got it," he said, swinging the window up on its hinge. He slipped through the window's opening before his friend could say a word. Staring up from the security of the basement floor, Curtis whispered, "Ain't nothin' down here but us chickens—come on in."

His chunky friend had a more difficult time squeezing through the window. Finally forcing his way through, he tumbled into the basement with a loud thump, crashing into a water pail on his way.

"Damn, Atwood, why don't you just announce we're here?" said Curtis, helping him to his feet.

Atwood Wilson brushed himself off, checking to make sure he hadn't broken anything. "This was a dumb idea."

"You won't think so when we got us a gun."

"Then let's find ourselves one and get the hell out of here. I'm startin' to feel like I'm gonna puke."

They duck-waddled their way across the concrete floor to a stairway near the middle of the basement. "Think she might keep a gun down here?" asked Atwood, looking around the room.

"Nah, I'm bettin' on upstairs myself." Curtis's voice had a sudden cockiness.

They started up the basement steps, hesitating at every creak. At the top of the stairs, Curtis pushed back a flimsy, hollow wooden door, and they found themselves looking into Nadine Kemp's sparsely furnished kitchen with the sink and the only window in the room directly in front of them. A badly abused butcher-block counter-top flanked one side of the sink while an avocado-colored 1950s-vintage gas range buttressed the other. The only other furnishing in the room was a dainty-looking, marble-topped soda-fountain table with rusted wrought-iron legs. Curtis walked over to the sink to find it filled with half a dozen cups, some still partially full of coffee. A coffeepot rested cockeyed on a back burner of the range. Curtis picked the empty pot up and shook it.

"Looks deserted," said Atwood.

"Good sign." Curtis scanned the room. "Wanna check the place out together or split up?"

"Together," Atwood answered hastily.

"Bedrooms first." Curtis headed boldly toward the hallway just to the left of the kitchen. They worked their way down the hallway side by side until they found a bedroom. A lumpy-looking double bed with an antique brass headboard and a small oak chest of drawers filled the cramped little room. Curtis rushed over to the chest, opening and closing drawers and tossing clothes helter-skelter across the room. When he pulled three successive pairs of frilly-looking silk panties from the bottom drawer, he started giggling. "Maybe we should take a pair of these with us."

Atwood shook his head in protest. "Thought we were after guns."

Atwood's admonition redirected Curtis. He finished searching the bedroom with professional thief-like preci-sion before nodding for Atwood to follow him across the hall to a second bedroom. They ransacked the room quickly, but the only weapon they found was a rusty hunting knife.

They moved to the dining room, where they tossed silverware around haphazardly and sent dishes crashing to the floor. Exasperated, Curtis slipped a couple of silver spoons into his pocket, ready to call it a day. "We can check the basement for guns on our way out." Poking out his lower lip, he looked around and added, "I could've swore she would've had some guns around somewhere."

"Guess you were wrong. Let's split."

As they headed back down the hallway, Curtis noticed the barely ajar door to a room they had missed. "Shit, we skipped the bathroom," he said, noticing the unmistakable octagonal floor tile of a bathroom just beyond the doorway. "Let's check it out." As he swung back the door a clogged-up-sewer kind of stench hit him head on. "Damn, somebody forgot to flush." Pinching his nostrils together, he moved around the corner into the small L-shaped room with Atwood glued to his side.

They both caught sight of Nadine Kemp at the same moment. She was perched on the toilet, a look of concentration frozen on her face, pink panties looped around her ankles. A red-ringed bullet hole, no larger than a pencil eraser, occupied the center of her forehead as her bloodshot eyes stared back at them, wide open in cold admonition at their trespass. Curtis let out a wail, pivoted in something slippery, and broke into a run. Atwood had turned to run after his first glimpse of the dead woman and was already halfway down the hallway. In seconds they were both through the front door, down the porch steps, and into the street, screaming and streaking for home.

Chapter 25

Whitaker Rodgers leaned into the mammoth six-foot-high road-grader blade and chipped away with a surveyor's stake at the stubborn clump of mud lodged between the heel and sole of his boot. For the past fifteen minutes he had been shouting over the grader's engine drone, talking diamond mining strategy with Evelyn Coleman. They were dressed in matching mud-splattered, ankle-length yellow rain slickers and wide-brimmed safari hats that sagged limply over their ears. The dreary, overcast Colorado skies had opened up first thing that morning, ushering in a cold, steady drizzle that hadn't let up all day, and the temperature had dropped into the mid-40s. The fog from Whitaker's breath streamed megaphone-style out in front of his face.

Against his mother's orders, Whitaker had plucked half a dozen pieces of earth-moving equipment from Pandeco's oil drilling operations in southern Colorado and moved them to the Devil's Backbone excavation site. Whitaker's act of defiance was a solid sign to Evelyn that he actually could stand up to his mother when money was on the line. If the kimberlite fields were as rich as Whitaker claimed, she knew they'd find a few more twenty-carat diamonds like the one Hambone Dolbey had stumbled onto less than a quarter of a mile from where they stood.

Evelyn removed her hat, squeezed out a stream of water, and put it back on, brim bent back seafarer-style. "We need to start pumping up more than worthless rock from these kimberlite pipes," she said, shouting over the engine noise. She pulled her slicker collar up and snapped it tight around her neck.

Whitaker tossed the surveyor's stick he had been using to clean his boots toward a nearby fifty-foot-wide gouge in the earth. "It'll come. There's more than one twenty-carat diamond around here waiting to be excavated."

Whitaker knew Hambone Dolbey had found the twenty-carat diamond in a kimberlite field that had mysteriously bubbled up from the earth. He hadn't been able to pinpoint the site, but he suspected that the diamond-rich kimberlite pipes, as they were known in the mining industry, had to be somewhere very close to Trapper's Lake. He had pressed Dolbey to give him the exact location of his find and had even demanded it when he gave Dolbey the money for an easement across his land. But Dolbey had taken the money and then dynamited the easement road to the lake once Whitaker started constructing it, saying the agreement they had struck was just to see how serious Whitaker was about mining diamonds, and now that he knew, he wanted a piece of the action.

Dolbey had suckered him twice and probably would have again if Evelyn hadn't stepped in and threatened him with litigation that she told him would not only cause him to lose his land but possibly force him to spend the rest of his life living in a cardboard box. Evelyn had offered him $10,000 to get lost or find himself swept away by the legal system's undertow. Hambone had had the matter under advisement when he died, never realizing, as Evelyn and Whitaker did, that he had found the diamond on his land, not theirs.

Whitaker adjusted his slicker collar, thinking about the changes Hambone Dolbey had put him through. "I know one thing," he said, turning to Evelyn. "We better hit pay dirt quick before my mother declares this whole project a bust."

Evelyn didn't want to hear Whitaker's backsliding. She had kissed up to Virginia Rodgers as much as she ever intended to. "You're going to have to cut the cord sooner or later, Whit. If you don't, we'll both suffocate. We may need her backing to keep this project moving, but just remember, if worst comes to worst, everyone responds to intimidation."

Whitaker grimaced and turned away from the wind. "She's my mother, Evelyn, or have you forgotten? Besides, she doesn't respond well to pressure."

"Everyone responds to pressure, Whitaker."

Whitaker thought for a moment before kicking a

softball-sized clump of mud in frustration. "What do you think it will get us, a couple more pieces of junk equipment like this?" He pointed at the idling grader in disgust.

"I'm not sure, but I'm betting sooner or later we'll have to push."

Whitaker leaned away from the road-grader blade and took a long, hard look at Evelyn. One thing Evelyn didn't understand about him or his mother was that they were the kind of people who never took a social or economic step backward. Pressuring his mother into further backing a money-draining mining venture that he had had trouble selling her from the start would only result in her putting the clamps on the whole operation.

"Why the stare?" said Evelyn.

"Just searching for answers."

"They're here for the taking." Evelyn eased over to him, slipped her hand into his slicker, and began slowly stroking the inside of his thigh.

"That's not always the answer."

Annoyed, she pulled her hand away. "Do you have a better one?"

"Not one that's going to solve our problem any faster."

Evelyn turned her lip up in a pout, jammed both hands back under her slicker and glared right through Whitaker.

"Mother'll come around. We just need to unearth something more than kimberlite slag to show her the operation's real potential."

"And until then?"

"We keep pushing dirt on the strength of the Pandeco name and her letter of credit."

"Maybe next we can offer to pitch in with picks and shovels."

Before he could respond, Whitaker heard the sound of a vehicle and looked up to see a muddy pickup truck banging across the rutted road toward them. The truck bounced and squeaked its way for another quarter mile until the driver finally pulled up next to them. A big man with oily, pockmarked skin jumped out of the truck and rose slowly to his full six-foot-five-inch height. His face was flushed with excitement. "We've got something back up at the lake." His words were directed more at Evelyn than Whitaker.

Whitaker looked at Evelyn, a glimmer of satisfaction forming on his face. "What did I tell you?" he said matter-of-factly, as if he'd been down the road they were about to travel before.

Evelyn relaxed the bear hug she had on herself, and a torrent of rain streamed down the front of her slicker. "Let's check it out."

They squeezed into the front seat of the pickup with the driver and prepared for the bone-jarring mile-and-a-half ride back up to Trapper's Lake. As the truck gained speed, Whitaker nudged the driver. "Think we've got something you can measure in carats?"

"Maybe. But there could be a problem with where we're digging."

The look of excitement quickly drained from Whitaker's face. "What?"

"We pulled some serious gemstone-looking rock out of the pipes we've been digging this week over on the far south side of the lake. I knew when we started excavating that we were pretty close to the property line. It's possible the pipe we're pulling from may not be on your land."

"Oh," said Whitaker, glancing at Evelyn, feigning surprise.

Eyeing the driver and then turning to Whitaker, Evelyn whispered, "Looks like we might need one of my kind of pushy solutions after all, especially considering that woman Nadine Kemp's recent demands. She wants more money."

"Don't worry, I've already settled with her," said Whitaker, watching Evelyn's perplexed expression and then breaking into a self-satisfied smile as they bumped their way up a slippery five percent grade toward Trapper's Lake and the northern face of the Devil's Backbone.

Chapter 26

CJ couldn't recall throwing up so many times in his life. His head was throbbing, his sinuses were pulsing, and his eyes felt as if they had been welded into their sockets. He knew he was in bed at Mavis's and that someone had tried to kill him, but he couldn't remember how he had gotten there or how long he had been in bed.

The room wasn't spinning as it had been earlier, but everything was out of focus. He had been playing a game with himself, trying to remember things that had occurred as far back as childhood, just to make certain he didn't have amnesia. One minute he could remember specifics, like being pulled from the bottom of a pile during a high school football game. The next minute he couldn't remember his address. The thing he couldn't seem to get out of his mind, no matter how hard he tried, was the sound of Flora Jean screaming as she dragged him from the garage. He could only vaguely remember being taken to the hospital and being examined, and someone slipping what he thought must have been an oxygen mask over his face. But mostly he remembered throwing up.

He closed his eyes, trying to concentrate, hoping he was having a bad dream. When he opened them again Mavis was standing at the foot of the bed, holding a tray with a bowl of oatmeal, one of his least favorite foods, and a tumbler filled with orange juice.

Trying to mask her concern, Mavis forced a smile. "You must have dozed off again." She set the tray down on the cedar chest in front of her, walked around to CJ, and softly stroked his cheek.

A confused look spread across CJ's face. "How long have I been here?"

"Since Julie and I brought you home from Denver General about noon."

CJ eased up in the bed, trying his best to peer around Mavis at the clock on the nightstand. A battery of sharp pinpricks shot through his right eye and he rested back on his pillow. "What time is it?"

"Just past eight."

"Missed a few minutes, I guess." He reached out and squeezed Mavis's hand.

Mavis squeezed back. "Try most of yesterday and today."

They held hands without saying a word until CJ finally reached up and gingerly felt the right side of his head. In addition to the knot on his ear, there was now a fleshy swelling above it. Realizing that he could barely get his hand around the swelling, he sighed and patted himself down to make certain that everything else was still in place.

Satisfied that he was in one piece, he ignored a strange sudden dizziness and moved to swing his legs out of bed. Before his feet hit the floor he broke into a series of dry heaves that sent him slumping forward. Mavis slipped an arm behind him and adjusted the pillows behind his back, supporting him until the convulsions subsided. Relieved that the episode was over, she slipped a cold compress that had been chilling on the nightstand across his forehead and leaned him back into bed. Unable to hide the fact that she was frightened, she sat down on the edge of the bed and stared blankly out into the room.

In a voice laced with guilt she said, "I should've left you in the hospital."

"Glad you didn't. You know how I hate those places."

"When they said you didn't have a skull fracture, I decided you'd be better off here with me, but——"

"But nothing. You made the right decision." He reached over and squeezed her arm reassuringly.

Mavis looked down at him, her eyes welling up with tears. "Sometimes you scare me to death, CJ."

"Good thing my head's harder than whatever I got popped with," said CJ, hoping to take the edge off the conversation.

Mavis grimaced. "It was a tire iron. You could have been killed."

"Lucky for me their aim was off."

"Please don't joke. They tried to finish you off with carbon monoxide. I've been worried sick. And to make matters worse, while you've been drifting in and out of dreamland, I've had two visits from Denver's finest, serious-looking spit-and-polish cops who wanted to question you about a link between your assault and one on Cicero Vickers. They weren't very happy when I told them they'd have to come back." She paused and gave CJ a piercing stare. "You never told me that someone had tried to kill Cicero or that he was in a coma at Denver General struggling for his life."

Mavis's lower lip quivered until CJ ran his hand reassuringly along the hairline above her temple. An image of Bobby Two-Shirts's mysterious sister standing over him dressed in leather biker's garb with a gas mask and a tire iron in her hand flashed through his mind. Now he understood the reason for the dry heaves: a whopping dose of carbon monoxide. "Cicero will be all right." The words came out slowly and apologetically, as if he didn't believe them himself.

Mavis removed the compress from CJ's head and replaced it with a fresh one. "You're too old for these kinds of games, CJ."

"I just do what I know how."

Mavis swallowed hard, fighting back the urge to comment. She told herself to be thankful that at least CJ had cut back on the number of bounty-hunting jobs he was taking and that he had quit tweaking the inferiority complex of every street thug in Five Points by telling anyone who would listen that what the little hoods needed was a wartime tour of duty to set them straight. But she suspected that no matter what she said, CJ would continue to do what he had always done—all because he would never stop trying to rid the world of the kind of person that he knew he could so easily have become. She stood up from the edge of the bed and walked back for the tray she had placed on the cedar chest. "Your oatmeal's getting cold."

"How come no grits?" said CJ, trying to lighten things up.

"Too much salt. Doctor's orders." Mavis flipped down the stubby legs on the bed tray and placed it over CJ's lap. CJ inched up in the bed and spooned up a dollop of oatmeal. "Can't always believe what the doctors say." He swallowed the oatmeal with a frown, ready for another spoonful, when a voice from the doorway said, "Or lawyers."

Julie Madrid had stepped into the room with a large, rumpled-looking man at her side. CJ tried to focus on the man, but the room suddenly started spinning. He lost his grip on his spoon, and it fell to the tray table with a dull thump. In the time it took for the room to stop spinning, he realized the man with Julie was Carlton Pritchard, the Weld County sheriff.

Julie, now standing with Pritchard at the foot of the bed, shot an apologetic look toward Mavis. "The sheriff said he needed to talk to CJ right now."

Mavis gave Pritchard a helpless, *why now* kind of look.

"Evening, Floyd, Ms. Sundee." Pritchard slipped into a relaxed parade-rest stance. "Sorry to bother you at a time like this, but I figured your patient here would understand." He looked at Mavis for some glimmer of approval. Seeing none, he continued, "It's important to move quickly when you've got a murder on your hands."

Puzzled by Pritchard's timing, CJ said, "You're a little late on the Dolbey case, aren't you, Sheriff?"

"Maybe, but I'm here on a different matter. Yesterday a couple of boys broke into Dolbey's girlfriend's house. Nadine Kemp, you must know her. The boys found her in her bathroom with a bullet in her forehead. When we searched the house we found a note to you beneath a blotter on her desk. I was hoping you could interpret it for me." Pritchard reached into his shirt pocket, pulled out a dinner napkin, and handed it to CJ.

CJ studied the handwriting on the napkin. *I think the threats are coming from Hambone's son. Call Floyd.* His telephone number was scrawled along the bottom of the napkin.

"I didn't know you and Ms. Kemp were such good friends," said Pritchard, reaching to take the napkin back. "What's more, after our talk at the Stampede I didn't think you'd still be sniffing around the fringes of the Hambone Dolbey case." Pritchard began twirling the gray, wide-brimmed Stetson he was holding. When CJ didn't answer, he stopped and in a cold, authoritative tone said, "Guess you won't mind me sniffing back."

Adjusting himself in bed, CJ prepared for the long sniffing session he knew was about to follow.

Chapter 27

Aaron Baptiste slipped a dog-eared copy of *Patterson's Field Guide to Rocks and Minerals* and the soggy relief map he had been studying into his back pocket beneath his poncho and patted them for good luck. He was following the sagging fence line that his father had told him marked the northern boundary of his fifty-five-acre tract of land near the Devil's Backbone. The rough terrain and a driving rainstorm had reduced his progress to a crawl, but in two hours of trekking through the muck, negotiating his way around slippery car-sized boulders, and shinnying up and down the rocky hillsides, he knew he was inching closer to nailing down what was rightfully his.

He stopped to get his bearings and wiped his mud-

and rain-splattered face with the back of his leather work glove before continuing his trek along what remained of a rickety barbed-wire fence. His thoughts suddenly turned to his father, Hambone Dolbey.

He hadn't liked the loudmouthed, boastful man who had wedged his way into his life six months earlier, straining an already troubled relationship with his mother. It bothered him even more that he and the man who turned out to be his father had such an amazing physical resemblance: short, stocky, and fuzzy-haired, with wide-set, bulging eyes and such thick thigh muscles that their pants never fit. From the very beginning Hambone had been an interloper, a bad dream come to life whom he had planned to teach a lesson until he learned about the diamonds and his father's plan to mine kimberlite on an otherwise worthless plot of land in Colorado north of a rock outcropping called the Devil's Backbone. After that he had played his role as the dutiful son well enough to get his father not only to show him a twenty-carat diamond he had plucked from the site but to confide the general location the diamond had come from.

He had seen the diamond only once. During one of Hambone's unannounced Wyoming visits that always made his mother, Rebecca, a nervous wreck, Hambone had pulled the diamond out from the same shine rag he used to polish his boots. It was the size of a peach pit and still uncut. When he had asked Hambone how he knew the unimpressive, colorless-looking rock was really a diamond, Hambone had replied, "I have a friend who's into rocks and jewelry; she guarantees it." That's when Aaron had learned of Nadine Kemp. It wasn't until later that he learned Hambone had promised Nadine a share of the profits from all the diamonds he planned to mine. He never told his father that he had no intention of sharing what was rightfully his with Nadine Kemp.

Rushing to pick up his pace, Aaron lost his footing and stumbled to his knees into a puddle lined by jagged rocks. He rose to a half-crouch to find his Levis ripped and both knees bleeding. "Motherfuck," he mumbled, brushing off his bloody knees with the sleeve of his poncho. Assured that the damage was minor, he gripped the remaining strand of barbed wire in the sagging fence to his right, pulled himself up, and continued walking, tired, sore, cold, and angry.

Winded, he worked his way over a rocky rise and found himself staring down a fifteen percent grade at a choppy lake. He smiled as he watched the water rise and break into brown foamy caps. He knew from what Hambone had told him that somewhere in the vicinity of the lake were diamonds.

The fence line he had been following had finally petered out. Facing directly into a gusting thirty-five-mile-per-hour wind, he closed one eye, stuck out his thumb, and ran an imaginary line from the edge of the lake to where the fence line stopped. He stood still for a moment, checking his bearings, then broke into a relaxed, easy grin. He'd need a survey to be certain, but from his rough calculations it appeared as though he and the lake were on the same side of the fence line, which meant the diamond fields had to be on Hambone's property.

Hambone had told him that the land around the lake was rich with kimberlite, and now it was time to find out for himself. He leaned back against the knobby hump of a boulder, pulled his field guide out of his pocket, and reread the pages he had dog-eared. The bold heading at the top of the page read *Diamonds.*

He ran his finger across the page, mouthing the words in italics: *Brilliant crystal structures formed at great depth in the earth's subcrustial iron-magnesium magmas. Diamonds are ferried to the surface in volcanic kimberlite lavas.* Just reading the words gave him a rush. He flipped to the next page, laughing out loud when he reached the underlined paragraph that described the rare sites worldwide where diamonds occurred. *Sporadic diamonds can be found only in gold placers in the eastern United States and California. The world's heavier and harder diamonds are mined from original rocks only in Siberia, South Africa, Australia, and Arkansas.* "Bullshit!" he shouted, stomping his run-down logger's boots in the muddy pool at his feet. "Bullshit!" he screamed again, pointing down toward the muddy lake. He slipped the field guide back into his jeans pocket, eased his contour map out, and carefully unfolded it. The fully opened three-by-three-foot map sagged in the middle from the pelting rain.

He eyed the map, then the disappearing fence line, and finally the lake again and again until he was satisfied that he had his landmarks straight. Then, standing on tiptoe and shading his eyes, he zeroed in on the tail of the Devil's Backbone in the distance. He looked from the prehistoric-looking rock outcropping to the contour map over and over until his head felt dizzy and his nose dribbled mucus.

Satisfied that he had aligned his coordinates properly in accordance with what Hambone had hinted were the defining landmarks that pinpointed the diamond fields, he folded the map back up, patted it dry, and slipped it into his pocket as he started working his way down the steep hillside. On his way down the rocky incline, he kept an eye trained on the most prominent of the jagged spines in the Devil's Backbone, just as Hambone had said he should if he wanted to arrive at the site where he had unearthed his twenty-carat diamond. Halfway down the hillside he lost his balance and nearly tumbled, but he never lost sight of his point of reference. Three hundred yards from the lake he stopped in a treeless clearing and rechecked his reference points one last time. The lake was a good fifty yards within the limit of the imaginary boundary line he had drawn from the prominent spine of the Devil's Backbone and the projected path of the downed fence line, which meant the kimberlite deposits and the diamonds were positively on his father's property.

Now he was on his own. A mudflat and a heavily treed hillside along the western boundary of the lake seemed to be where his coordinates were directing him. As he approached the mudflat, he found himself negotiating football-field-size excavations in the earth, gouges that he hadn't seen from his rain-impeded vantage point above the flat. Realizing that the flat was being mined, he flew into a rage. "You have no right! You have no right!" he shouted, zigzagging his way around the craters. Negotiating his way around a hole pooled with rain, he suddenly found himself on the blind side of a sloping pit and face-to-face with a mammoth drab-brown excavator whose tires were buried up to the rims in three feet of mud. The Pandeco corporate logo was prominent on the excavator's door. Furious, he stopped and patted down his poncho. Then, reaching beneath it and into the pocket of his lumber jacket, he pulled out a .38 and fired point blank at the tire closest to him. The tire let out a mournful hiss, and the excavator sank another half-foot before listing to the right.

"You're a dead motherfucker now." He slogged his way through the mud to within a few feet of the other rear tire and punctured the knobby-looking rubber with a second shot. He did the same for the two front tires until the excavator rested a full foot lower in the mud than it had when he arrived. He slipped the gun back beneath his poncho and into his jacket pocket as a post-ejaculative smile formed on his face.

Satisfied that he had accomplished his mission, he reached back under his poncho, pulled out a Polaroid camera, and snapped a series of twelve photographs as he slowly turned a full 360 degrees. Then, slipping the camera back into his pocket, he turned to focus on the lake's choppy waters before walking across the mudflat toward the water's edge. He paced back and forth several times before he finally dropped to one knee and grabbed a handful of mud. He looked back toward the Devil's Backbone reference point and smiled, knowing that he would now be able to fend off claims by anyone who said the property wasn't his. Then he pulled a surveyor's stake out of his poncho pocket, pressed it into the ground, stood up, and buried the stake almost to the hilt with the heel of his boot. For the time being he had seen all he needed to. He would have to think about what to do next.

He turned abruptly and headed back across the mudflat in the direction from which he had come. On his way out of the area he stopped at one of the shallower excavation sites and picked through what he knew from his field guide and his father's lengthy descriptions had to be exposed kimberlite. He didn't expect to stumble across a gem right then; he just wanted to experience what raw diamond ore felt like in his hands. He knew that soon he would be able to break away from his mother and his lifelong Wyoming incarceration. He foraged in a few more of the pits before turning to leave. On his way back up the rocky hillside he began thinking about how he was going to deal with Whitaker Rodgers, the man Hambone had told him was trespassing on their land.

He decided the only way to deal with a trespasser was the way his grandfather always had, face-to-face. Suddenly he began to shiver as the wind and steady drizzle he had been facing for most of the day turned into a gale-force downpour. He picked up his pace as he climbed and felt for his .38, wanting to make certain it was still in place. As he headed farther away from the diamond fields and back parallel to the Devil's Backbone, he began chuckling to himself, thinking that he couldn't remember a single time in his life that his grandfather ever dealt with a trespasser without a gun in his hand.

Chapter 28

Two days of being confined to bed were all CJ could take, especially because for at least half that time he had been repeatedly second-guessing himself, trying to determine how someone had been able to ambush him in his own garage. The fact that Mavis was busy ministering to him hand and foot didn't help matters. It only served to emphasize the fact that although he hated to admit it, he was as vulnerable as anyone else in the world.

He hadn't been dizzy for twelve hours, and his dry heaves had subsided. After five rounds of oatmeal and four of boiled, skinless chicken, he would have given anything for a bowl of gumbo with a side order of collard greens or a fried catfish platter. And he kept telling himself that if Mavis forced him to drink another glass of either orange juice or water, his bladder was going to spring a leak.

He looked around Mavis's bedroom, studying the delicately stenciled light blue wallpaper pattern and eyeing the decidedly feminine accents and expensive Western period pieces. In addition to trying to erase the ambush from his memory, he wanted to push Sheriff Pritchard's two-hour interrogation out of his mind. His conversation with Pritchard had been formal, polite, and anything but pleasant. After emphasizing how sorry he was to hear about the assault and explaining how disturbed he was to have to bother CJ under the circumstances, Pritchard had pointedly told CJ that if he continued to stick his nose into an ongoing murder investigation, he would make sure that he saw some jail time.

In the course of their one-sided conversation, CJ was able to learn that Pritchard had also questioned Morgan and Dittier about Nadine Kemp's murder and that Morgan had told Pritchard about the whole Rebecca Baptiste–Hambone Dolbey affair and about Hambone's son. When Pritchard pressed CJ on the issue of just why Nadine Kemp had wanted to contact him about threats from Hambone's son, CJ had answered honestly that he didn't know. He didn't tell Pritchard that he was hoping to find the answer to that question through Billy DeLong, who was checking the issue out in Wyoming.

He had found it odd that not once during their conversation did Pritchard mention Whitaker Rodgers, Pandeco Oil, or Rodgers's diamond mining operation, nor did he mention how they might relate to the deaths of Hambone Dolbey or Nadine Kemp. He had the feeling that deep down, the politician inside the sheriff had Pritchard dancing around any issues that related to Rodgers, probably because of Rodgers's political clout. Fortunately, CJ didn't have the same restrictions. Pritchard had left CJ with a warning to butt out of the Hambone Dolbey case, an admonition not to repeat anything he had just been told about the circumstances of Nadine Kemp's death and a wish for a speedy recovery.

CJ had managed to catch a half-hour of sleep before two Denver detectives rushed in on Pritchard's heels to question him about the assault and inform him that a criminalist had checked his garage from top to bottom and they were awaiting the results. They were neither as polite nor as thorough as Pritchard, and when they left he was convinced that the difference between big-city cops and small-town police was that the big-city types had computerized Jell-O for brains and a list of programmed insults built into their heads.

The only good thing that had come out of his meeting with local and regional law enforcement was that Julie had taken pity on him and agreed to take another bar exam study break and run a financial check on Rodgers. He knew Julie had a law school classmate who worked part time at a 17th Street brokerage house and could spit out a financial spreadsheet on Rodgers and his company in less time than it took for Sheriff Pritchard to get back to Greeley. He sat up in bed and massaged the knot on his ear and the swelling on the side of his head. With Mavis down the street at Mae's for the first time in two days and Julie off on her assignment, he was alone in the house.

He swung his legs out of bed and sat on the edge, staring across the room and out the window. Outside it was overcast, and a light drizzle was falling. He wondered whether Bobby Two-Shirts's sister was waiting outside, hoping for a second chance at him. He knew she had to be one hell of a calculating cuss to have ambushed him and vengeful enough to never let go without settling the score.

He watched the rain dribble from the eaves above the two dormer windows onto the shake shingles below and thought about Bobby Two-Shirts's warning to him. "She'll kill you for sure," had been Bobby's exact words. Words that he recalled being uttered less as a threat than as some ritualistic promise. He felt for the knot above his ear again as if he needed to remind himself that Bobby Two-Shirts's sister was playing for keeps. *Kill or be killed,* he thought, remembering a credo he had heard his gunnery chief repeat hundreds of times during his second tour of Vietnam. He watched the rain continue to fall until he felt drowsy and surprisingly cold. Then, swinging his legs back into bed, he sank back into Mavis's overstuffed down pillows and drifted off to sleep.

The first thing he did on awakening two hours later was jump out of bed and stand up straight in an attempt to judge whether his equilibrium had returned. Through twenty quick rounds of leaping up and then sitting back down he never once felt dizzy. In the midst of a second set of leaps, Julie walked into the room without him noticing. She paused just beyond the doorway, uncertain what CJ's gyrations were about. "You on some kind of new street drug I should know about?" she said, realiz-

ing as CJ continued his calisthenics that he was trying to
check his balance.

CJ tugged at the front of his T-shirt. "I'll be on
something soon if I don't get a shower and out of these
gamey things fast."

Julie walked across the room, shaking her head. "I
thought you were on orders from the doctor and Mavis
to stay in bed for the next few days."

"I'm about to cheat."

"Not a good idea." Julie shot him a disapproving
stare.

"I feel fine." He threw his arms into the air tri-
umphantly.

The expression on Julie's face changed to one of
disbelief as she tapped the back edge of the manila
folder she was holding against an outstretched palm. "I
didn't track down this information on Rodgers and Pandeco Oil so you could rush out on the streets and get
yourself brained again."

"I don't intend to. Besides, you're mixing up kum-
quats and cantaloupes. Rodgers didn't brain me, and that
little garage incident isn't related to either him or his
company. It goes back to me pissing off a little bond-
skipping weasel named Bobby Two-Shirts and his sister."

Julie looked puzzled. She had missed most of what
was going on in CJ's office during the past week because
she had been studying.

"I'll tell you about them later. For now I just need
the straight skinny on my drugstore-cowboy friend."

Julie clutched the folder to her chest. "If I tell you,
will you promise to pass the information on to that sher-

iff who was here and lay off playing James Bond until your head solidifies?"

"Can't. I told Morgan and Dittier I'd see this Dolbey thing through."

"Loyalty's a great trait, CJ, real akin to stubbornness. Quit fooling yourself. You're playing this thing out for Calvin Jefferson Floyd. Somehow, chasing down the bad guys lights your fire. I just hope it doesn't end up getting you killed."

CJ looked down at the floor, avoiding eye contact with Julie. He knew she was right. In an attempt to skirt the issue, he said, "I'm no more stubborn than you, counselor."

"Don't lay that counselor shit on me, CJ. This is serious business."

"You're starting to sound like Mavis."

Julie took a step back and angrily slammed the folder she was holding down on the nightstand. "I don't see how she puts up with you."

Suddenly feeling dizzy, CJ took a quick gulp of air, hoping Julie wouldn't notice. "Maybe she likes a challenge."

"I'm not going to stand here and argue with you." Julie nodded toward the folder. "You've got the information you wanted—use it in good health. I'm going back downstairs to make myself some tea. Maybe it'll settle my stomach." Turning to leave, she added, "And don't think I didn't catch your little gasp." She left in what CJ jokingly liked to call one of her Puerto Rican fireball huffs.

Waiting for the new surge of dizziness to subside, CJ sat on the edge of the bed, thinking about how he would smooth things over with Julie. When his head finally stopped spinning he reached for the folder she had left behind. It was still damp from the nervous sweat on Julie's hands. Flipping the folder open, he found a legal tablet with Julie's handwriting and a front-page note to *Check out pages 11 and 16 of the enclosed prospectus.* Beneath the legal pad was a stock-offer prospectus dated eleven months earlier that outlined a joint-venture diamond mining exploration project between Pandeco Oil and a company called Gemstone Mining Ltd.

CJ flipped through the delicate tissue-paper-thin pages of the prospectus, stopping on page eleven. A third of the way down the page the joint venture's six principals were listed. Three of the names he recognized immediately: Whitaker Rodgers, Virginia Rodgers, and Evelyn Coleman. Whitaker was listed as Gemstone's president, Evelyn as vice-president and treasurer. Below each person's name was a brief résumé summarizing his or her professional background and experience.

CJ reached for a pen on the nightstand, circled the three names, and continued reading. For the next twenty minutes he plowed through the prospectus, but when he finished he was nearly as confused about what the document said as when he had started. He didn't realize until he flipped beyond the first page of the legal pad that Julie had summarized things for him in a note: *In case you missed it, here's the beef: About a year ago Whitaker Rodgers and Evelyn Coleman set up a diamond mining company, Gemstone Mining Ltd., using $600,000 backed by personal assets. Together they own 51 percent of Gemstone's stock. The project has the blessing of Rodgers's mother, CEO of Pandeco Oil, who in ex-*

*change for 20 percent of Gemstone's stock pledged to
put Pandeco's borrowing strength behind the venture
with a 2 million dollar letter of credit for a share of future diamond mining profits to be paid to Pandeco at a
later date. There's a two-year timeline kicker on the
agreement before the letter of credit comes due. The only
asset that Gemstone seems to own is listed on page 16
and is described as extensive kimberlite reserves in
north-central Colorado on a 3,000-acre tract of land
just northeast of Loveland in a region known as the
Devil's Backbone. There's no mention of Hambone Dolbey in the document, and everything in the prospectus
seems to be kosher.*

Julie had signed her name and drawn a happy face
next to it. Beneath the happy face were two additional
lines of print. *Two hours of personal billable time, $250.
Consultation with William Harris, stockbroker, Pipper
Jeffrey, at $125 per hour, total $625.* A lightly penciled
X had been drawn through the bill along with the words,
I just love being a lawyer.

CJ placed the folder on the nightstand feeling as
guilty as he had in years. Julie had not only tried to remind him of his own vulnerability but had also taken
time out from her studies to get him the information he
needed, and he had run her off. He shook his head at his
stupidity, mulling over the serious fence-mending he had
in store. Now convinced that Dolbey's and Nadine
Kemp's deaths were linked to Whitaker Rodgers's diamond mining venture, he knew he needed to tease out
the killer's motive. What if Hambone's supposedly
worthless tract contained a cache of diamonds? A wind-
fall like that would certainly have been grounds for mur-

der, especially if you were an only surviving son like the Baptiste kid Billy DeLong was checking on.

He thought for a moment about what each of the joint-venture partners had to lose, starting with Virginia Rodgers. Even if the kimberlite reserves turned out to be worthless, she and Pandeco Oil were home free because her offer of collateral was no more than a promise of future financial support in the form of a letter of credit. On the other hand, Whitaker Rodgers stood to lose $300,000, and Evelyn Coleman the same—reason enough to kill in his book.

CJ pulled his hands out from behind his head and thought back to how Nadine Kemp had described Hambone Dolbey's land. "A worthless patch of land up near the Devil's Backbone," had been her exact words. He suspected that if he were ever going to piece together what was now a double murder puzzle, he'd not only have to run down Whitaker Rodgers but also probably have to visit the Devil's Backbone mining site. But it would have to be after his dizzy spells subsided and he found out what Billy had discovered about the shovel-wielding Baptistes. CJ wasn't ready to dismiss the fact that the Baptistes had their own set of reasons for wanting to see Hambone Dolbey dead. What he couldn't figure out was why they would have wanted to kill Nadine Kemp.

He swung out of bed and reached for the phone on the nightstand. When it took him longer than usual to remember Billy's Wyoming phone number, he found himself thinking back to what Julie had said about his stubbornness. Maybe he was pursuing the Hambone Dolbey case in order to prove to himself that come hell or high water, nothing slowed him down. Then again, maybe he was doing it to help out a couple of old friends. It didn't really matter. He was in the hunt till the end. Finally recalling Billy's number, he punched it in, knowing that as shaky as he felt he might need someone to cover his rear, and there was no one better than a case-hardened mountain goat of a Wyoming cowboy like Billy DeLong.

He let the phone ring twenty times before hanging up and mouthing, "Shit." Frustrated at the sudden kink in his game plan, he decided to move on to plan B and try to track Whitaker Rodgers down. He headed for the bathroom to shave and shower, realizing that it was the first time in two days that Mavis had been more than a few steps from his side. When she had rushed out to open the restaurant that morning, he had suddenly realized that he needed her more than ever. Mavis had left a thermos of decaf on the nightstand along with a heaping bowl of fruit and half a dozen freshly baked breakfast muffins that Flora Jean had dropped off on her way to work. Mavis had left him in a rush but not before giving him a warm, lingering kiss, pulling his hand up between her breasts, and promising him with a wink that if he rested like he was supposed to all day, that evening when she returned home she'd have her own special remedy for his lightheadedness.

He patted down his face with a damp, baby-soft, lemony-smelling washcloth and watched his reflection in the bathroom mirror, frowning at the size of the swelling above his ear. Ignoring the swelling, he pulled out a drawer to the left of the sink and smiled at the familiar sight of his electric shaver, suddenly feeling surprisingly secure. He palmed the shaver and plugged it in. As the razor head made its first pass through his stubby two-day growth of beard, he glanced back into the mirror.

It wasn't until he had almost finished shaving that CJ realized he wasn't watching his own reflection but concentrating instead on the objects reflected in the room behind him: Mavis's bed, the chest of drawers, the paintings on the wall. He stopped shaving, suddenly gripped by the uneasy feeling that someone could be lurking in the bedroom, ready to spring out and finish the job they had started in his garage. He turned to look behind him as the shaver's high-pitched hum recharged his memory, somehow reminding him of the sound of incoming choppers in the steamy jungles of Vietnam. He stood staring back into the mirror, shaver vibrating in his hand, until the image disappeared. Then, in a cold sweat, he turned back to shaving, knowing he had just wrestled with genuine fear, an enemy he hadn't encountered in a long, long time.

Chapter 29

Whitaker Rodgers was standing in the doorway of his secretary's office looking as though he'd been gored by a bull. His hair was matted, his temples were pounding, and his nose was running as it always did when he felt pressured or found himself in the midst of sex.

Rodgers's voice quivered as he waved his arms spastically at his secretary. "Forward all my calls to voice mail unless it's urgent. If my mother stops by, tell her I went to check on things up at the Devil's Backbone and I'll be in touch this evening." He patted down all four of his pockets, making certain he had all his keys. Satisfied that he did, he pulled a wrinkled handkerchief from his front pocket, dabbed awkwardly at his runny nose, and looked across the room toward Evelyn Colcman, his eyes screaming for help. Evelyn was seated, thumbing through a copy of *Newsweek,* content not to expend a single ounce of energy until Whitaker was fully prepared to leave.

"Are we forgetting anything?" asked Rodgers, stuffing the handkerchief back into his pocket.

Peering over the edge of the magazine, Evelyn pushed her reading glasses up on her nose. "Not that I can think of." It was the third time Whitaker had asked her the same question, and she was on the verge of screaming for him to get a grip. He had every right to be on edge, since he had just learned from one of the field engineers up at their diamond mining site that the tires on one of their earth excavators had been riddled by bullets the previous day. The engineer had sworn that he had also seen someone walking the northern property line the same day. His message had Whitaker so agitated that he wasn't thinking straight.

Evelyn was used to Whitaker overreacting. It was just one of the things he did. But the incident had her edgy as well. Unlike Whitaker, she continued to hide her apprehension as she always did, acting as nonchalant as possible. Worried that Whitaker would end up doing something stupid and derailing their entire Gemstone plan, she had agreed to accompany him back up to the Devil's Backbone. She wasn't looking forward to slogging through acres of rain-soaked muck searching for goblins, ghosts, or the increasing number of people Whitaker seemed to be convinced were out to muscle in on his diamond bonanza. But she had her own invest-ment to protect, and she knew she couldn't trust Whitaker with that. Perturbed and irritable, she scratched her arm and silently cursed the Gore-Tex-lined field gear she was wearing, gear that always seemed to make her overheat and itch.

"We'll be better prepared for the weather this time," said Whitaker, glancing down at Evelyn's waterproof boots, then his own.

Evelyn nodded and forced a smile, acknowledging that Whitaker's quick preparation for the elements had nonetheless been thorough.

"Who do you think would be traipsing around up there checking out boundaries and blasting away at our equipment?"

Evelyn shrugged. "Beats me."

Whitaker glanced toward his secretary to make certain she wasn't following the conversation too closely. Satisfied that she wasn't, he walked across the room and sat down next to Evelyn. His voice now a whisper, he said, "It had to be somebody connected to Dolbey."

"That would be my guess."

"Could have been those two rodeo-bum friends of his," whispered Whitaker.

"Or that girlfriend of Dolbey's. What's her name?"

"Nadine Kemp," said Whitaker. "How could you forget the name of someone who tried to put the screws to us for twenty grand?"

"Spaced it, I guess. Maybe the ten thousand you finally gave her to keep her mouth shut about our little problem with property boundaries helps keep her name a little more fresh in your mind," said Evelyn.

Whitaker frowned. "That's water under the bridge. You should be glad that's all it cost us. Just remember, the little shrew was out to screw Dolbey, not us. We got the easement, didn't we, and we're mining every day. That's all that counts."

"I guess so," said Evelyn. It bothered her that she and Whitaker had paid the Kemp woman $1,500 a month for close to a year to keep her mouth shut about the fact that they were not simply crossing Dolbey's property with their equipment but also excavating on his land. She had never understood why Dolbey himself hadn't protested, but always suspected that it was because he didn't care if they dug up the whole county, since he alone knew where the Devil's Backbone diamond deposits were.

"Let's go," said Whitaker. He snapped the buttons closed on his field jacket, then fumbled around in one of the jacket pockets. "I'm doubly prepared for our trespasser if he shows today."

Evelyn shot him a quizzical look.

Breaking into an impish grin, he turned the jacket pocket out toward her, flashing the butt of a nickel-plated .38. He shot a quick, guilty glance toward his secretary before snapping the pocket flap closed.

Evelyn's eyes narrowed in astonishment. "I don't believe you, Whitaker. You're playing with fire."

Whitaker's expression turned somber. "No, just playing for keeps." He patted his pocket for good luck and motioned for Evelyn to follow him toward the door.

CJ was pacing back and forth in front of Flora Jean's desk, telling himself that the pounding in his head would pass soon. "Try him again," he said, snapping at Flora Jean.

Flora Jean dutifully dialed Whitaker Rodgers's number for the seventh time in the past few minutes. "Same as before. Keeps rolling over to voice mail."

"Damn." CJ gritted his teeth and sat down in one of the sawed-off short-legged chairs he usually reserved for clients, chairs that were intended to make everything in the office, including the personnel, seem bigger. Misconnecting with Rodgers was making his headache worse.

On the cab ride to his office from Mavis's he had stopped at Gart Brothers Sports Castle and picked up a couple of trail and topo maps that detailed the lay of the land around the Devil's Backbone. With or without Rodgers's help, he had decided to check the property out for himself. The pixieish salesclerk who had waited on him had volunteered that she was in her final year of geology studies at the University of Colorado's Denver campus when he mentioned that he was looking for maps of the Devil's Backbone area. She had pointed the area out to him on a topo map and outlined in yellow a triangular zone between the Devil's Backbone and a small body of water known as Trapper's Lake. "I wish I were going with you," she had said, laying her highlighter aside, a look of lost adventure in her eyes. When he had offhandedly mentioned that he was heading up to the Devil's Backbone in search of diamonds, the clerk spent the next several minutes giving him a quick lesson on kimberlite extraction, how to spot a diamond, and where on the topo map she thought diamonds were most likely to be found. CJ had left the sports castle knowing two things for certain: he would have flunked geology 101, and the rock he had found in the water trough at the Stampede had very likely been kimberlite. He nearly had a relapse when he walked out of the sports castle and remembered there was a cab waiting. The $29 tab on the meter made him realize that he still wasn't thinking straight.

Flora Jean realized it too as she patiently studied CJ, expecting him to slump over in his chair any moment. "You're lookin' pretty mustard-faced to me. You sure that doctor of yours said it's okay for you to come back to work?"

"Sure." In truth he had been told to limit his activities to nothing more strenuous than getting up to go to the bathroom or lifting a fork for at least a week. Reflecting on the doctor's advice, he paused and asked himself why it was so important that he hit the streets. Especially considering the fact that there wasn't one nickel in it for him.

The answer boiled down to two simple things. One was principle. Lightheaded or not, he had made a promise to Morgan and Dittier, and he never reneged on promises he made to friends. The second reason had nothing to do with Hambone Dolbey. It related to the fact that very simply he didn't much enjoy being stalked. He had had enough of that in Vietnam. It made him feel paranoid, and he knew that if he wanted the feeling to disappear he would have to flush his adversary out. Bobby Two-Shirts's sister was going to see him on the street; he would make certain of it, because he didn't want to spend a second more than he had to glancing over his shoulder, wondering who was there.

Realizing that he may have answered Flora Jean's question too abruptly, he added, "The doctors gave me a clean bill of health. Think I'd be here if they hadn't?"

Flora Jean eyed CJ suspiciously, but the look of seriousness on his face made her decide against challenging his response. "Want me to try that Rodgers guy again?"

"Might as well."

"Mind if I try it my way this time?"

"Be my guest."

"Got a number at that company of his besides the one we been dialing?"

CJ fished in his pocket, pulled out a cache of papers and business cards, and fumbled through them until he found the card of the PR person who had given him the ten-cent tour of Pandeco Oil before easing him out the door. "Try this one." He tossed the card on Flora Jean's desk.

Covering the receiver with her free hand, Flora Jean dialed the number on the card. Then, suddenly grinning, she said, "You say this whole thing's about diamond mining. Ain't that a kick. Heck, I thought they only mined them kind of rocks in Africa." Before she could add another comment, someone answered, "Public Relations, Pandeco Oil."

Flora Jean was suddenly all business. "This is Lauren Postens, Channel 2 news," she said, sounding as official as a news bulletin. Lauren Postens, Denver's only black television investigative reporter, had a profile higher than most Colorado politicians. Even the governor was reported to be wary of her, and it was common knowledge that if she ever called and announced, "This is Lauren Postens," in her patented, slow, Texas hill-country drawl, you were in serious trouble. "I'm doin' a story on Colorado diamond mining. I understand your company's heavily involved." Flora Jean cleared her throat, hoping to sound even more official. "I'd like to speak with Mr. Whitaker Rodgers if I could."

"I'm sorry, you'll have to speak with his secretary," came a nervous voice on the other end of the line.

"Could you transfer me?" said Flora Jean, Texas twang rock-solid.

"Certainly."

Flora Jean looked up at CJ and smiled as she was being transferred.

"Hello, Whitaker Rodgers's office," said a new, more authoritative woman's voice.

"Lauren Postens here, Channel 2 news. I'd like to speak with Mr. Rodgers."

"May I ask what it's in reference to?"

"Diamonds, sugar, diamonds."

"I'm afraid Mr. Rodgers doesn't do interviews related to that. But I'm sure our public relations department can help you."

Flora Jean broke into a wide grin. "I think he'll want to speak to me. I understand that his diamond mining company has an unwritten rule about not hiring minorities. Sounds real country club to me."

"That's preposterous."

"My sources claim otherwise. I'm certain Mr. Rodgers would like to clear things up before I go any further with my investigation."

There was a moment of dead-air silence before the secretary responded, "He's out of the office until tomorrow."

"I can't sit on this until then."

There was another brief pause, the kind that occurs when someone isn't quite prepared to think on her feet.

"You might try him at this number." The secretary rattled off the phone number so fast Flora Jean almost missed it. When Flora Jean turned the number jotted on a memo pad toward CJ, the northwest Colorado 970 area code told him that Whitaker Rodgers was more than likely up at the Devil's Backbone mining site. "Thank you very much," said Flora Jean, winking at CJ. "You've been a big help."

In a mousy kind of voice that said *I hope I didn't do something wrong,* the secretary said, "You're welcome," and immediately hung up.

Before CJ could say anything, Flora Jean was dialing the new number.

"Gemstone field office," answered a gruff-voiced man.

A crackle of static shot through the line, followed by a roll of thunder, unnerving Flora Jean. "I'd like to speak to Mr. Rodgers, please," she said, trying to regain her composure.

"He's out in the field. Any message?"

"One second, please." Flora Jean turned to CJ, her hand cupped over the receiver. "The man on the line says Rodgers is out in the field. Wanna leave a message?"

"No."

"I'll call back later," said Flora Jean.

"Better make it before six, toots. After that he's headed back for Denver."

"Sure thing," said Flora Jean. Furious at being called toots, she slammed down the receiver. "Looks like you won't land your big fish today unless you hook him before six. That's when he heads back to Denver. Got any idea where he's at?"

"I'm betting he's trying to pluck a few diamonds out of the earth." CJ glanced at his watch. "One thing for certain, I've got almost six hours to find out if I'm right."

"Wherever he's at, it's stormin' like hell," said Flora Jean. "There was enough static on the line to fry your hair."

CJ stood up, obviously unsteady on his feet. "That's good to know." The words echoed inside his head.

"You don't look up to negotiatin' this on your own," Flora Jean said, sliding her chair across the alcove.

CJ dropped into the chair with a deadweight thump. "Thanks." He paused to catch his breath before resting back in the chair. "No need to worry. I've got backup." He remained half slumped in the chair, breathing heavily for the next couple of minutes before standing up and heading for his office. At the doorway he stopped and looked back at Flora Jean. "That was one hell of a con job you did on the phone. You should've been an actress."

"Who says I ain't?" Flora Jean broke into an impish smile that made CJ wonder what other skills she might be hiding.

CJ closed his office door and half shuffled over to the chair behind the desk. Gritting his teeth, he tried to remember Billy DeLong's phone number. When it finally came to him, he dialed the number hastily, fearing it would disappear again.

Billy picked up on the first ring. "DeLong."

"Where the hell have you been?"

"Running back and forth between here and that Baptiste place," said Billy, immediately recognizing CJ's voice. "I've been trying to keep a close watch on it like you asked me to."

CJ shook his head as if he were trying to shake off a punch. Easing back in his chair, he massaged both temples as he tried to come to grips with the fact that his mind was acting like a sieve. "What've you got?" he asked finally, regaining his composure.

"Plenty. For one, we got a problem kid named Aaron Baptiste, who from what I dug up had one hell of a reason to dispense with dear ol' dad—money. Second, we got that fidgety mother of his, Rebecca, who answered just about every question I put to her the first time I dropped by to visit and then immediately disappeared. Ain't seen hide nor hair of her for a day and a half. And the white pickup that was there the first time I dropped by is gone."

"Anything else?"

"Besides the fact that Rebecca's father and brother are dead, natural causes by the way, a sheriff's car out of Greeley swung by the place earlier today. A big guy got out and went over the place with a fine-toothed comb. I was watching him with binocs from a hillside to the north. He carted away a stack of branding irons, and believe it or not, the guy was damn near a dead ringer for that sheriff we butted heads with a couple of years ago over in Steamboat Springs. Had the same baggy-pants, lop-eared-dog kind of look."

"It was the same guy all right, Carlton Pritchard," said CJ, wondering if Pritchard had stumbled across Hambone Dolbey's murder weapon.

"I knew it."

CJ checked his watch, anxiously rolling his tongue

around the inside of his mouth. "Can you meet me over near Greeley by four? We can hook up at Lisa Darley's place," CJ added, picking a spot he knew Billy had been to before.

"If I haul ass and pretend I'm at Indy."

CJ suddenly clutched his stomach. "Hang on for a second." He laid down the receiver, slid the chair out from behind his desk, reached for a nearby wastepaper basket, and threw up into it. He heaved into the basket a second time and then sat up rigidly in the chair, staring at the wall until his stomach stopped gurgling. Exhausted, he picked the phone back up and mumbled, "I'm back."

"What the hell was that? Sounded like somebody throwing up."

"It was—me."

"You okay?"

"Yeah, just a little out of sync from an encounter with a tire iron. Tell you about it later."

"Maybe we should put this thing off."

"Can't. I promised Morgan and Dittier I'd find Dolbey's killer. On top of that, there's somebody out there riding my ass who I need to flush out."

"I see." Billy shook his head, confused at CJ's lopsided logic.

CJ nudged the trash can away from him with the toe of his boot. "How about bringing some firepower with you on your way down? I've got a feeling it's the only thing the person riding my ass'll understand."

"He must be a bad MF," said Billy, already running a quick list of weapons through his head.

"She," said CJ, setting the record straight. "And don't get caught in any speed traps on your way."

"I won't." Then, sounding as if the world had somehow flipped on its axis, Billy added, "A woman, now don't that take the cake."

"See you by four." CJ cradled the receiver and glanced at the pool of vomit in the wastebasket, then spun his chair around to check out his rogues' gallery. There were only four photos of women mixed in among the ninety photographs. Two of the women had been mean, sour people, filled with hatred for the world. One had been an unfortunate, drugged-out loser, treading her way along in life's undertow until it swallowed her whole, and one had been a bunco artist out to scam the world. None of the four had tried to kill him, and other than the fact that they had been women, he didn't remember much about them at all.

He had no idea what rage was driving Bobby Two-Shirts's sister. Maybe it had something to do with what his uncle used to call the *same-egg voodoo of twins.* Maybe she just liked cracking people's heads with tire irons. Whatever the case, he was tired of thinking about her dogging his ass. He spun his chair back around slowly and pulled out the middle drawer in his desk to the sound of a loud stomach rumble. Shoving a half-used ream of paper aside, he reached for the snub-nosed .38 in the drawer's upper right-hand corner. He didn't like the possibility of having to shoot someone, especially a woman, but if it came down to it and his life was on the line, he knew he could. He pulled the .38 out of the drawer, checked the magazine to make certain it was full of cartridges, and slipped the gun into his pocket.

Chapter 30

hree days of rain had finally petered out into an intermittent drizzle and persistent fog that hugged the valley floor below the Devil's Backbone. Whitaker Rodgers could barely make out the spines of the craggy outcropping in the distance as he and Evelyn Coleman trudged along a mucky trail that had mud cresting over their boot tops with each new step. The idea of having to fight her way through another half-hour's worth of muck to get to Trapper's Lake had Evelyn second-guessing why she had agreed to come along with Whitaker.

"What makes you think we'll find any diamonds near the lake? Most of our kimberlite finds have been further to the east."

"Let's just say I have a hunch," said Whitaker.

Accustomed to a more scientific-minded Whitaker, Evelyn shot him a puzzled look. "Do you know something I don't?"

Whitaker stopped and stared back at her without answering the question. "I just want to see if I'm right before the day's over. Let's keep moving."

Evelyn forced back a frown and jerked her foot out of a suction cup of mud only to step back down into a blob of coffee-ground ooze that left her momentarily immobile.

Whitaker trudged ahead, unaware of Evelyn's predicament and oblivious to the fact that someone was watching them from a hillside two hundred yards away.

CJ stood in the driveway next to his Bel Air staring at Flora Jean, shaking his head in disbelief. "Why the hell didn't you stop him?"

"I couldn't," said Flora Jean, hunkering beneath her umbrella. "He came barreling down the driveway like a bat out of hell."

CJ shaded his eyes and peered intently into the misty rain and up Delaware Street as if he expected the Jeep to suddenly reappear. After a few seconds he slammed his fist into his palm. "Shit." He was about to go back inside and call the cops to report a stolen vehicle when he looked back up the driveway and noticed the hint of a shadow just beyond the open garage door. He drew his .38 and began walking slowly up the driveway, his mind filled with visions of Bobby Two-Shirts's sister. He was less than ten feet away from the door when a dripping wet Dittier Atkins stepped out from the corner he had been hiding in. Dittier shoved his hands up defensively, mouthing the words, "Don't shoot, don't shoot."

CJ lowered the .38, certain that the horrified look on Dittier's face matched his own. "What the shit's going on, Dittier? You damn near scared me to death."

Dittier didn't budge until he saw the .38 disappear into the pocket of CJ's ankle-length range duster. Then, with a look of guilt spreading across his face, he slowly and methodically signed, "I helped Morgan hot-wire the Jeep so he could go up to where they're mining diamonds and find Hambone's killer."

The only words CJ recognized for sure were Jeep and mining diamonds. But they were enough to tell him where Morgan was headed. He slammed his palm against his forehead, wondering how Morgan had found out about the diamonds, until he remembered Lisa's fax.

Coming to grips with the fact that standing there second-guessing himself wasn't going to solve the problem, CJ draped his arm over Dittier's shoulder and walked the still stunned rodeo clown back down the driveway to where Flora Jean was standing. "This is my friend Dittier Atkins. Think I scared him half to death. How about taking him inside, drying him out, and driving him over to Mae's for a meal and something to settle his nerves."

"Right now?" said Flora Jean.

"An hour of downtime won't put us out of business."

Flora Jean looked at Dittier and then back at CJ. "Where're you headed?"

"To try and catch up with an old bull rider before he does something stupid." CJ looked back down the driveway toward the garage and shook his head. "Means I've gotta take the Bel Air out in this slop."

"It's not like it's battery acid," said Flora Jean.

"But it's close." With his range coat flapping in the breeze, CJ headed for the garage. Inside, he called Mavis from his shop phone to let her know what he was up to, only to learn that she wasn't expected back at Mae's for at least an hour. He left a message that he would be out for a while and he'd call back. Frustrated at missing Mavis, CJ shed his coat, slipped into the Bel Air, stashed his .38 in the glove compartment, and backed out of the garage and down the driveway.

He nosed the Bel Air toward Speer Boulevard, thinking that maybe he should have let Mavis know where he was headed, but since she would certainly hear what he was up to from Flora Jean, and he planned to be back before dark, he decided to leave things as they were and gunned the Bel Air onto Speer. As he eased past the southern fringe of lower downtown Denver and finally onto I-25, a sudden spell of dizziness hit him and a stabbing pain shot through his right eye. He eased off the accelerator and asked himself, *What the hell am I doing?* just as a flatbed semi loaded down with galvanized conduit sped past him, sending a fantail of grimy water slamming into the Bel Air's windshield. In the time it took him to turn the wipers on high, the dizziness disappeared, and so did his justification for backing away from looking for Morgan. He pushed the Bel Air back up to sixty-five, and soon he was kicking his own spray of water into the windshield of the vehicle behind him, a tailgating pickup that had been following him ever since he turned onto Speer Boulevard.

Chapter 31

Aaron Baptiste had upgraded the firepower he had used to shoot out the excavator's tires, replacing it with the .45 he now had jammed into his jacket pocket and an infield semiautomatic rifle. Taking a break from two hours of tracking the erratic movements of Whitaker Rodgers and Evelyn Coleman, he was leaning on the rifle's muzzle, catching his breath. He had watched Whitaker and Evelyn zigzag their way around the margins of Trapper's Lake and then angle across his father's fifty-five-acre tract until they were now fifty yards from the last craggy facet in the tail of the Devil's Backbone. He couldn't decide if they were looking for something in particular or simply disoriented in the foggy mist.

What he knew for certain was that they were trespassing on land that by birthright now belonged to him. Deciding he had had enough of playing cat and mouse, he pulled the butt of his rifle out of the mud, wiped it off on his jeans, and moved out of the shadow of the pine trees where he had been hiding to confront the two trespassers.

The muscles in Evelyn Coleman's face were sagging and heavy dark circles rimmed her eyes. "I don't care about searching through any more kimberlite, Whitaker, or about land rights or even diamonds. I'm exhausted and chilled to the bone. I've had enough for today—let's go home."

Wheezing noticeably, Whitaker stopped and took a gulp of air. "This is the last site I want to check out, promise." He worked his way up to within twenty feet of one of the five-story-tall rocky facets in the Devil's Backbone. "Then we'll call it quits." He looked back and motioned for Evelyn to follow him.

Dead on her feet, she followed him up the short incline, certain that just as with the last half-dozen sites that Whitaker had sworn would yield a diamond bonanza, she was going to be disappointed again.

Celeste Deepstream had parked her pickup in a roadside ravine to watch for CJ to come back down the gravel road that led to the Riverside Veterinary Clinic. The truck's motor was running and the defroster blasting, but the moisture from her heavy breathing had the pickup's windows almost completely fogged. She wiped away the windshield fog with a mass of napkins and tossed them aside on the front seat next to her. She wasn't quite sure how she was going to take care of Floyd, but she knew he had done her a favor by driving into the sparsely populated canyon lands leading up to Estes Park. She relaxed in her seat and turned up the volume on her tape deck, proud of the fact that she had tailed Floyd all the way from Denver without his knowledge. As the ecclesiastical harmonies of Tchaikovsky's *Romeo and Juliet* filled the cab, she closed her eyes to enjoy the hypnotic power of a form of music she had never known prior to college. As the sounds of the suite moved past the allegro section and toward the powerful crescendo, she realized that she had reached a point of no return. She glanced down at the dozens of tapes in her cassette box on the floor, then at the pistol next to it, knowing that she had the entertainment capacity to wait Floyd out for the rest of the night.

Chapter 32

Lisa kneaded her lower lip between her front teeth, trying to control her anger as she paced back and forth in front of CJ and Billy DeLong, who were scrunched down in two of her undersized cane-backed chairs next to one another, looking just like apprehended high school truants. Billy was staring intently at the wall in front of him. CJ's eyes were glued to the floor.

Lisa stopped pacing suddenly and looked directly at CJ. "Sometimes I swear you think you're still in Vietnam." She shook her head in disgust. "Look at you. The side of your head's puffed up like a balloon, you come in here begging for pain pills to take the edge off a migraine, and you've got my Uncle Morgan combing the hillsides up by the Devil's Backbone for a killer." She looked up at the ceiling and sighed. "You promised you wouldn't let him get involved in this mess, CJ."

"I'm sorry. It just happened," said CJ, still eyeing the floor, unwilling to ask Lisa whether it was her slip of the tongue that had sent Morgan on his mission.

Lisa looked over at Billy for his explanation. Less accustomed than CJ to Lisa's straightforwardness, Billy shrugged his shoulders and said, "Me too." Billy had shown up ahead of CJ, lumbered up to the horse barn where Lisa had just finished feeding Geronimo, and bellowed, "CJ here yet?" unaware of Morgan's theft of CJ's Jeep. CJ drove in ten minutes later, and he had been trying to explain his way out of a hole ever since.

Lisa leaned back against the edge of her desk, drummed her fingers on the desktop, and peered again at CJ. "First you say that Whitaker Rodgers might have killed Dolbey. Then you tell me maybe it was Dolbey's girlfriend, and finally, to confuse the issue totally, you say maybe it was some estranged kid of his. I don't care about any of that, CJ. I only care about my uncle."

"So do I," said CJ, finally looking up. The stern look on CJ's face was a look Lisa had seen before. A foggy, lost-in-space kind of stare that surfaced when CJ's temper was about to get the better of him. "Okay," she said hesitantly. "What do you plan to do?"

"Go find Morgan."

"On your own? Without the police?"

"You got a better plan?"

Lisa was about to offer one but hesitated, unsure of whether to risk pushing CJ's temper beyond the threshold. Looking perplexed, she finally answered, "No."

CJ stood up and tried to ignore the pain behind his right eye, but standing only made it worse. "Guess we better get started," he said, heading for the door, nodding for Billy to follow.

"Wait." Lisa walked around behind her desk, pulled out the bottom drawer, and tossed a bottle of extra-strength Tylenol to CJ.

CJ shagged the bottle in midair. "Thanks."

"Remember your promise. You won't let Morgan get hurt."

CJ nodded as he popped two Tylenol, and he and Billy walked out the door.

It was a couple of minutes before Lisa heard Billy's beast of a truck grind to a halt down the lane from her office. She watched Billy raise the hood and tinker with the engine for a while, then heard CJ scream *Fuck* as Billy slammed the hood, took something bulky from the pickup's bed, and headed with CJ toward the Bel Air. She watched the Bel Air disappear down the lane, then walked back into her office, picked up the phone, and dialed the Weld County sheriff's office. It took her the better part of five minutes to convince the slow-talking deputy on the other end of the line that he should drop what he was doing and head up to the Devil's Backbone. She was still seated at her desk a few minutes later, nursing an ice-cold cranberry juice cocktail, when Morgan strolled into the outer office, a doleful look of frustration on his face. After several false starts trying to avoid explaining the fact that he had stolen CJ's Jeep, he told Lisa that for the past half-hour he had unsuccessfully tried to find the route up to Hambone Dolbey's Devil's Backbone property without success. He couldn't quite understand why Lisa had run across the room to embrace him as though she hadn't seen him in years, or why she mumbled as she did, "Oh my God, I shouldn't have called the sheriff."

Chapter 33

CJ missed the narrow pothook of a turn onto Hambone Dolbey's land three times before Billy spotted a couple of cow-trail–looking tracks that snaked their way off the highway and into a cluster of lodgepole pines. Unwilling to subject the Bel Air to an off-road shakedown cruise, CJ pulled onto the shoulder and had Billy get out of the car and follow the tracks into the trees to check out the terrain. When Billy returned, his threadbare old canvas hunting jacket was covered with pine needles and dew and he was carrying his Stetson in his hand. "Muddy as a pigsty out there," he said, smacking on a fresh wad of gum. Then, stomping the mud off his boots, he added, "There's a road just beyond the pines that heads up toward what has to be a mile-long string of the ugliest-lookin' rocks I've ever seen. Reminds me of the business edge of my fish-gutting knife."

"The Devil's Backbone," said CJ.

"What?"

"That's what they call the rock outcropping you spotted."

Billy nodded, clutching his chin. "Name makes sense."

CJ killed the Bel Air's engine. "That's probably where Morgan's headed, hoping to hook up with Whitaker Rodgers." CJ had filled Billy in on the entire Hambone Dolbey and Bobby Two-Shirts sagas on their way up from Denver.

"Turn the engine back on, CJ. This ain't no time for thinking about your car getting a little muddy."

CJ eyed the mud line three-quarters of the way up Billy's boots. "A little mud!"

"Hell, man, we got a murderer on the loose and probably some she-wolf dogging our asses. Besides that, you told Lisa you'd get Morgan out of this mess." Billy glanced over the seat back at the rifle and shotgun he had taken out of his pickup before they left Lisa's. "Time to get this show on the road. The sooner we do, the sooner we get to watch the soaps." He smiled, pulled three fresh sticks of gum from somewhere beneath his rain slicker, chomped down, and began working them into his wad.

Reluctantly, CJ turned the Bel Air's engine back on. "You know what I think of that gum-smacking habit of yours?" he said, cutting his eyes at Billy.

"Sure do, but since it keeps me off the spirits, your opinion don't matter."

CJ thought about the lifelong string of problems his uncle and Billy had experienced because of their drinking. Billy had been fortunate enough to get the alcohol monkey off his back. CJ's uncle hadn't. CJ nudged the Bel Air's accelerator and headed for the clump of pines, violating an oath he had made to himself years before to never subject the Bel Air to the indignities of mud, road salt, gravel roads, or snow.

As the Bel Air broke beyond the tree line, the steady drizzle and a low-hanging fog bank made it impossible for CJ or Billy to realize that they had been followed, or for CJ to see that the Bel Air was already caked with mud.

Disoriented, dog-tired, and infuriated because after foraging all day he hadn't found a single excavation site worthy of further scrutiny for diamonds, Whitaker Rodgers had returned to his field operations trailer. He was searching for a map that he knew clearly delineated the Trapper's Lake kimberlite fields and the boundary line between his property and Hambone Dolbey's. When he had parked the trailer on a barren patch of land eight months earlier and stared up at the Devil's Backbone, he had considered the craggy outcropping a good-luck omen. But so far he and Evelyn had spent close to a million dollars of their money unearthing nothing more than thousands of tons of worthless kimberlite and a few Indian artifacts, and he had amassed a fortune in corporate debt that he knew his mother would choke on if she knew about it.

Evelyn was sitting in an idling Blazer a quarter of a mile down the road, having refused to walk up the hill to the trailer, saying that she preferred the truck's warmth to a drafty old trailer. So he had left her pouting and shivering and made his way up to the trailer alone.

Unable to find the missing map, Whitaker realized it was close to his six P.M. departure time. He decided to take a momentary break and have a drink before heading for Denver. He walked over to an old-fashioned orange crate, the trailer's makeshift liquor cabinet, and mixed himself a double-strength Seven and Seven. He had just plunked down in a chair next to a rickety two-by-four and plywood desk when CJ barged through the trailer door and announced, "Damn, you're a hard man to find." CJ had slipped up behind the trailer on foot via a back hillside, avoiding detection by Evelyn Coleman, leaving Billy behind to deal with her.

Stunned and frightened, Whitaker sprang up from his chair, knocking his drink over in the process. "What the fuck?" It took him a moment to realize who CJ was.

"No need for such language, Whitaker. I'm just here to ask some questions and try to straighten a few things out."

"You're trespassing, Floyd."

"Haven't you noticed it's foggy outside? I got lost."

"Then lose your way out of here or I'll call the sheriff." Whitaker glanced at the phone on the desktop beside him.

"Have at it. Maybe it'll give you a chance to explain to him why you're trespassing on Hambone Dolbey's land."

"You're stupid, Floyd. For your information, I've got an easement."

"Funny. I always thought an easement meant you had a right-of-way. On my way up here, even with the fog, I spotted excavation craters big enough to house the foundation for a skyscraper. I'd say you've stumbled off your easement a few times."

"I'd say you'd better get the hell out of here."

"I'll do that, but first I want the answers to a couple of very simple questions."

"Like?"

"Like, did you kill Dolbey?"

Whitaker smiled, ignoring the question.

"Smile all you want to, Rodgers. I've seen documents that prove you had plenty of reasons. Does the name Gemstone Mining ring a bell?"

Rodgers's smile faded, replaced by a spiteful glare. "Public information, Floyd. It's been in the papers. You're making one hell of a mistake."

"Maybe. But I'll risk it. Like the risk you're taking with this diamond mining thing, hoping to put millions in your pocket."

"In case you haven't noticed, Floyd, I run a company already worth millions."

"I have noticed. I've also noticed you have a mother. Been wondering if she shares your diamond mining dreams."

"I run things at Gemstone," said Rodgers angrily.

"Sounds to me like you're trying to convince yourself."

The annoyed look on Rodgers's face suddenly disappeared as he reached into his jacket pocket, pulled out his .38, and aimed it squarely at CJ's chest. "I could shoot you on the spot for trespassing."

"Or get your ass kicked trying."

Whitaker fired a round at CJ's feet. Before he could

square the gun back up, CJ rushed him, jamming his head into Rodgers's midsection and sending the .38 spinning across the floor. Gasping for air, Rodgers hooked CJ around the neck and tried to bulldog him to the floor. CJ shook him off and, legs churning, planted a shoulder beneath Rodgers's rib cage and drove him into the back wall of the trailer. Rodgers landed two chops to CJ's neck before CJ finally grabbed him by the hair and slammed his head into the wall. CJ was about to give Rodgers a second bell ringer when he suddenly heard the throaty sound of a diesel engine behind him. He relaxed his grip to follow the sound, and Rodgers's head slumped to the right. As he stood up to try to place the direction of the familiar grating sound, the trailer's metal shell suddenly flew back over his head like a pressurized bottle cap, and CJ found himself staring into the headlights of a front-end loader. Blinded by the lights, he dove to the floor.

"You're trespassing," someone called out from the loader's cab.

"Second time I've heard that today," CJ shouted.

Aaron Baptiste slipped his rifle off the seat beside him, stepped out on the loader's booster step, and aimed the rifle toward CJ. He had steadied the rifle on his shoulder when a shotgun blast shattered the side window of the cab. Billy DeLong pumped a second blast into the cab's metal housing as Aaron jumped from the loader and fled, rifle in hand, into the fog.

Billy chased him down a hillside, squeezing off two more rounds before Aaron disappeared into a thicket of serviceberries, boulders, and waist-high skunk cabbage. Winded, Billy stopped, reloaded, and scanned the thicket for the better part of two minutes before dejectedly walking back up the hillside.

Shotgun still at the ready, he walked directly into the glare of the loader's headlights, and then, stumbling over the trailer's damaged cinderblock foundation and up onto what remained of the subfloor, he headed over to check on CJ. "You okay?" he said, giving CJ the once-over.

"Yeah." CJ dusted himself off, picked up Rodgers's gun, and walked toward where Rodgers lay moaning. "What about our friend in the loader?" he said, kicking himself for having left his .38 in the Bel Air's glove compartment.

"Chased him a bit and dusted his heels with some lead, but he was running like a deer. Didn't look to me to be much more than an overgrown kid," said Billy.

"He was bold enough to point a rifle my way. In my book that makes him a man," said CJ, pulling Rodgers to his feet, and wondering if they'd just had a close encounter with Aaron Baptiste.

Chapter 34

The flashing red and blue lights atop the two Weld County sheriff's cruisers gave the foggy valley below the Devil's Backbone an eerie, psychedelic glow. The cars were parked nose to tail in front of what remained of Whitaker Rodgers's field operations trailer. The bucket of the front-end loader hovered just above the hood of the first car, where CJ, still seeing double from his collision with Rodgers, was seated in the rear seat talking to Sheriff Pritchard, trying to convince him to release Billy DeLong. Billy was handcuffed, hands behind his back, in the front seat of the second cruiser. A tall, lanky sheriff's deputy was standing outside the cruiser with his hand on the butt of his gun, eyes glued to Billy, daring him to move. Whitaker Rodgers sat behind Billy, slumped over with his head in his hands. The deputy turned from Billy for a moment to eye the loader bucket, puzzled at how unscathed the bucket appeared after delivering its death blow to the trailer.

Sheriff Pritchard leaned forward in his seat, taking the weight off a chronically painful right hip, and stared at CJ. "You know, Floyd, if that trailer had been single-unit construction you might have ended up dead at the bottom of a gully instead of just a little dizzy."

CJ shook his head, trying to clear the cobwebs. "That wouldn't be wishful thinking on your part, would it, Sheriff?"

"Don't tweak me, Floyd. I can cuff you along with your friend DeLong over there if need be."

"Ease up on Billy, Sheriff. He was just trying to help me out of a jam. Our vanishing front-end loader operator's the one who needs to be handcuffed."

"DeLong was the one blasting away with a shotgun when I drove up on the scene, and he's going to take a ride back to Greeley cuffed until I straighten this mess out."

"You can straighten it out right now. Just have another chat with your buddy Rodgers. He pulled a gun on me just before the front-end loader man popped the trailer top."

"Whitaker says you were trespassing and he needed to defend himself."

"My ass. Tell you this, though, if I'd been feeling a hundred percent, I might've cracked his head open."

"Good thing you didn't," said Pritchard, realizing that CJ meant what he had just said. He fidgeted in the seat, seeking relief from his throbbing hip, and looked out into the fog and back down the road.

"You say you saw a Blazer with a woman in it half a mile down the road? Funny, I never saw one on the way up."

"It was there."

"You sure? Fog does funny things up here."

"One thing for sure, it didn't swallow a truck. I'd say she split. Could be the flashing lights on your cruisers made her nervous."

"Could be." Pritchard craned his head out the window at his deputy. "Hey, Charlie, you see a vehicle parked by the road on your way up here? Seems Floyd here thinks we drove right past one."

"Nope," said the deputy, walking over to the window.

"Maybe she left before you charged up San Juan Hill," said CJ.

Pritchard ignored CJ and barked at his deputy, "Let's wrap it up here and head back down the hill. We'll check out Floyd's vanishing Blazer theory on our way. If need be, you can come back up and check things out in the morning."

"Fine by me," said the deputy, shooting a glance back toward the second cruiser and Whitaker Rodgers. "Rodgers seems to be either hurt or sick. He hasn't pulled his head out of his hands since I helped him into the back seat."

"Send him over here with me," said Pritchard, moving to get out of the back seat. "I'll perk him up."

The deputy walked over to the cruiser, opened the rear door, and tapped Whitaker Rodgers on the shoulder. "Let's move it, Rodgers. You're riding with the sheriff."

Whitaker, who hadn't missed one word of the exchange between Pritchard and the deputy, pulled his head out of his hands and looked up. "You sure you didn't see a Blazer back down the road? A lady would have been behind the wheel."

"Sorry."

Whitaker walked over and slipped into the front seat of the other cruiser, wondering why Evelyn would have left him behind, as Sheriff Pritchard slipped behind the wheel.

Eyeing Rodgers, CJ gritted his teeth and rigidly pushed both hands into the seat, proud of the fact that with Mavis's help he was learning to control his hair-trigger temper. A few years earlier, sheriff or no sheriff, he would have retaliated against someone stupid enough to have pulled a gun on him.

"Glad you could join us," said Pritchard, aiming his words straight into Whitaker's ear. "I was hoping to hear the rest of your version of what happened up here on our way back to Greeley."

"What's wrong with my version?" asked CJ, his voice resonating with anger.

Pritchard glanced over the seat back. "I'll do the talking, Floyd. Just sit back there and be quiet unless you're asked a question." He started the car, stared out into the fog, and began turning the cruiser around.

On their way down the hillside they drove by the Bel Air, splattered from hood to tailfin with mud. "Don't hit my ride," said CJ as the police cruiser narrowly missed kissing the side of the Bel Air.

"Wouldn't think of it," said Pritchard. "Can't speak for my deputy, though."

CJ's head shot backward, his eyes glued to the Bel Air until the car behind him had cleared it. During the rest of the ride down the rutted road he kept his eyes peeled for another vehicle but never saw one.

When they reached the highway, Pritchard spoke up. "Have a few questions for you, Whitaker. Simple ones that need straight answers. Hope you'll oblige."

"I'm listening," said Rodgers, glancing back at CJ, who had leaned forward into the grill that separated them. Pritchard shot CJ an irritated glance before continuing. "What do you know about a kid named Aaron Baptiste?"

"Never heard of him before."

"What about you, Floyd?"

"Never heard of him before either," said CJ, hoping his tone of voice wouldn't give away the fact that he was lying and hoping that Billy wasn't in the other car saying something that would later contradict everything he told the sheriff.

It was the last question the sheriff asked CJ during the rest of their ride to Greeley. His remaining questions were directed to Whitaker Rodgers. CJ learned three things from their exchanges. Rodgers's oil and gas exploration business was on shakier financial footing than he had guessed; the sheriff was indeed looking into whether Rodgers was mining illegally on Hambone Dolbey's land; and although the sheriff didn't know as much about the Aaron Baptiste–Hambone Dolbey connection as CJ did, Pritchard had his finger squarely on the pulse of the case.

As they turned off Highway 34 and headed for the sheriff's office, no one in either car paid any attention to the fact that a third vehicle, the same pickup that had followed CJ up from Denver, had latched onto their caravan as they left the Devil's Backbone.

Chapter 35

After two separate thirty-minute interrogations, Sheriff Pritchard released CJ and Billy with a stern warning to stay away from the Hambone Dolbey and Nadine Kemp murder investigations. CJ used the pay phone in the jail lobby to ask Lisa if Morgan had ever shown up. When CJ announced who he was, Lisa said, "Talk to Morgan," and passed the phone on without another word. In short order, CJ convinced Morgan to come get him so he could go retrieve the Bel Air, but he had a suspicion that Lisa might not ever speak to him again once she found out where Morgan was headed.

By the time CJ, Billy, and Morgan got back to the Bel Air, it was approaching midnight. Flashlight and surveyor stick in hand, CJ had already picked a three-inch-thick coating of russet-colored mud from two of the car's wheel wells when Billy tapped him on the shoulder and said, "Just gonna pick up more mud on our way down."

Billy's comment made CJ realize that maybe his head injuries had him thinking a little less than straight. He stood up from what he was doing, reached into the pocket of his duster, and tossed Billy the keys to the Bel Air. "Why don't you drive? I've got some thinking to do on the way back down this fricking hill." Then he nodded for Morgan to follow in the Jeep.

The bumpy ride back down didn't help his throbbing head, but it did give CJ a chance to think about something Whitaker Rodgers had said to the sheriff during their ride back to Greeley. It had been a remark about packing in Pandeco's oil and gas exploration business for diamond mining because it really wasn't paying its way. The comment had CJ wondering if Rodgers's Gemstone Mining partner, Evelyn Coleman, felt the same and whether Virginia Rodgers shared her son's feelings about the business that had made her wealthy.

When Billy brought the Bel Air to a stop at the bottom of the hill, CJ said, "Think you can check on Rebecca Baptiste and that kid of hers on your way back home? Sure would like to know exactly where the two of them fit into this."

Billy stroked his chin. "Easy enough. Long as I can take your Jeep."

"You got it," said CJ as Morgan approached them from the Jeep.

"Anything you want me to check out?" asked Morgan, leaning against the Bel Air, eager to help.

Remembering Lisa's directive, CJ was about to say, *Nothing,* but he knew Morgan would be crushed. "Yeah, there is," he said, looking over the seat back and smiling. "I've got a bunch of PR fluff on Whitaker Rodgers, his mother, and a woman named Evelyn Coleman that I tossed in the trunk the same morning I got love-tapped with that tire iron. Photographs, phone numbers, addresses, the whole shooting match. You can look through it on your way home. When we get back to Denver, I want you and Dittier to stake out the two women's places, see if they're home, and let me know how easy it would be for me to drop in unexpectedly, guess-who's-coming-to-dinner-like, for a visit."

"Done," said Morgan.

"And Morgan, not one word of this to Lisa, ever."

Smiling, Morgan clamped his thumb and forefinger over his lips as CJ reached out the window and ran his flashlight beam down the length of the Bel Air, eyeing its coat of mud. "After I drop you off, I think I'll stop by a car wash and give the Bel Air a bath."

Morgan walked around the car, let Billy exit, and slipped in on the other side. "Good idea."

"Later," said Billy, heading for the Jeep. "Call you when I have something on the Baptistes."

It was two forty-five A.M. when CJ headed up the back stairway of his apartment. He had garaged the freshly washed Bel Air after giving it a bath that had cost him $10 in quarters. He thought about calling Mavis, but didn't, deciding the cross-examination he knew he was going to receive could wait until morning. After slipping off his range coat, removing his boots, and peeling off his soggy jeans, he debated whether to jump into the shower. Although he hadn't felt dizzy in hours, his stomach felt woozy and both ears were buzzing. He decided to pass on the shower in favor of sleep. Ignoring the buzzing, he sat down on the edge of his bed and set the alarm clock on the nightstand for seven A.M. Then, exhausted and muscle-weary, with mud still plastered to his ankles, he slipped into bed and drifted off to sleep.

Chapter 36

Morgan jump-started CJ's day the next morning with a phone call a few minutes before seven. "Floyd," answered CJ, unsure of whether his grogginess was from lack of sleep or his head injury.

"It's Morgan. I'm at a 7-Eleven over on University Boulevard. Had to race to get to a pay phone ahead of somebody else. Here's the story on your two oil ladies. The Coleman woman never came home last night; least-ways whatever she was drivin' never did. No vehicle to be found anywhere. Not in front of the house, in the drive-way, or in the garage, and me and Dittier sat outside the Washington Park address listed in the PR guide most of the night. A couple of lights inside the place never went off. Real strange. Never got to check on the Rodgers woman.

That Cherry Creek building of hers has got a security system like a prison. Me and Dittier checked out a couple of ways of easin' into both places, though, in case you want to take a crack. The weak link to the Coleman woman's place is the back door. Not even a deadbolt. As for the Rodgers woman's building, scootin' on your hands and knees, you can slip down the driveway between surveillance camera sweeps and into the underground garage in nothin' flat. But there's a security-guard booth at the entrance with a bank of phones inside. Don't think you'd want to get caught down there without an excuse. That's as much as we could get." Morgan paused and thought for a moment. "Been wonderin' since last night, though, why all the stakeout shenanigans? How come you just don't call 'em both on the phone?"

CJ smiled at Morgan's straightforward assessment. "Because I don't think either of them would volunteer to have a chat with me about why Whitaker Rodgers was so afraid of my bird-dogging that he pulled a gun on me, or why their little diamond mining company is busy excavating the shit out of somebody else's land."

"And you think a surprise visit will loosen their lips?"

"Can't hurt."

"Want me and Dittier to come along?"

"No. I want you both to stay clear. Three black men surprising a couple of unsuspecting white women, even if it's just to talk, could make us all front-page news."

"If you say so," said Morgan, sounding disappointed.

"Tell you what you can do, though. You can cruise by Whitaker Rodgers's house and see if anyone's there. He lives in the same Washington Park neighborhood as the Coleman woman. Easy enough address to remember,

100 South Gaylord. Call the office and let me know if
he's home. If I'm not in, leave a message with Flora
Jean. Who knows, his place may end up being my third
stop of the morning."

"Done," said Morgan, happy that he and Dittier
were back on the case.

"And Morgan, don't forget. Drive like you've got
some sense."

"Always." Morgan cradled the receiver with a smile
and glanced over at Dittier, who for most of the conversation had been standing by the pay phone eating peanuts. A
mound of peanut shells now encircled his feet. "Come on,
Dittier. We gotta go check on Whitaker Rodgers."

Dittier stuffed a half-empty bag of peanuts in his
pocket, then signed, with salt-coated fingers, "Where's
CJ headed?"

"To check out a couple of white women who don't
seem to want to talk."

Dittier broke into an impish grin as he and Morgan
crunched across the mound of peanut shells. "Maybe
they should learn to sign," he signed, licking the fingers
of his other hand clean.

Flora Jean was sitting at her desk struggling with
the shrink-wrap surrounding the half-dozen rap and R
and B tapes she had bought at a thirty-percent-off sale
the previous evening when CJ walked in. "Worse than a
damned pill bottle," she said, finally breaking the seal
and looking up at CJ. "How you doin' this morning after
your trip up north?"

"Dragging," said CJ, listing to the right.

"I can tell." Flora Jean set the tapes aside. "But you

best undrag yourself quick. You got two ladies really peeved." She picked up a stack of phone messages and waved them at CJ. "Four from Mavis and three from Julie. Can't say whether they're more mad or hurt."

CJ slapped his forehead and let his hand creep down his face. "Sort of figured I might've painted myself into a corner."

"More like dug yourself a pit. Hard to get a good woman on your side these days, and you got two. If I was you, I'd work a little harder at tryin' to keep it that way."

"How deep's the pit?"

"Deep. Julie's last message was, don't even think about calling her till she's done with her bar exams. Mavis just sounded fed up."

"Think I should call Mavis right now?"

"If you have a brain left in your head."

CJ headed for his office without responding, dizzy and dragging his right foot. Closing the door behind him, he wondered whether his strange gait was noticeable, unaware of the look of alarm on Flora Jean's face.

He slipped behind his desk and checked his watch. At eight forty-five he knew that Mavis would be nearing the end of the breakfast rush. When he picked up the receiver to call her at Mae's, the numbers on the face of the phone seemed strangely out of focus.

Thelma Larson, a gruff-voiced waitress who had worked at Mae's for over twenty years, picked up on the other end. "Mae's Louisiana Kitchen."

"Hello, Thelma, it's CJ. Let me speak to Mavis."

"Hold on a second while I track her down."

CJ felt a rush of relief until Thelma came back on the line.

"Says she's busy, and she'll have to call you back. Sounded pretty weak to me. You two on the outs?"

"I'm trying to find out."

Thelma laughed. "Take it from me, I'd be looking for a florist if I were you."

"Thanks for the advice."

"No problem. Been there myself. Anything else?"

"No, I'll call back."

"Later, then." Thelma hung up, leaving CJ wondering if he was in the kind of pit he'd never be able to climb out of. He cradled the receiver and stared out the bay window until Flora Jean buzzed him to say that Billy DeLong was on her other line. Trying his best to hide his mood, CJ picked up the receiver. "Billy, what's up?"

Billy was hunkered out of the Wyoming wind in a phone booth, smacking on a wad of gum and flipping the coin return in and out. "We got action up here. Thought you'd want to know about it. I'm fifteen minutes from the Baptiste place. A boy I'm guessing is the Baptiste kid rolled in early this morning in a muddy pickup, and ever since, he and his mama have been packing up everything in the house and loading it into a twenty-foot trailer. From the looks of the reddish mud caked all over the truck, I'd say he's the one who gave you the lift with the front-end loader up at the Devil's Backbone last night."

Billy's revelation caught CJ off guard. He wasn't sure whether to take off after the Baptistes or finish with his plans to confront Virginia Rodgers and Evelyn Coleman. "Think you can handle things up there if I nose around here in Denver for a while?" he finally asked.

"Don't see why not. From the looks of things they'll be packing up for a good little while."

"Keep an eye on them and check in with me if things get funky. If worst comes to worst, I can be there by one."

"Got you. Anything else?" asked Billy.

"No. Just watch your ass."

"Always," said Billy, hanging up.

Cradling the receiver, CJ pulled a piece of paper with Evelyn Coleman and Virginia Rodgers's addresses and phone numbers from his vest pocket and examined it before standing up and heading for the door. He walked past Flora Jean, trying his best to mask the fact that he was still dragging his foot.

"Where're you headed?" asked Flora Jean, trying not to stare.

"To check on a couple of diamonds in the rough."

"Sure you're up to it?"

"Save the sermon, Flora Jean."

"Suit yourself."

CJ walked out the front door, making a concerted effort not to drag his foot.

Flora Jean listened for CJ to back the Bel Air past the front porch before she reached into her desk drawer and grabbed her car keys and purse. She draped the bulky leather bag's strap over her shoulder and headed out the front door, keys in hand. CJ had already turned down 13th Avenue, headed for Speer Boulevard, as she raced toward her car, hoping she'd be able to catch up with him before he disappeared into the boulevard traffic. Feeling guilty about not stopping CJ before he left the office, she spun away from the curb, kicking up a trail of rocks, unaware that Billy DeLong was desperately trying to reach the office again, or that CJ was already being followed.

Chapter 37

Number One Country Club Place, a newly constructed seven-story condominium complex on the banks of Cherry Creek, had been built to house and pamper Denver's moneyed elite. The two hundred fifty *residences,* the name preferred by the building's tenants, ranged in price from $400,000 to $2,000,000. Virginia Rodgers's sixth-floor, four-thousand-square-foot, million-dollar piece of the rock overlooked the grassy knolls, sand traps, and water hazards of the Denver Country Club golf course and had an unobstructed view of the Front Range of the Rockies with Mount Evans as the centerpiece.

Virginia had just finished a late continental breakfast and stepped out onto the balcony of her residence to enjoy the first rays of sunshine after the three-day monsoon when CJ parked the Bel Air several blocks from her building on Cherry Creek Drive along the willowy southern shoulder of Cherry Creek. For most of the morning Virginia had been wondering why Whitaker hadn't shown up to meet her the previous evening as he had said he would. Disappointed and concerned, she was admiring the crystal-clear sixty-mile view when CJ duckwalked his way, undetected, down the driveway leading to her building's underground parking garage.

At the bottom of the driveway approach, security cameras and two four-foot-high wrought-iron motorized gates separated CJ from the entrance. It wasn't until he leaped over one of the gates that he saw the guard booth, and a sign on the wall next to a pay phone just beyond the booth that read, GUARD ON DUTY FROM 11 A.M. TO MIDNIGHT. RESIDENTS PLEASE USE YOUR SECURITY CARD FOR ENTRANCE AT ALL OTHER TIMES. Below the first two lines in much smaller print was a line reading, DELIVERIES—SEE SECURITY GUARD IN LOBBY FOR ADMITTANCE.

CJ had moved beyond the guard booth toward a carpeted elevator alcove ten yards into the garage when he heard an electronic hum and realized that the gate behind him was opening. With no time to run for cover, he hunkered into a corner of the alcove, hoping no one would step out of the elevator and see him. A few moments later, a bright red late-model Chevrolet rolled slowly past, the driver oblivious to his presence.

Suddenly CJ wasn't sure that his plan to talk to Virginia Rodgers was such a good one. He had an uneasy feeling that instead of sneaking around a parking garage, he should have been on his way to Wyoming to hook up with Billy and confront Aaron and Rebecca Baptiste. The fact that he was trespassing in an elite white world also had him wondering why he hadn't gone after Whitaker Rodgers instead of his mother. Thinking of what he was going to say to Virginia Rodgers, he heard a car door slam and the sound of footsteps. He slipped into a new hiding place behind a nearby car as the footsteps approached the elevator, holding his breath until he heard the familiar ding announcing the elevator's arrival.

He waited for a full minute after the elevator doors closed before easing up from his crouched position behind the car and heading into the depths of the garage, hoping that his plan to confront Virginia Rodgers would work—a plan that depended on finding her car. After walking down six aisles and turning up nothing, he spotted the nose of a gleaming silver Rolls-Royce Corniche with license plates that read PAN OIL just ahead of him. *Sometimes it just takes perseverance,* he thought. When he checked his watch he realized that he only had twenty minutes before the garage's security guard came on duty. He fumbled in his pocket for the slip of paper with Virginia Rodgers's phone number, then headed back toward the pay phone he had spotted earlier.

Before dropping a quarter into the coin slot he scanned the garage one last time. "Virginia Rodgers's residence," said a firm-voiced female on the second ring.

CJ leaned into the wall next to him and swallowed hard. "Mrs. Rodgers?"

"Yes."

"This is the garage. Got a problem down here with your Rolls."

"What is it?"

"Seems like somebody tried to break in. I'd appreciate it if you'd come take a look."

"I'll be right down. I'm headed out anyway."

"Thanks," said CJ, noting that Virginia Rodgers's I'm-in-charge tone of voice had never changed from the moment she answered the phone. He hung up and headed back toward the Rolls, satisfied that he had orchestrated that part of his plan without a hitch.

He was standing directly in front of the Rolls, smiling, when Virginia Rodgers exited the elevator clutching a Saks Fifth Avenue shopping bag in her right hand and with Evelyn Coleman at her side. The surprise of seeing both women caused CJ to briefly consider walking away until it hit him that ready or not, he now had the opportunity to kill two birds with one stone.

Virginia Rodgers recognized him the instant she turned down the aisle toward the Rolls. "Mr. Floyd," she said, puzzled, continuing toward him.

In as pleasant a voice as he could muster, CJ said, "Good morning," as both women stopped a few paces in front of him. With her car keys also clutched firmly in her right hand, Virginia adjusted the shopping bag and looked past CJ toward her car. "What's this all about? Has my car been vandalized?"

"No," said CJ, his tone apologetic. "I'm just trying to tie up some loose ends on a murder case." Before he could say anything else, a flash of the dizziness that had kept him confined to Mavis's bed for two days resurfaced, and he staggered.

Evelyn Coleman's eyes ballooned. "Call Security, Virginia, the man's drunk."

"Afraid not. Just a little dizzy from an encounter I had with Whitaker up at the Devil's Backbone last night. Sorry you missed the party."

"If you won't call Security, Virginia, I will," said Evelyn. "He's trespassing."

"She's right, Mr. Floyd. I think you should leave." Virginia walked around CJ, unperturbed, and popped the trunk on the Rolls open with her remote.

CJ followed her, hoping his dizziness had passed. "Funny someone should mention it. Trespassing, I mean. That's actually what I'm here about." He looked Virginia directly in the eye as she turned back toward him after placing her shopping bag in the trunk next to her golf clubs. "Are you aware that Gemstone Mining is excavating on land that isn't theirs?"

"That's Whitaker's project. I'd suggest you take it up with him."

"I tried, but he pulled a gun on me."

"Good thing I wasn't there," said Evelyn, slowly inching backward away from CJ. "I might've urged him to use it."

"Like he did with Nadine Kemp?"

Evelyn's voice rose in contempt. "Whitaker didn't kill the little witch."

"What about you?" said CJ.

Evelyn rolled her eyes. "Don't be absurd."

CJ glanced at Virginia for a response.

"Don't look at me. I didn't shoot her in the head."

CJ cocked both eyebrows. "What did you say?"

"I didn't shoot her," said Virginia.

"No. You said, 'I didn't shoot her in the head.' How did you know how she died?"

Virginia looked toward Evelyn, her eyes pleading for help. Evelyn's shocked expression told CJ that Virginia was on her own. Regaining her composure, Virginia said, "I heard it from Whitaker."

"Fine. I'll ask him. See if he backs you up. Good son that he is, though, I don't think he'll cover for you when it comes to murder." CJ turned back to Evelyn. "What's your version of the story?"

Her eyes half glazed, Evelyn responded slowly. "Whitaker never said anything to me about how the Kemp woman died."

"Then it was someone else who told me," said Virginia, staring intently into the trunk of the Rolls. "Yes, I'm sure it was."

CJ decided to press Virginia a step further. "One thing for sure, it couldn't have been Hambone Dolbey. You'd already killed him."

"Get out of here!" shouted Virginia, her shoulders shaking visibly. CJ turned back toward Evelyn. "Think you'd better go ahead and get Security, and while you're at it—"

Evelyn screamed, and CJ turned to find Virginia swinging an eight iron toward his head. When he threw up his arm to ward off the blow, Evelyn screamed again and bolted for the elevator as the sound of CJ's forearm cracking echoed down the aisle. Grabbing his arm, CJ dropped to one knee in agony, thinking that unlike Hambone Dolbey, he had been lucky enough to see the blow coming. He rolled beneath the car and out of the path of a second downswing that caught the back door of the Rolls. Then, extending his good arm, he grabbed Virginia by her ankle, tugged, and sent her sprawling across the floor.

She was attempting to get back up when CJ heard the sound of footsteps running toward them. Virginia was on one knee, bracing herself with the golf club, when he heard a male voice call out, "I'll take it from here." CJ cautiously stuck his head out from beneath the rocker panel of the Rolls to find Evelyn and a rotund, balding black man in a security guard's uniform staring down at him.

He and Virginia Rodgers stared up at the man in unison. It took a few seconds for CJ to realize that they were both staring at the same thing, the guard's meaty hand resting on the butt of his holstered .44 Magnum.

Chapter 38

The snooty Ichabod Crane–looking manager of Number One Country Club Place was close to having what CJ's uncle had always referred to as a *white folks' hissy*. Not only had the security of his building been violated, but for an hour the parking garage had been crawling with police and emergency medical technicians. And to top it off, even the residents were whispering that they had a murderer in their midst.

CJ was seated on a bench watching the manager pace back and forth while a Denver General Hospital EMT finished temporarily splinting CJ's fractured arm. Earlier, in the refreshment alcove just beyond them, CJ had watched a baby-faced Denver plainclothes detective briefly question Virginia Rodgers before politely whisking her away. At no time during the short interrogation was she ever handcuffed. He, on the other hand, had been cuffed and grilled for twenty minutes about what he had been doing in the garage, how he had gained entry, and why he had provoked the incident.

Three things saved CJ from being hauled off to jail: Evelyn Coleman's version of the events; CJ's broken-arm testimony to Virginia Rodgers's assault; and a call by the baby-faced cop to Sheriff Pritchard, who corroborated CJ's story that Virginia Rodgers was among a list of murder suspects. He had come away from the grilling with an order from the baby-faced cop to report to the University Hills police precinct to give a statement as soon as his injuries were treated, knowing, as he always had, that money and status afforded even murder suspects, like Virginia Rodgers, certain perks. Thrilled that he wasn't jail bound, he thought about another of his uncle's sayings: *Once in a while the law errs on the side of colored folks.*

Fed up with the manager's pacing, CJ finally said, "You're gonna blow a gasket, my man. Why don't you have a seat?"

"I can't. I'm too upset." The manager paused and lit a cigarette. "This incident will cast a lengthy shadow, mark my words." Then, after a short drag, he looked at CJ suspiciously and added, "I heard what you told those officers. Are you certain that our Mrs. Rodgers killed someone?"

"You hard of hearing? Didn't you hear her say so to that baby-faced cop?"

"As a matter of fact, I didn't. I only heard her say that she wished to speak to her lawyer, before the officer escorted her away."

"I'll be damned." CJ shook his head, amazed at how two people listening to the same conversation could hear such very different things. He waved off the EMT who had been working on his arm and stood up from the bench. The instant he did, his dizziness struck again.

The EMT sat him back on the bench and shook his head. "Like I've been saying all along, you need to take a ride to Denver General, my friend." He had tried earlier to press CJ to leave with him in an ambulance, but CJ had refused, saying there was no way in hell he was about to leave his Bel Air behind.

"I already told you. I'll take my car." Then, checking out the arm splint, CJ added, "Nice job."

The EMT shrugged and packed up his things. "My ambulance is parked right out front."

"So's my car," said CJ, stretching the truth.

"Maybe I'll see you at Denver General," said the EMT, fed up with CJ's stubbornness.

"Maybe." CJ skirted the quivering building manager and walked up the ramp to the garage cradling his broken arm and wondering if there had been something besides money that had driven Virginia Rodgers to commit two murders. On his way out, he asked a straggling cop where they had taken her.

"City jail," came the perturbed response.

As he headed down Cherry Creek Drive's sandy shoulder a family of mallards broke skyward from the thick willows at the water's edge, startling him. The brief adrenaline rush sent a bullet of pain arcing through his right temple that was so intense he decided that while he was at Denver General he had better have someone check out his lingering dizziness and headaches.

The Bel Air was parked next to a stand of stubby cottonwoods and five-foot-tall, insect-infested willows. When CJ stopped to pull his keys out of his pocket, he noticed the car's hood and windshield were covered with tree sap and aphids. He swiped a handful of bugs off the windshield, preoccupied with the fact that the Bel Air would now need another car wash, then slipped behind the wheel. He had just stuck the key into the ignition when a woman's voice behind him said, "You're just in time, Mr. Floyd. I was really starting to cramp up, hunkered down here on the floor." The woman eased up onto her knees.

CJ looked back into the stoic face of a beautiful woman and the barrel of the .357 Magnum she had angled off the seat back and aimed directly at his neck.

The woman smiled. "Celeste Deepstream. Bobby Two-Shirts's sister. Glad we finally got a chance to meet."

"We've met," said CJ, wondering how he was going to get out of his predicament. "In my garage."

"Don't know what you're talking about."

"Sure you do. Think hard. You tried to make love to me with a tire iron, remember?"

"You're hallucinating, my friend."

Surprised by Celeste's denial, CJ turned in his seat to try to get into a more defensive position.

Celeste nudged the barrel of the .357 into the nape of CJ's neck. "Stay facing forward. I'd hate to have to turn this beautiful car into a bloody mess. Just sit still while I slip into the front seat with you. I wouldn't want people wondering why I'm riding all alone in the back."

In the seconds it took CJ to consider whether he had enough time to pull away before Celeste could get up front, she was out of the back seat and onto the ground with her hand on the front door handle. As she pulled the door back and leveled the .357 at CJ's chest, Flora Jean Benson rose out of the willows behind her, grabbed Celeste around the neck in a choke hold, and sent her slumping to her knees and the .357 skidding across the sand.

Coughing and wheezing, Celeste broke free and lunged for the gun just as Flora Jean kicked it out of reach. Dropping to the ground, Flora Jean then jammed a knee across the back of Celeste's neck and ground her face into the sand.

The only thing CJ could think of as he bolted to help and watched Flora Jean stretch to retrieve the .357, was that she now had herself a permanent job.

With gun in hand, Flora Jean said, "After the way your foot dragged your butt out of the office, I figured you needed a little watchin' over. Good thing, too. Because I saw your lady friend here latch on to you when you headed down Speer. When you parked and she parked, so did I. Then I just hung in the willows swattin' bugs, waitin' to see what would develop." Flora Jean handed the gun to CJ and smiled. "Wasn't expectin' anything like this."

Chapter 39

It was nearly four o'clock when the Denver General Hospital neurologist attending CJ finished jotting his progress notes on CJ's medical chart. CJ had a fresh cast on one arm and Flora Jean's arm hooked in the other. Flora Jean hadn't left his side for more than fifteen minutes since they had arrived at DG, and although she wouldn't admit it, CJ knew that, like him, she was exhausted.

After Celeste's bungled murder attempt, CJ had run back to the parking garage and convinced the lone remaining cop that he had a serious problem just up the street. The cop had reluctantly followed him back to the Bel Air to find Celeste handcuffed to the steering wheel and Flora Jean standing beside her outside the car giving her a look that said, *I dare you to move!* It was another thirty minutes before an investigative unit arrived on the scene. After sorting things out and taking CJ's and Flora Jean's preliminary statements, a detective had carted Celeste off as she continued to insist, despite CJ's protests, that she had never assaulted CJ in his garage.

CJ and Flora Jean spent the next hour at the University Hills police substation answering questions, and then headed for Denver General, where CJ spent the rest of the afternoon getting the once-over by a team of doctors who pinpricked, probed, scanned, and imaged what seemed like every square inch of his body. Except for a short break after an MRI when he made a phone call to Sheriff Pritchard, CJ was never out of sight of a Denver General staff member. He came back from the call with such a perplexed look on his face that Flora Jean was fearful that he had had a stroke. The doctors continued palpating, probing, and asking questions for another hour until, after failing to determine the specific cause of CJ's dizziness and headaches, they concluded that he was suffering the aftereffects of what they termed a severe trauma-induced concussion, and advised him to go home, drink plenty of fluids, and spend the next week in bed. CJ and Flora Jean left the hospital with CJ shaking his head and wondering how much the space-age medical workup and the old-fashioned advice would end up costing him.

With Flora Jean at the wheel of the Bel Air, they were on their way back to Cherry Creek to pick up her car when CJ said, "Do me a favor. Before we get your car I want you to head over to Washington Park."

"What?" said Flora Jean, one eyebrow arched in disbelief.

"Head to Washington Park. It's only a little out of the way. After that, I promise we'll call it a day."

"The doctor said you need to go home and rest."

"It can wait a few more minutes."

"It's your life," mumbled Flora Jean with a shrug as she turned on University Boulevard, and headed south toward Denver's old established Washington Park neighborhood.

Several blocks later, CJ finally said, "I need to deal with something that's been bothering me all afternoon. I'll let you know where to stop." He directed her through a couple of turns until she brought the Bel Air to a stop in front of a quaint-looking stucco bungalow. "This is it. I'll only be a few minutes."

"I'm coming with you."

"Why?"

"Because."

"No need."

"Sorry, Macho Man. I'm coming anyway."

"Shit," said CJ, moving to get out of the car as Flora Jean slipped out on the opposite side.

"Who lives here?" she said as they walked up the sidewalk.

"Someone who needs to answer some questions," said CJ. He rang the doorbell several times before the front door swung back just enough for him to make out Evelyn Coleman. She was dressed in a crisp-looking khaki outfit and riding boots.

"Mr. Floyd. What brings you to Wash Park?"

CJ forced a smile. "Believe it or not, a headache and a few mumblies that don't quite fit in their pegs."

Evelyn swung the door fully open and straddled the doorway, eyeing Flora Jean suspiciously. "I'm not sure I can assist you with your problem."

"Well, let me give you some help. After I left you at the parking garage this morning I bumped into a woman I was sure tried to brain me with a tire iron last week. Only problem is, she claims that she didn't."

"Oh."

"Lucky for her, I spent the better part of the afternoon wrapped in the arms of modern medicine. While I was getting probed from A to Z, I had plenty of time to consider why the woman just might have been telling the truth and to also think about who might've cold-cocked me if it wasn't her."

"I'm listening," said Evelyn, stoic-faced.

"I kept telling myself it had to be someone who had a hell of a lot to lose. Someone who didn't want me digging too deeply into Hambone Dolbey's murder, and very likely the same person who killed Nadine Kemp."

"That would be Virginia Rodgers."

"That's what I thought until I was cooling my heels inside an MRI imager with forty-five minutes of nothing to think about except the events of the past week. While I was thinking, I remembered what the Weld County sheriff had actually told me about Nadine Kemp's murder. Believe it or not, it came back to me, almost word for word. It could have been that I misconstrued what he had said when he dropped in on me to tell me that Nadine had been murdered. Especially since my head was still a marshmallow from that tire iron episode I mentioned. But trapped inside that imager I remembered that after the sheriff slipped and told me that Nadine had been shot in the head, he emphasized that the circumstances of her death weren't being released to anyone.

"So when I took a break from the doctors trying to magnetize me, I called the sheriff and asked him if he had ever told anyone else besides me how Nadine Kemp had been killed. After a few not-so-pleasant exchanges, I finally explained why I needed to know the answer, and he reluctantly admitted that he had told Whitaker that Nadine had been shot in the head. That meant that Virginia Rodgers was probably telling me the truth this morning when she said Whitaker had told her how Nadine Kemp had died. I'm betting Whitaker also told you, and to cover your own guilt and shift suspicion to Virginia, you lied."

Evelyn shrugged. "Why would I lie about something like that?"

"Let's see," said CJ, stroking his chin. "Why do people lie? I'm wagering Virginia Rodgers did it for the same reason she came after me with a golf club, to protect her son, who she thought might have killed two people. I'm guessing you lied for the same reason you actually committed those murders. Diamonds! And I'm betting you tried to brain and then gas me in my garage because you were afraid that somehow I might find you out."

"Prove it."

"That's not my job. It's the DA's. But I'm wagering that when Whitaker and his mother get together to save their own skins, the chickens will come home to roost.

Besides, blood's thicker than water any day o. ..e week."

CJ realized immediately why Evelyn stepped back out of the doorway and tried to slam the door in his face, but it wasn't until later that he understood why someone who had been so cool up to that point would run. The size twelve-and-a-half boot he planted squarely between the door frame and the door prevented the door from closing, so Evelyn's sprint back into the house was barely a few feet ahead of his and only inches ahead of Flora Jean's. Just as Evelyn reached a towering, inlaid-walnut living room divider bookshelf, Flora Jean grabbed her by the collar and slammed her spine-first into the floor. As Evelyn lay moaning, CJ picked up a phone on a nearby coffee table and dialed 911.

Cradling the phone, he walked over to where Flora Jean had Evelyn lying face down on the floor with a knee planted in the small of her back. "Learn that in the marines?" asked CJ, taking a seat in one of Evelyn's leather-bound chairs and pulling out a cheroot.

"Second week of basic training. Works like a charm," said Flora Jean with a smile.

The gun that the police found in the room divider, wedged between a copy of *Roadside Geology of Colorado* and *War on the West,* told CJ why Evelyn had raced back into the house. It also proved to be the beginning of her undoing. The slow but certain ballistics examination of the fully loaded .32 caliber pistol matche‚ that of the bullet that had killed Nadine Kemp, and ‚ though Evelyn never admitted to killing Hambon‚ Nadine, or trying to kill CJ, a partial thumbprint th‚

lice eventually lifted from one of the legs on the work-bench in CJ's garage matched hers and placed her at the scene of CJ's assault. They also found a logbook in the same bookcase as the .32 that detailed six months of Hambone Dolbey's comings and goings between Na-dine's house and the diamond fields of the Devil's Back-bone, but they never found a branding iron.

Two weeks later, when CJ called the Denver district attorney's office to ask how they were doing at piecing together a case against Evelyn Coleman for his at-tempted murder, he was told in a less than apologetic tone by a junior assistant DA, "The Weld County DA wants the Coleman woman for the Kemp and Dolbey murders. Take your place in line."

When CJ asked why the attempt on his life had ap-parently been deemed unimportant, there was silence on the other end of the line; a haunting silence that lingered the whole time he was trying to recuperate.

Chapter 40

ort Garland, the famous southeastern Colorado outpost Kit Carson commanded during 1866 and 1867, marked the halfway point of CJ and Mavis's long-delayed vacation trip to Santa Fe. A warm midafternoon breeze swept across the compound as CJ backed away from the squat mud-brown adobe fortress to take a wide-angle photograph of Mavis standing near the entrance. As he stared through the lens his thoughts suddenly turned to Cicero Vickers and the concept of fairness. Cicero had died two weeks earlier as a result of the beating he had received from Celeste Deepstream. Bobby Two-Shirts, on the other hand, survived his suicide attempt, but since his sister was now facing a murder charge, he was go to have to learn to make it on his own. In the time it for the shutter to snap and for CJ to reframe the picture, he had a split second of dizziness, his first in weeks, and fairness seemed a more abstract concept than it ever had. He took several steps backward, remembering that his doctors had told him he might very well have dizzy spells for months; then he heard Mavis shout, "You're going to back out into the highway if you keep it up."

He stopped, snapped three slightly different photos in rapid succession, and recased the camera. As he walked back toward Mavis he had the feeling that rehashing the past had made him dizzy. When Mavis looped her arm into the crook of his elbow just above his cast, he feigned pain, grumbling, "Ouch."

Mavis knew the ploy. "No babying from me, Mr. Floyd. My touch didn't seem to hurt last night."

CJ smiled and thought about how sweet their lovemaking had been the previous evening. "It's taken you two weeks to cut me some slack," he said, draping his arm over Mavis's shoulder.

"Three weeks if you consider the fact that you spent pretty close to seven days in bed."

"Each one a day in hell when you count Sheriff Pritchard's visits, the endless parade of Denver's finest through my apartment, and Whitaker Rodgers calling every hour that first day pestering the hell out of me to help get his mother off the hook."

"She's off, isn't she?"

"For murder. But not for securities and exchange aud, illegal mining activities, criminal trespass, and a f-dozen other major legal infractions. My guess is ven with her money and connections, she and that drugstore-cowboy son of hers are looking at doing a little time."

"Did anybody ever find any diamonds?"

"Sure did. Pritchard found a fishing creel full in a crawl space beneath Nadine Kemp's house last week. Told me so himself after he thanked me for my continuing cooperation and warned me to stay the hell out of his jurisdiction." CJ broke into a broad smile. "From what my in-house lawyer, Julie, tells me, the diamonds and Dolbey's land will go to his next of kin, a loose-cannon son of his named Aaron Baptiste."

"Strange turn of events," said Mavis. "Tell me about the son."

"There's not a lot to tell except that before we landed Evelyn Coleman, I wasn't all that sure the kid hadn't killed his old man. Billy tracked him damn near up to Yellowstone before I called him off. Looks like at least one person stands to strike it rich."

"Glad you and Julie patched things up. Of course your stubbornness didn't help any," said Mavis, virtually ignoring CJ's story about Billy's Yellowstone trek.

"Me too," said CJ, not caring to rehash his reconciliation with Julie. It had taken a week's worth of pleading phone calls, three deliveries of a dozen roses, and a promise that under no circumstances would he ever again interrupt her studying for the bar to turn the tide.

Mavis moved CJ's arm to a secure position around her waist. "When will Julie hear if she passed the bar?"

"In a few more weeks. But she's already acting like she's passed. I know she has a meeting today to try to negotiate a deal with Cicero Vickers's sister to rent space in his building."

"A lawyer wedged in among you Delaware Street bail-bonding types?"

"Julie can hold her own. I wouldn't worry."

Mavis nodded in agreement. "I hope she won't ever end up defending people like Evelyn Coleman."

"Hope not. But even with Oliver Wendell Holmes defending her, I don't think Ms. Coleman stands a snowball's chance in hell of skirting the fact that she killed Nadine Kemp. Turns out Nadine was putting the bite on Evelyn to the tune of $1500 a month to keep her mouth shut about the fact that she and Whitaker were mining on Hambone Dolbey's land. Pritchard has photocopies of the canceled checks. Guess Evelyn just got tired of ponying up. Pinning Hambone Dolbey's murder on her will be harder, but that's why they have prosecutors and we pay taxes."

"A little glib, aren't we, Barrister?"

"No, just truthful." CJ bent down and gave Mavis a lingering kiss.

"Another one of those feeling-guilty kisses Flora Jean warned me about?"

"No," said CJ, recalling how three weeks earlier he'd had Flora Jean fax Mavis a "please forgive me" letter of apology every other working hour for two days straight. And how, when Mavis didn't respond, Flora Jean finally called her to say that if she didn't forgive CJ he was going to end up dying from guilt.

"Flora Jean's one hell of a loyal lady. You need to keep her around."

"Till the day I swear off sweet potato pie," said CJ, miling briefly before solemnly adding, "Besides, I owe r my life." He walked over and retrieved a wicker picnic basket from the grassy knoll where he and Mavis had enjoyed lunch earlier.

When he returned Mavis slipped her hand into his and led him back toward the Bel Air. As CJ placed the basket in the trunk, Mavis noticed a rusted Kansas license plate wrapped in see-through plastic that had been wedged in front of the spare tire. She picked up the plate and examined it. "Nineteen-fourteen, scarce. Pretty poor condition for your taste, though, isn't it?"

Shaking his head, CJ said, "Morgan and Dittier gave it to me, along with a cord of cherry wood. Partial payment for finding Dolbey's killer. It's going into my first-of-state collection. The condition doesn't matter."

"Partial payment?"

"That's right. Feel beneath the edge of the tire."

Mavis felt along the rubber until she found a dirty wad of cotton. She pulled it out and stripped back the layers until the face of Morgan's championship Cheyenne Frontier Days belt buckle was clearly visible. "CJ, you can't keep this."

"I had to or cost myself a friendship. I told Morgan I'd pick up a belt for it in Santa Fe. He and Dittier expect to see me wearing the buckle when we get back. I also promised Morgan I'd bring back a peace offering for Lisa. Neither one of us is back on her good side yet."

Mavis nodded understandingly and placed the license plate and belt buckle back in place. CJ closed the trunk lid, pointed toward the highway, and said, "Santa Fe or bust," as they walked along opposite sides of the car and settled into the Bel Air's front seat. Turning on the engine, he then reached across Mavis and slipped a B. B. King tape out of the glove compartment. Mavis gently smacked the top of his hand. "How about letting me pick the music for a change? Remember your promise last night, fifty-fifty."

CJ shrugged and handed the tape over. Mavis slipped it back into the glove box, then reached down into the purse at her feet and pulled out a handful of tapes. "Try this one," she said, handing CJ the tape on the bottom.

CJ slipped the tape into the tape deck and turned up the volume as he pulled off the shoulder and onto the highway. They were already doing sixty when Bob Seger began his classic rendition of "Against the Wind." CJ didn't back off the accelerator until he was doing eighty-five and Mavis had snuggled up next to him as the Bel Air knifed into the wind toward Santa Fe.

PRIME CRIME FROM
DONALD E. WESTLAKE

☐ THE AX
0-446-60608-1, $6.99 US/$9.99 CAN.

☐ BABY, WOULD I LIE?
0-446-40342-3, $5.99 US/$7.99 CAN.

☐ DON'T ASK
0-446-40095-5, $5.50 US/$6.99 CAN.

☐ KAHAWA
0-446-40343-1, $5.99 US/$7.99 CAN.

☐ SMOKE
0-446-40344-X, $6.50 US/$8.99 CAN.

☐ WHAT'S THE WORST THAT COULD HAPPEN?
0-446-60471-2, $6.50 US/$8.99 CAN.

AVAILABLE WHEREVER WARNER BOOKS ARE SOLD